Freeman Wills Crofts (1879–1957), the son of an army doctor who died before he was born, was raised in Northern Ireland and became a civil engineer on the railways. His first book, *The Cask*, written in 1919 during a long illness, was published the summer of 1920, immediately establishing him as a master of detective fiction. Regularly outselling Agatha Christie, it was with his fifth book that Crofts introduced iconic Scotland Yard detective, Inspector Joseph French, who would feature in no less than thirty books over the next three decades. He was a founder member of the Detection Club and was elected a Fellow of the Royal Society of Arts in 1939. Continually praised for his ingenious plotting and meticulous attention to detail—including the intricacies of railway timetables—Crofts was once dubbed 'The King of Detective Story Writers' and described by Raymond Chandler as 'the soundest builder of them all'.

Also in this series

Inspector French's Greatest Case
Inspector French and the Cheyne Mystery
Inspector French and the Starvel Hollow Tragedy
Inspector French and the Sea Mystery
Inspector French and the Box Office Murders
Inspector French and Sir John Magill's Last Journey

By the same author

The Cask
The Ponson Case
The Pit-Prop Syndicate
The Groote Park Murder
Six Against the Yard *
The Anatomy of Murder *

*with other Detection Club authors

FREEMAN WILLS CROFTS

Inspector French's Greatest Case

COLLINS
CRIME
CLUB

COLLINS CRIME CLUB

An imprint of HarperCollins*Publishers*
1 London Bridge Street
London SE1 9GF
www.harpercollins.co.uk

This paperback edition 2016

First published in Great Britain
by Wm Collins Sons & Co. Ltd 1924

A catalogue record for this book is
available from the British Library

ISBN 978-0-00-819058-3

Set in Sabon by Palimpsest Book Production Limited, Falkirk, Stirlingshire

Printed and bound in Great Britain by Clays Ltd, St Ives plc

MIX
Paper from
responsible sources
FSC
www.fsc.org   FSC™ C007454

INTRODUCTION

Meet Chief-Inspector French

I have been asked to tell you something about Chief-Inspector Joseph French of the Criminal Investigation Department of New Scotland Yard. I shall do my best, but I thought it would give you a better idea of him if I were to bring the man himself to the microphone. So with a good deal of trouble I have persuaded him to come, and he'll speak to you himself. But I have put him in the next room for the moment, lest his ears should burn from my introduction.

As he's not here, then, I may say that he's really quite a good fellow at heart. He's decent and he's straight and he's as kindly as his job will allow. He believes that if you treat people decently—you'll be able to get more out of them; and he acts on his belief. Politeness is an obsession with him, and he has well earned his nickname of 'Soapy Joe.' He's far from perfect, but I have known him now for many years, and I don't wish for a better friend.

But I have to admit that he's not very brilliant: in fact, many people call him dull. And here I'll let you into secret history. Anyone about to perpetrate a detective novel must first decide whether his detective is to be brilliant and a 'character,' or a mere ordinary humdrum personality. When French came into being there seemed two good reasons for making him the second of these. One was that it represented a new departure; there were already plenty of 'character' detectives, the lineal descendants, most of them, of the great Sherlock. The other reason was much more important. Striking characteristics, consistently depicted, are very hard to do.

I tried therefore to make French a perfectly ordinary man, without peculiarities or mannerisms. Of course he had to have *some* qualities, but they were to be the ordinary qualities of ordinary fairly successful men. He was to have thoroughness and perseverance as well as a reasonable amount of intelligence: just the qualities which make for moderate success in any walk of life.

From this it follows that he does not leap to his conclusions by brilliant intuition. He begins a case by going and looking for information in those places in which he thinks information is most likely to be found. When he gets the information he swots over it until he grinds out some sort of theory to account for the facts. Very often this turns out to be wrong, but if so, he simply tries again till he thinks of something better.

French I made an inspector of the Yard rather than a private detective because I hoped in this way to gain realism. But at once a horrible difficulty loomed up: I knew nothing about Scotland Yard or the C.I.D. What was to be done? The answer was simple. I built on the great rock which sustains so many of my profession: if I knew nothing of my subject, well, few of my readers would know any more.

As a matter of fact I have found this rock not quite so steadfast as I had hoped. It has been pointed out to me that French has at times done things which would make a real inspector of the Yard shudder. He has consistently travelled first-class on railways, particularly in sleeping-cars. He has borrowed bicycles from local police-officers without paying for their hire. He has undertaken country inquiries without his attendant sergeant. And many other evil things has he done. Fortunately, now that he has become a chief-inspector he is seeing the error of at least some of his ways and being more careful to live up to his great traditions.

French is a home bird, and nothing pleases him more than to get into his slippers before the fire and bury himself in some novel of sea adventure. He is married, but unlike Dr Watson he is the husband of only one wife. On occasion his Emily helps him with his cases. But this is only when he is more utterly stuck than usual. Otherwise he doesn't think it decent—or perhaps worth while—to worry her with shop. I have been wondering whether he has children. It's like a dream to me that in one book children were mentioned, and that in another their existence was denied. But as I can't find either reference, I can only note the point as one to be avoided.

French's job at the Yard is distinctly comfortable, particularly since he was made a chief-inspector. His promotion was decided on for a somewhat unusual reason. It was not because of his work or of what his superiors thought of him, but because so many people mentioned in letters that his promotion was long overdue. The customer, of course, is always right.

Not only, indeed, is French's job at the Yard comfortable,

but he enjoys very considerable advantages over his colleagues. Two in particular are so striking as to give him an almost unique position.

The first is that he must necessarily succeed in his cases. He may become utterly discouraged and pessimistic—indeed, he does so at regular intervals. This, however, is merely a concession to the reader, who must often be feeling equally bored and wearied. But if French is discouraged it is his own fault. He knows very well—or he would know if he applied his own methods of reasoning—that he wouldn't have been put into a book if he were going to fail. Success does not come at once—the value of suspense in a book cannot be overlooked—but that it will come, and that not later than about page three hundred, he is well aware.

His second great advantage over his colleagues really arises out of the first. It is that definitely he will find all the clues that he wants. He is bound to find them, because they have been laid down specially for that purpose, and he is led up to them in such a way that he could not avoid seeing them even if he wished to. These clues which he will find, moreover, are exactly those which lead to the solution of his problem, though naturally he does not see this at first. A decent interval always occurs between the picking up of the clue and the realization of its significance. This is necessary, as otherwise the book would run out too short.

This plan of finding just the clues necessary to lead the investigator to the correct conclusion seems to me such an extraordinarily good way of conducting an inquiry that I offer the idea, quite freely, to the heads of Scotland Yard.

I said that French had two advantages over his colleagues

at the Yard, but really he has three. He cannot be killed. He cannot even be seriously injured. The reason, of course, is that he will be wanted for the next book. So if anyone fills the room with petrol vapour and attempts to light it, as was done at Newhaven, French will, if he thinks hard, know that either the person will not light the petrol, or that if he does it won't burn. If the criminal he is attempting to arrest withdraws the pin from a Mills's bomb he is carrying he will know, again if he thinks, that either he will be able to hold the lever down, or that the bomb will prove a dud. Of course, under such distressing circumstances he never does think, as otherwise he couldn't register the amount of terror which is the reader's right and proper due.

I'm afraid I've talked too much about French, but it's really because I think a lot of him. However, with your permission I'll call him now. I give a shout that would wake the dead, and he appears.

'Yes, what is it?' he asks.

'Speak to these good folk, will you?' I say.

He approaches the microphone in a hesitating way and, clearing his throat, begins deprecatingly: 'Well, I'm very glad to be able to talk to all these kind friends, and to say it's a proud day in my life when—'

I stop him. Goodness knows where he would otherwise get to. I ask him to tell how he solves his cases.

This is more in his line. He gives a little laugh, and starts off in his normal voice.

'Huh, yes, I can do that. The answer is that I don't—not always. But I'll tell you ladies and gentlemen how I make things look pretty well: I just don't mention the failures. Sir Mortimer and the boys at the Yard may know about them—as a matter of fact, they do; but you don't. That's my thoughtfulness for you, of course: I don't want to worry you with anything that's not just absolutely so.'

'But,' I tell him, 'you know you usually do succeed. They would like to hear your methods.'

'Well,' he explains, 'I have two principal ways. Either I get a good clue or I have a stroke of luck. And you may take it from me that the luck's the best way. It saves endless trouble and difficulty.'

The stream of his inspiration seems to come to an end, and I start him off again.

'You've been in one or two tight corners,' I suggest. 'You might tell them about your worst five minutes.'

He warms to it. 'At the Yard we do get occasional nasty turns, but of course they're all in the day's work. Since you've asked me, I think my worst was in the case I just heard you speak of—Did you know the door wasn't shut? I mean the case in which two financiers were murdered on an abandoned yacht off Newhaven, and a lot of diamonds were missing. You may remember it. Well, a man called Nolan was my suspect, though I couldn't prove his guilt. But I thought there was just a chance that I might be able to make him commit himself. So I laid a trap for him. I pitched him a yarn that made him think he'd left a clue on his launch, in the hope that he'd try to destroy the launch and we could take him in the act.

'The launch was lying in Newhaven Harbour, and the next night Sergeant Carter and I took cover on the wharf and settled down to watch. It was a wet night, and we got our fill of it. But it was worth it. About three in the morning we saw Nolan creeping down and slipping aboard. We followed him as close as we dared. He disappeared into the little engine-room. I crept after him to the door and peeped in. He was working with a torch, and you can imagine my feelings when I watched him take the missing diamonds from a hiding-place and put them in his pocket. This, of course, was all the proof I could have wanted. But then things grew nasty. He flooded the place with petrol and put a canister on the floor with a clock attached. So I thought it was about time to make a move.

'As a matter of fact, it was past the time. Before I could do anything he had flashed his torch on me, and I found myself looking into the wrong end of a pistol. He spoke quite quietly. He said he had feared a trick, but that he had gone through with the thing on chance. He said that as long as I lived he was in danger of being hanged. Therefore he was going to kill me. If he could get away afterwards himself, he would; if not, we would die together.

'You'll understand that I could do nothing, for if I'd made a move he'd have fired, and if he'd fired, the whole place would have gone up in a sheet of flame. It was nasty, and no mistake.'

French pauses, and I prompt him again.

'Tell them how you escaped.'

'Ah, that was where my bit of luck came in. Carter was behind me, and Nolan didn't see him. So Carter nipped on deck, lowered himself over the side, and shot Nolan through the porthole. He got him in the hand, but the flame from the gun didn't get in, so there was no fire. But Nolan was desperate, and in spite of his wound he went for me all out. I tripped over a pipe and fell with my side against the motor. I broke some ribs, but managed to hold off Nolan till Carter got back and pulled him off.'

'And after that you think you can be killed! French, my dear fellow, you're a humbug!'

He grins, and indicates pointedly that he is now due at the Yard. So I have to let him go.

FREEMAN WILLS CROFTS
1935

CONTENTS

Murder!

The back streets surrounding Hatton Garden, in the City of London, do not form at the best of times a cheerful or inspiring prospect. Narrow and mean, and flanked with ugly, sordid-looking buildings grimy from exposure to the smoke and fogs of the town and drab from the want of fresh paint, they can hardly fail to strike discouragement into the heart of anyone eager for the uplift of our twentieth century civilisation.

But if on a day of cheerful sunshine the outlook is thus melancholy, it was vastly more so at ten o'clock on a certain dreary evening in mid-November. A watery moon, only partially visible through a damp mist, lit up pallidly the squalid, shuttered fronts of the houses. The air was cold and raw, and the pavements showed dark from a fine rain which had fallen some time earlier, but which had now ceased. Few were abroad, and no one whose business permitted it remained out of doors.

Huckley Street, one of the narrowest and least inviting in the district, was, indeed, deserted save for a single figure.

Though the higher and more ethical side of civilisation was not obtrusive, it was by no means absent. The figure represented Law and Order, in short, it was that of a policeman on his beat.

Constable James Alcorn moved slowly forward, glancing mechanically but with practised eye over the shuttered windows of the shops and the closed doors of the offices and warehouses in his purview. He was not imaginative, the constable, or he would have rebelled even more strongly than he did against the weariness and monotony of his job. A dog's life, this of night patrol in the City, he thought, as he stopped at a cross roads, and looked down each one in turn of the four dingy and deserted lanes which radiated from the intersection. How deadly depressing it all was! Nothing ever doing! Nothing to give a man a chance! In the daytime it was not so bad, when the streets were alive and fellow creatures were to be seen, if not spoken to, but at night when there was no one to watch, and nothing to be done but wait endlessly for the opportunity which never came, it was a thankless task. He was fed up!

But though he didn't know it, his chance was at hand. He had passed through Charles Street and had turned into Hatton Garden itself, when suddenly a door swung open a little way down the street, and a young man ran wildly out into the night.

The door was directly under a street lamp, and Alcorn could see that the youth's features were frozen into an expression of horror and alarm. He hovered for a moment irresolute, then, seeing the constable, made for him at a run.

'Officer!' he shouted. 'Come here quickly. There's something wrong!'

Alcorn, his depression gone, hurried to meet him.

2

'What is it?' he queried. 'What's the matter?'

'Murder, I'm afraid,' the other cried. 'Up in the office. Come and see.'

The door from which the young man had emerged stood open, and they hastened thither. It gave on a staircase upon which the electric light was turned on. The young man raced up and passed through a door on the first landing. Alcorn, following, found himself in an office containing three or four desks. A further door leading to an inner room stood open, and to this the young man pointed.

'In there,' he directed; 'in the Chief's room.'

Here also the light was on, and as Alcorn passed in, he saw that he was indeed in the presence of tragedy, and he stood for a moment motionless, taking in his surroundings.

The room was small, but well proportioned. Near the window stood a roll-top desk of old-fashioned design. A leather-lined clients' arm-chair was close by, with behind it a well-filled bookcase. In the fireplace the remains of a fire still glowed red. A table littered with books and papers and a large Milner safe completed the furniture. The doors of this safe were open.

Alcorn mechanically noted these details, but it was not on them that his attention was first concentrated. Before the safe lay the body of a man, hunched forward in a heap, as if he had collapsed when stooping to take something out. Though the face was hidden, there was that in the attitude which left no doubt that he was dead. And the cause of death was equally obvious. On the back of the bald head, just above the fringe of white hair, was an ugly wound, as if from a blow of some blunt but heavy weapon.

With an oath, Alcorn stepped forward and touched the cheek.

'Cold,' he exclaimed. 'He must have been dead some time. When did you find him?'

'Just now,' the young man answered. 'I came in for a book, and found him lying there. I ran for help at once.'

The constable nodded.

'We'd best have a doctor anyway,' he decided. A telephone stood on the top of the desk, and he called up his headquarters, asking that an officer and a doctor be sent at once. Then he turned to his companion.

'Now, sir, what's all this about? Who are you, and how do you come to be here?'

The young man, though obviously agitated and ill at ease, answered collectedly enough.

'My name is Orchard, William Orchard, and I am a clerk in this office—Duke & Peabody's, diamond merchants. As I have just said, I called in for a book I had forgotten, and I found—what you see.'

'And what did you do?'

'Do? I did what anyone else would have done in the same circumstances. I looked to see if Mr Gething was dead, and when I saw he was I didn't touch the body, but ran for help. You were the first person I saw.'

'Mr Gething?' the constable repeated sharply. 'Then you know the dead man?'

'Yes. It is Mr Gething, our head clerk.'

'What about the safe? Is there anything missing from that?'

'I don't know,' the young man answered. 'I believe there were a lot of diamonds in it, but I don't know what amount, and I've not looked what's there now.'

4

'Who would know about it?'

'I don't suppose anyone but Mr Duke, now Mr Gething's dead. He's the chief, the only partner I've ever seen.'

Constable Alcorn paused, evidently at a loss as to his next move. Finally, following precedent, he took a somewhat dog's-eared notebook from his pocket, and with a stumpy pencil began to note the particulars he had gleaned.

'Gething, you say the dead man's name was? What was his first name?'

'Charles.'

'Charles Gething, deceased,' the constable repeated presently, evidently reading his entry. 'Yes. And his address?'

'12 Monkton Street, Fulham.'

'Twelve—Monkton—Street—Fulham. Yes. And your name is William Orchard?'

Slowly the tedious catechism proceeded. The two men formed a contrast. Alcorn calm and matter of fact, though breathing heavily from the effort of writing, was concerned only with making a satisfactory statement for his superior. His informant, on the other hand, was quivering with suppressed excitement, and acutely conscious of the silent and motionless form on the floor. Poor old Gething! A kindly old fellow, if ever there was one! It seemed a shame to let his body lie there in that shapeless heap, without showing even the respect of covering the injured head with a handkerchief. But the matter was out of his hands. The police would follow their own methods, and he, Orchard, could not interfere.

Some ten minutes passed of question, answer, and laborious caligraphy, then voices and steps were heard on the stairs, and four men entered the room.

'What's all this, Alcorn?' cried the first, a stout, cleanshaven man with the obvious stamp of authority, in the same phrase that his subordinate had used to the clerk, Orchard. He had stopped just inside the door, and stood looking sharply round the room, his glance passing from the constable to the body, to the open safe, with inimical interest to the young clerk, and back again to Alcorn.

The constable stiffened to attention, and replied in a stolid, unemotional tone, as if reciting formal evidence in court.

'I was on my beat, sir, and at about ten-fifteen was just turning the corner from Charles Street into Hatton Garden, when I observed this young man,' he indicated Orchard with a gesture, 'run out of the door of this house. He called me that there was something wrong up here, and I came up to see, and found that body lying as you see it. Nothing has been touched, but I have got some information here for you.' He held up the notebook.

The newcomer nodded and turned to one of his companions, a tall man with the unmistakable stamp of the medical practitioner.

'If you can satisfy yourself the man's dead, Doctor, I don't think we shall disturb the body in the meantime. It'll probably be a case for the Yard, and if so we'll leave everything for whoever they send.'

The doctor crossed the room and knelt by the remains.

'He's dead all right,' he announced, 'and not so long ago either. If I could turn the body over I could tell you more about that. But I'll leave it if you like.'

'Yes, leave it for the moment, if you please. Now, Alcorn, what else do you know?'

A few seconds sufficed to put the constable's information at his superior's disposal. The latter turned to the doctor.

'There's more than murder here, Dr Jordan, I'll be bound. That safe is the key to the affair. Thank the Lord, it'll be a job for the Yard. I shall 'phone them now, and there should be a man here in half an hour. Sorry, Doctor, but I'm afraid you'll have to wait.' He turned to Orchard. 'You'll have to wait, too, young man, but the Yard inspector probably won't keep you long. Now, what about this old man's family? Was he married?'

'Yes, but his wife is an invalid, bedridden. He has two daughters. One lives at home and keeps house, the other is married and lives somewhere in town.'

'We shall have to send round word. You go, Carson.' He turned to one of the two other members of his quartet, constables in uniform. 'Don't tell the old lady. If the daughter's not there, wait until she comes in. And put yourself at her disposal. If she wants her sister sent for, you go. You, Jackson, go down to the front door and let the Yard man up. Alcorn, remain here.' These dispositions made, he rang up the Yard and delivered his message, then turned once more to the young clerk.

'You say, Mr Orchard, that no one could tell what, if anything, is missing from the safe, except Mr Duke, the sole active partner. We ought to have Mr Duke here at once. Is he on the 'phone?'

'Gerard, 1417B,' Orchard answered promptly. The young man's agitation had somewhat subsided, and he was following with interest the actions of the police, and admiring the confident, competent way in which they had taken charge.

The official once again took down the receiver from the top of the desk, and put through the call. 'Is Mr Duke there? . . . Yes, say a superintendent of police.' There was a short silence, and then the man went on. 'Is that Mr Duke? . . . I'm speaking from your office in Hatton Garden. I'm sorry, sir, to tell you that a tragedy has taken place here. Your chief clerk, Mr Gething, is dead . . . Yes, sir. He's lying in your private office here, and the circumstances point to murder. The safe is standing open, and—Yes, sir, I'm afraid so—I don't know, of course, about the contents . . . No, but you couldn't tell from that . . . I was going to suggest that you come down at once. I've 'phoned Scotland Yard for a man . . . Very good, sir, we shall be here when you come.' He replaced the receiver and turned to the others.

'Mr Duke is coming down at once. There is no use in our standing here. Come to the outer office and we'll find ourselves chairs.'

It was cold in the general office, the fire evidently having been out for some time, but they sat down there to wait, the superintendent pointing out that the furniture in the other room must not be touched. Of the four, only the superintendent seemed at ease and self-satisfied. Orchard was visibly nervous and apprehensive and fidgeted restlessly, Constable Alcorn, slightly embarrassed by the society in which he found himself, sat rigidly on the edge of his chair staring straight in front of him, while the doctor was frankly bored and anxious to get home. Conversation languished, though spasmodic attempts were made by the superintendent to keep it going, and none of the quartet was sorry when the sound of footsteps on the stairs created a diversion.

Of the three men who entered the room, two, carrying black leather cases, were obviously police constables in plain clothes. The third was a stout man in tweeds, rather under middle height, with a cleanshaven, good-humoured face and dark blue eyes which, though keen, twinkled as if at some perennially fresh private joke. His air was easy-going and leisurely, and he looked the type of man who could enjoy a good dinner and a good smoke-room story to follow.

'Ah, Superintendent, how are you?' he exclaimed, holding out his hand cordially. 'It's some time since we met. Not since that little episode in the Lime-house hairdresser's. That was a nasty business. And now you've some other scheme for keeping a poor man from his hard-earned rest, eh?'

The superintendent seemed to find the other's easy familiarity out of place.

'Good-evening, Inspector,' he answered with official abruptness. 'You know Dr Jordan?—Inspector French of the C.I.D. And this is Mr Orchard, a clerk in this office, who discovered the crime.'

Inspector French greeted them genially. Behind his back at the Yard they called him 'Soapy Joe' because of the reliance he placed on the suavity of his manners. 'I know your name, of course, Doctor, but I don't think we have ever met. Pleased to make your acquaintance, Mr Orchard.' He subsided into a chair and went on: 'Perhaps, Superintendent, you would just give me a hint of what this is all about before we go any further.'

The facts already learned were soon recited. French listened carefully, and annexing the constable's notebook, complimented that worthy on his industry. 'Well,' he beamed on them, 'I suppose we'd better have a look round inside before Mr Duke turns up.'

The party moved to the inner room, where French, his hands in his pockets, stood motionless for some minutes, surveying the scene.

'Nothing has been touched, of course?' he asked.

'Nothing. From what they tell me, both Mr Orchard and Constable Alcorn have been most circumspect.'

'Excellent; then we may go ahead. Get your camera rigged, Giles, and take the usual photos. I think, gentlemen, we may wait in the other room until the photographs are taken. It won't be long.'

Though French had tactfully bowed his companions out, he did not himself follow them, but kept prowling about the inner office, closely inspecting its contents, though touching nothing. In a few minutes the camera was ready, and a number of flashlight photographs were taken of the body, the safe, every part of both offices, and even the stairs and hall. In the amazing way in which tales of disaster travel, news of the crime had already leaked out, and a small crowd of the curious hung, open-mouthed, about the door.

Scarcely had the camera been put away, when the proceedings were interrupted by a fresh arrival. Hurried steps were heard ascending the stairs, and a tall, thin, extremely well-dressed old gentleman entered the room. Though evidently on the wrong side of sixty, he was still a handsome man, with strong, well-formed features, white hair, and a good carriage. Under normal circumstances he would have presented a dignified and kindly appearance, but now his face was drawn into an expression of horror and distress, and his hasty movements also betokened his anxiety. On seeing so many strangers, he hesitated. The inspector stepped forward.

'Mr Duke, sir? I am Inspector French of the Criminal Investigation Department of New Scotland Yard. I very much regret to confirm the news which you have already heard, that your head clerk, Mr Gething, has been murdered, and I fear also that your safe may have been burgled.'

It was evident that the old gentleman was experiencing strong emotion, but he controlled it and spoke quietly enough.

'This is terrible news, Inspector. I can hardly believe that poor old Gething is gone. I came at once when I heard. Tell me the details. Where did it happen?'

French pointed to the open door.

'In here, sir, in your private office. Everything is still exactly as it was found.'

Mr Duke moved forward, then on seeing the body, stopped and gave a low cry of horror.

'Oh, poor old fellow!' he exclaimed. 'It's awful to see him lying, there. *Awful!* I tell you, Inspector, I've lost a real friend, loyal and true and dependable. Can't he be lifted up? I can't bear to see him like that.' His gaze passed on to the safe. 'And the safe! Merciful heavens, Inspector! Is anything gone? Tell me at once, I must know! It seems heartless to think of such a thing with that good old fellow lying there, but after all I'm only human.'

'I haven't touched the safe, but we'll do so directly,' the inspector answered. 'Was there much in it?'

'About three-and-thirty thousand pounds' worth of diamonds were in that lower drawer, as well as a thousand in notes,' groaned the other. 'Get the body moved, will you, and let us look.'

French whistled, then he turned to his men.

'Get that table cleared outside there, and lift the body on to it,' he ordered; then to the doctor he added, 'Perhaps, Doctor, you could make your examination now?'

The remains were lifted reverently and carried from the

11

room. Mr Duke turned impatiently to the safe, but the inspector stopped him.

'A moment, sir, if you please. I am sorry to ask you to stretch your patience a little longer, but before you touch the safe I must test it for finger prints. You see the obvious necessity?'

'I would wait all night if it would help you to get on the track of the scoundrels who have done this,' the old gentleman answered grimly. 'Go on in your own way. I can restrain myself.'

With a word of approval, Inspector French fetched one of the cases brought by his assistants, and producing little boxes of French chalk and of lampblack, he proceeded to dust over the smooth portions of the safe, using white powder on a dark background and *vice versa*. On blowing off the surplus powder, he pointed triumphantly to a number of finger prints, explaining that the moisture deposited from the skin held the powder, which otherwise dropped off. Most of the marks were blurred and useless, but a few showed clearly the little loops and whorls and ridges of thumbs and fingers.

'Of course,' French went on, 'these may all be quite useless. They may be those of persons who had a perfect right to open the safe—your own, for instance. But if they belong to the thief, if there was one, their importance may be incalculable. See here now, I can open this drawer without touching any of them.'

Mr Duke was clearly at the end of his patience, and he kept fidgeting about, clasping and unclasping his hands, and showing every sign of extreme impatience and uneasiness. As the drawer opened, he stepped forward and plunged in his hand.

'Gone!' he cried hoarsely. 'They're all gone! Thirty-three thousand pounds' worth! Oh, my God! It means ruin.' He covered his face with his hands, then went on unsteadily. 'I feared it, of course. I thought it must be the diamonds when the officer rang me up. I have been trying to face it ever since. I shouldn't care for myself. It's my daughter. To think of her exposed to want! But there. It is wicked of me to speak so who have only lost money, while poor old Gething has lost his life. Don't mind me, Inspector. Carry on. What I want most now is to hear of the arrest of the murderer and thief. If there is anything I can do to help in that, command me.'

He stood, a little stooped and with haggard face, but dignified even in his grief. French in his pleasant, kindly way tried to reassure him.

'Now, you don't need to give up heart, sir,' he advised. 'Diamonds are not the easiest things to dispose of, and we're right on to the loss at once. Before the thief can pass them on we shall have all the channels under observation. With any ordinary luck, you'll get them back. They were not insured?'

'Part of them only. About nineteen thousand pounds' worth were insured. It was my cursed folly that the rest were not. Gething advised it, but I had never lost anything, and I wanted to save the money. You understand our trade has been difficult since the war, and our profits were not the same as formerly. Every little has counted, and we have had to economise.'

'At worst, then, that is £14,000 gone?'

'If the insurance companies pay in full, that is all, besides the thousand in notes. But, Inspector, it is too much. To meet my share of the loss will beggar me.' He shook his

13

head despondently. 'But never mind my affairs in the meantime. Don't, I beg of you, lose any time in getting after the criminal.'

'You are right, sir. If, then, you will sit down there for a few minutes I'll get rid of the others, and then I shall ask you for some information.'

The old gentleman dropped wearily into a chair while French went to the outer office. The policeman who had been sent to inform Gething's family of the tragedy had just returned. French looked at him inquiringly.

'I called, sir, at the address you gave me,' he reported. 'Miss Gething was there, and I told her what had occurred. She was considerably upset, and asked me if I could get a message to her sister and brother-in-law at 12 Deeley Terrace, Hawkins Street, in Battersea. I said I would fetch them for her. The brother-in-law, name of Gamage, was from home in Leeds, being a traveller for a firm of fur dealers, but Mrs Gamage was there and I took her across. It seemed the old lady had wanted to know what was up, and Miss Gething had told her, and she had got some kind of stroke. They asked me to call a doctor, which I did. The two daughters say they can't get across here on account of being occupied with the mother.'

'So much the better,' French commented, and having added the names and addresses of Mr and Mrs Gamage to his list, he turned to the doctor.

'Well, Doctor,' he said pleasantly, 'how do you get on?'

The doctor straightened himself up from his position over the corpse.

'I've done all I can here,' he answered. 'I don't think there's any doubt the man was killed instantaneously by the blow on the head. The skull is fractured, apparently by some heavy, blunt weapon. I should think it was done from behind while the old fellow was stooping, possibly working at the safe, though that, perhaps, is your province.'

'I'm glad of the hint anyway. Now, gentlemen, I think that's all we can do tonight. Can your men remove the body, Superintendent? I want to stay for a moment to take a few measurements. You'll let me know tomorrow about the inquest? Mr Orchard, you might stay a moment also; there is a question or two I want to ask you.'

The superintendent had sent one of his men for a stretcher, and the remains were lifted on and carried slowly down to the waiting taxi. With an exchange of good-nights, the local men withdrew, leaving Inspector French, Mr Duke, Orchard, and the two plain-clothes men from the Yard in charge of the premises.

2

The Firm of Duke and Peabody

When Inspector French ushered the clerk, Orchard, into the inner office, they found Mr Duke pacing the floor with an expression of utter mystification imprinted on his features.

'I say, Inspector, here's a puzzle,' he cried. 'I happened to look behind the safe door, and I find it has been opened with a key. I thought at first it had been broken or forced or the lock somehow picked. But I see it is unlocked.'

'Yes, I noticed that, sir,' French answered. 'But I don't follow you. What is the mystery about that?'

'Why, the key, of course. To my certain knowledge there were only two keys in existence. One I keep on my ring, which is chained to my belt and never leaves me day nor night. There it is. The other is lodged with my bankers, where no one could possibly get at it. Now, where did the thief get the key that is now in the lock?'

'That is one of the things we have to find out,' French replied. 'You may perhaps think it strange, but a point of that kind, which at first seems to deepen the mystery, often proves a blessing in disguise. It provides another point of attack, you understand, and frequently it narrows down the area of inquiry. You haven't touched the key, I hope?'

'No. I remembered what you said about finger prints.'

'Good. Now, gentlemen, if you will please sit down, I want to ask you a few questions. I'll take you first, Mr Orchard. I have your name, and your address is Bloomsbury Square. Now tell me, is that your home?'

The young fellow answered the questions without hesitation, and French noted approvingly his direct glance and the evident candour with which he spoke. The Bloomsbury Square address, it appeared, was that of a boarding house, the clerk's home being in Somerset. He had left the office at about half-past five that afternoon, Mr Gething being then almost ready to follow. Mr Gething was usually the last out of the office. Orchard had noticed nothing unusual in his manner that day, though for the last two or three weeks he had seemed somewhat moody and depressed. Orchard had gone from the office to Liverpool Street, where he had caught the 5.52 to Ilford. There he had had supper with a friend, a man called Forrest, a clerk in a shipping office in Fenchurch Street. He had left about 9.30, getting back to town a little before 10.00. The rain had stopped, and as he did not get as much exercise as he could have wished, he resolved to walk home from the station. Hatton Garden was but little out of his way, and as he approached it he remembered that he had left in his desk a book he had changed at the library at lunch time. He had decided to call in and get it, so as to read for a while before going to sleep. He had done so, and had found Mr Gething's body, as he had already explained. The outer street door had been closed, and he had opened it with his latch key.

Both the office doors were open, that between the landing and the outer office and that of Mr Duke's room. The lights were on everywhere, except that in the outer office only the single central bulb was burning, the desk lamps being off. He had seen no one about the offices.

French, having complimented the young fellow on his clear statement, bade him good-night and sent him home. But as he passed out of the room he whispered to one of his men, who promptly nodded and also disappeared. French turned to Mr Duke.

'That seems a straightforward young fellow,' he observed. 'What is your opinion of him?'

'Absolutely straightforward.' The acting partner spoke with decision. 'He has been with me for over four years, and I have always found him most conscientious and satisfactory. Indeed, I have been very fortunate in my whole staff. I think I could say the same of them all.'

'I congratulate you, Mr Duke. Perhaps now you would tell me something about your firm and your various employees.'

Mr Duke, though still extremely agitated, was controlling his emotion and answered in calm tones.

'The business is not a large one, and at the present time is virtually controlled by myself. Peabody, though not so old as I am, has been troubled by bad health and has more or less gone to pieces. He seldom comes to the office, and never undertakes any work. The junior partner, Sinnamond, is travelling in the East, and has been for some months. We carry on the usual trade of diamond merchants, and have a small branch establishment in Amsterdam. Indeed, I divide my own time almost equally between London and Amsterdam. We occupy only these two rooms which you have seen. Our staff in the outer office consists, or rather consisted, of five, a chief and confidential clerk, the poor man who has just been killed, a young man called Harrington, who is qualifying for a partnership, Orchard, a girl typist, and an office boy. Besides them, we employ an outside man, a traveller, a Dutchman named Vanderkemp. He attends sales and so on, and when not on the road works in the Amsterdam branch.'

Inspector French noted all the information Mr Duke could give about each of the persons mentioned.

'Now this Mr Gething,' he resumed. 'You say he has been with you for over twenty years, and that you had full confidence in him, but I must ask the question, Are you sure that your confidence was not misplaced? In other words, are you satisfied that he was not himself after your diamonds?'

Mr Duke shook his head decisively.

'I am positive he was not,' he declared warmly and with something of indignation showing in his manner. 'I should as soon accuse my own son, if I had one. No, I'd stake my life on it, Gething was no thief.'

'I'm glad to hear you say that, Mr Duke,' the other returned smoothly. 'Now, then, your office staff eliminated, tell me is there anyone that you suspect?'

'Not a creature!' Mr Duke was equally emphatic. 'Not a single creature! I can't imagine anyone who would have done such a thing. I wish I could.'

The inspector hesitated.

'Of course, sir, you understand that if you were to mention a name it would not in any way bias me against that person. It would only mean that I should make inquiries. Don't think you would be getting anyone into trouble.'

Mr Duke smiled grimly.

'You needn't be afraid. If I had any suspicion I should be only too glad to tell you, but I have none.'

'When, sir, did you last see your late clerk?'

'About half-past four this evening. I left the office at that time, about an hour earlier than usual, because I had a business appointment for a quarter to five with Mr Peters, of Lincoln's Inn, my solicitor.'

'And you did not return to the office?'

'No. I sat with Mr Peters for about half an hour, then as my business was not finished and he wanted to square up for the night, we decided to dine together at my club in Gower Street. It was not worth while going back to my own office, so I want straight from Peters' to the club.'

'And you did not notice anything peculiar about Mr Gething?'

'Not specially on that night. He seemed absolutely as usual.'

'How do you mean, not specially on that night?'

'He had been, I thought, a little depressed for two or three weeks previously, as if he had some trouble on his mind. I asked when first I noticed it if there was anything wrong, but he murmured something about home troubles, about his wife not being so well—she is a chronic invalid. He was not communicative, and I did not press the matter. But he was no worse this afternoon than during the last fortnight.'

'I see. Now, what brought him back to the office tonight?'

Mr Duke made a gesture of bewilderment.

'I have no idea,' he declared. 'There was nothing! Nothing, at least, that I know of or can imagine. We were not specially busy, and as far as I can think, he was well up to date with his work.'

'Is there a postal delivery between half-past four and the time your office closes?'

'There is, and of course there might have been a telegram or a caller or a note delivered by hand. But suppose there had been something important enough to require immediate attention, Gething would never have taken action without consulting me. He had only to ring me up.'

'He knew where you were, then?'

'No, but he could have rung up my home. They knew there where I was, as when I had decided to dine at the club, I 'phoned home to say so.'

'But were you in your club all the evening? Excuse my pressing the matter, but I think it's important to make sure the man did not try to communicate with you.'

'I see your point. Yes, I stayed chatting with Mr Peters until almost 9.30. Then, feeling tired from a long day's thought about business, I decided a little exercise would be pleasant, and I walked home. I reached my house a minute or two after ten.'

'That seems conclusive. All the same, sir, I think you should make sure when you reach home that no call was made.'

'I shall do so certainly, but my parlourmaid is very reliable in such matters, and I am certain she would have told me of any.'

Inspector French sat for a few seconds lost in thought, and then began on another point.

'You tell me that you had £33,000 worth of diamonds in the safe. Is not that an unusually large amount to keep in an office?'

'You are quite right; it is too large. I consider myself very much to blame, both for that and in the matter of

21

the insurance. But I had not meant to keep the stones there long. Indeed, negotiations for the sale of the larger portion were actually in progress. On the other hand, it is due to myself to point out that the safe is of a very efficient modern pattern.'

'That is so, sir. Now can you tell me who, besides yourself, knew of the existence of those stones?'

'I'm afraid,' Mr Duke admitted despondently, 'there was no secret about it. Gething knew, of course. He was entirely in my confidence about such matters. Vanderkemp, my outdoor man, knew that I had made some heavy purchases recently, as he not only conducted the negotiations, but personally brought the stones to the office. Besides, there were letters about them, accessible to all the staff. I am afraid you may take it that everyone in the office knew there was a lot of stuff there, though probably not the exact amount.'

'And the staff may have talked to outsiders. Young people will brag, especially if they are "keeping company," as the Irish say.'

'I fear that is so,' Mr Duke agreed, as if deprecating the singular habits of the young.

The inspector changed his position uneasily, and his hand stole to his pipe. But he checked himself and resumed his questioning. He obtained from Mr Duke a detailed list of the missing stones, then turned to a new point.

'About that thousand pounds in notes. I suppose you haven't got the numbers?'

'No, unfortunately. But the bank might know them.'

'We shall inquire. Now, Mr Duke, about the key. That is another singular thing.'

'It is an amazing thing. I absolutely cannot understand where it came from. As I said, this one never leaves, nor has left, my personal possession, and the other, the *only* other one, is equally inaccessible in my bank.'

'You always personally opened or closed the safe?'

'Always, or at least it was done by my instructions and in my presence.'

'Oh, well, that is not quite the same thing, you know. Who has ever opened or closed it for you?'

'Gething; and not once or twice, but scores, I suppose I might say hundreds of times. But always in my presence.'

'I understand that, sir. Anyone else besides Mr Gething?'

Mr Duke hesitated.

'No,' he said slowly, 'no one else. He was the only one I trusted to that extent. And I had reason to trust him,' he added, with a touch of defiance.

'Of course, sir. I recognise that,' French answered smoothly. 'I am only trying to get the facts clear in my mind. I take it, then, that the deceased gentleman was the only person, other than yourself, who ever handled your key? It was not within reach of anyone in your house; your servants, for example?'

'No, I never let it lie about. Even at night I kept it attached to me.'

The inspector rose from his chair.

'Well, sir,' he said politely, 'I'm sorry to have kept you so long. Just let me take your finger prints to compare with those in the safe, and I have done. Shall I ring up for a taxi for you?'

Mr Duke looked at his watch.

'Why, it is nearly one,' he exclaimed. 'Yes, a taxi by all means, please.'

Though Inspector French had said that everything possible had been done that night, he did not follow Mr

Duke from the building. Instead, he returned to the inner office and set himself unhurriedly to make a further and more thorough examination of its contents.

He began with the key of the safe. Removing it by the shank with a pair of special pincers, he tested the handle for finger prints, but without success. Looking then at the other end, a slight roughness on one of the wards attracted his attention, and on scrutinising it with his lens, a series of fine parallel scratches was revealed on all the surfaces. 'So that's it, is it?' he said to himself complacently. 'Manufacturers don't leave keys of valuable safes half finished. This one has been cut with a file, and probably'—he again scrutinised the workmanship—'by an amateur at that. And according to this man Duke, old Gething was the only one that had the handling of the key—that could have taken a wax impression. Well, well; we shall see.'

He locked the safe, dropped the key into his pocket, and turned to the fireplace, soliloquising the while.

The fire had still been glowing red when the crime was discovered shortly after ten o'clock. That meant, of course, that it had been deliberately stoked up, because the fire in the outer office was cold and dead. Someone, therefore, had intended to spend a considerable time in the office. Who could it have been?

As far as French could see, no one but Gething. But if Gething were going to commit the robbery—a matter of perhaps ten minutes at the outside—he would not have required a fire. No, this looked as if there really was some business to be done, something that would take time to carry through. But then, if so, why had Gething not consulted Mr Duke? French noted the point, to be considered further in the light of future discoveries.

But as to the identity of the person who had built up the fire there should be no doubt. Finger prints again! The coal shovel had a smooth, varnished wooden handle, admirably suited for records, and a short test with the white powder revealed thereon an excellent impression of a right thumb.

The poker next received attention, and here French made his second discovery. Picking it up with the pincers in the same careful way in which he had handled the key, he noticed on the handle a dark brown stain. Beside this stain, and sticking to the metal, was a single white hair.

That he held in his hand the instrument with which the crime was committed seemed certain, and he eagerly tested the other end for prints. But this time he was baffled. Nothing showed at the places where finger marks might have been expected. It looked as if the murderer had worn gloves or had rubbed the handle clean, and he noted that either alternative postulated a cold-blooded criminal and a calculated crime.

He continued his laborious search of the room, but without finding anything else which interested him. Finally, while his men were photographing the prints he had discovered, he sat down in the leather-covered arm-chair and considered what he had learned.

Certainly a good deal of the evidence pointed to Gething. Gething knew the stones were there. According to Duke, no one else could have got hold of the key to the safe to make an impression. Moreover, his body was found before the safe with the latter open. All circumstantial evidence, of course, though cumulatively strong.

However, whether or not Gething had contemplated robbery, he had not carried it through. Someone else had the diamonds. And here the obvious possibility recurred to him which had been in his mind since he had heard the superintendent's first statement. Suppose Orchard was the man. Suppose Orchard, visiting the office in the evening, arrived to find the safe open and the old man stooping over it. Instantly he would be assailed by a terrible temptation. The thing would seem so easy, the way of escape so obvious, the reward so sure. French, sitting back in the arm-chair, tried to picture the scene. The old man bending over the safe, the young one entering, unheard. His halt in surprise; the sudden overwhelming impulse to possess the gems; his stealthy advance; the seizing of the poker; the blow, delivered perhaps with the intention of merely stunning his victim. But he strikes too hard, and, horrified by what he has done, yet sees that for his own safety he must go through with the whole business. He recalls the danger of finger prints, and wipes the handles of the poker and of the drawer in the safe from which he has abstracted the diamonds. With admirable foresight he waits until the body grows cold, lest an examination of it by the policeman he intends to call might disprove his story. Then he rushes out in an agitated manner and gives the alarm.

Though this theory met a number of the facts, French was not overpleased with it. It did not explain what Gething was doing at the safe, nor did it seem to fit in with the personality of Orchard. All the same, though his instruction to his man to shadow Orchard had been given as an obvious precaution inevitable in the circumstances, he was glad that he had not overlooked it.

Another point occurred to him as he sat thinking over the affair in the leather-lined chair. If Orchard had stolen the stones, he would never have risked having them on his person when he gave the alarm. He would certainly have hidden them, and French could not see how he could have taken them out of the building to do so. A thorough search of the offices seemed therefore called for.

The inspector was tired, but, late as it was, he spent three solid hours conducting a meticulous examination of the whole premises, only ceasing when he had satisfied himself beyond possibility of doubt that no diamonds were concealed thereon. Then, believing that he had exhausted the possibilities of the scene of the crime, he felt himself free to withdraw. Dawn was appearing in the eastern sky as he drew the door after him and set off in the direction of his home.

3

Gathering the Threads

The fact that he had been out all the previous night was not, in Inspector French's eyes, any reason why he should be late at his work next day. At his usual time, therefore, he reached New Scotland Yard, and promptly engaged himself in the compilation of a preliminary report on the Hatton Garden crime. This completed, he resumed direct work on the case.

There were still several obvious inquiries to be made, inquiries which might almost be called routine, in that they followed necessarily from the nature of the crime. The first of these was an interview with the other members of the Duke & Peabody staff.

An Oxford Street bus brought him to the end of Hatton Garden, and soon he was once more mounting the staircase to the scene of his last night's investigation. He found Mr Duke standing in the outer office with Orchard and the typist and office boy.

'I was just telling these young people they might go home,' the principal explained. 'I am closing the office until after the funeral.'

'That will be appreciated by poor Mr Gething's family, sir. I think it is very kind of you and very proper too. But before this young lady and gentleman go I should like to ask them a question or two.'

'Of course. Will you take them into my office? Go in, Miss Prescott, and tell Inspector French anything he wants to know.'

'I'm afraid you won't be able to do quite so much as that, Miss Prescott,' French smiled, continuing to chat pleasantly in the hope of allaying the nervousness the girl evidently felt.

But he learned nothing from her except that Mr Duke was a very nice gentleman of whom she was somewhat in awe, and that Mr Gething had always been very kind to her and could be depended on to let her do whatever she wanted. Neither about the clerk, Orchard, nor the pupil, Harrington, was she communicative, and the office boy, Billy Newton, she dismissed as one might a noxious insect, a negligible, if necessary, evil. Mr Gething had been, as far as she could form a conclusion, in his usual health and spirits on the previous day, but she thought he had seemed worried and anxious for the past two or three weeks. As to herself, she liked the office, and got on well with her work, and was very sorry about poor Mr Gething. On the previous day she had gone straight from the office, and had remained at home with her mother during the entire evening. French, satisfied she had told him all that she knew, took her finger prints and let her go.

From Billy Newton, the precocious office boy, he learned but one new fact. Newton, it seemed, had been the last to leave the office on the previous evening, and before Mr Gething had gone he had instructed him to make up the fire in the chief's office, as he, Gething, was coming back later to do some special work. The boy had built up a good fire and had then left.

When French returned to the outer office, he found a new arrival. A tall, good-looking young man was talking to Mr Duke, and the latter introduced him as Mr Stanley Harrington, the clerk-pupil who was qualifying for a partnership. Harrington was apologising for being late, saying that on his way to the office he had met an old schoolfellow of whom he had completely lost sight, and who had asked him to accompany him to King's Cross, whence he was taking the 9.50 a.m. train for the north. The young man seemed somewhat ill at ease, and as French brought him into the inner office and began to talk to him, his nervousness became unmistakable. French was intrigued by it. From his appearance, he imagined the man would have, under ordinary circumstances, a frank, open face and a pleasant, outspoken manner. But now his look was strained and his bearing furtive. French, with his vast experience of statement makers, could not but suspect something more than the perturbation natural under the circumstances, and as his examination progressed he began to believe he was dealing with a normally straightforward man who was now attempting to evade the truth. But none of his suspicions showed in his manner, and he was courtesy itself as he asked his questions.

It seemed that Harrington was the nephew of that Mr Vanderkemp who acted as traveller for the firm. Miss Vanderkemp, the Dutchman's sister, had married Stewart Harrington, a prosperous Yorkshire stockbroker. Stanley had been well educated, and had been a year at college when a terrible blow fell on him. His father and mother, travelling on the Continent, had both been killed in a railway accident near Milan. It was then found that his father, though making plenty of money, had been living up to his income, and had made no provision for those who were to come after him. Debts absorbed nearly all the available money, and Stanley was left practically penniless. It was then that his uncle, Jan Vanderkemp, proved his affection. Out of his none too large means he paid for the boy's remaining years at Cambridge, then using his influence with Mr Duke to give him a start in the office.

But shortly after he had entered on his new duties an unexpected complication, at least for Mr Duke, had arisen. The principal's daughter, Sylvia, visiting her father in the office, had made the acquaintance of the well-mannered youth, and before Mr Duke realised what was happening the two young people had fallen violently in love, with the result that Miss Duke presently announced to her horrified father that they were engaged. In vain the poor man protested. Miss Duke was a young lady who usually had her own way, and at last her father was compelled to make a virtue of necessity. He met the situation by giving the affair his blessing, and promising to take Harrington into partnership if and when he proved himself competent. In this Harrington had succeeded, and the wedding was fixed for the following month, the partnership commencing on the same date.

French questioned the young fellow as to his movements on the previous evening. It appeared that shortly after reaching his rooms on the conclusion of his day's work in the office, he had received a telephone message from Miss Duke saying that her father had just called up to say he was detained in town for dinner, and, being alone, she wished he would go out to Hampstead and dine with her. Such an invitation from such a source was in the nature of a command to be ecstatically obeyed, and he had reached the Dukes' house before seven o'clock. But he had been somewhat disappointed as to his evening. Miss Duke was going out after dinner; she intended visiting a girls' club in Whitechapel, run by a friend of hers, a Miss Amy Lestrange. Harrington had accompanied her to the East End, but she would not allow him to go in with her to the club. He had, however, returned later and taken her home, after which he had gone straight to his rooms.

Skilful interrogation by French had obtained the above information, and now he sat turning it over in his mind. The story hung together, and, if true, there could be no doubt of Harrington's innocence. But French was puzzled by the young man's manner. He could have sworn that there was *something*. Either the tale was not true, or it was not all true, or there was more which had not been told. He determined that unless he got a strong lead elsewhere, Mr Harrington's movements on the previous night must be looked into and his statements put to the test.

But there was no need to let the man know he was suspected, and dismissing him with a few pleasant words, French joined Mr Duke in the outer office.

'Now, sir, if you are ready we shall go round to your bank about the key.'

They soon obtained the required information. The manager, who had read of the robbery in his morning paper, was interested in the matter, and went into it personally. Not only was the key there in its accustomed place, but it had never been touched since Mr Duke left it in.

'A thousand pounds in notes was also stolen,' French went on. 'Is there any chance that you have the numbers?'

'Your teller might remember the transaction,' Mr Duke broke in eagerly. 'I personally cashed a cheque for £1000 on the Tuesday, the day before the murder. I got sixteen fifties and the balance in tens. I was hoping to carry off a little deal in diamonds with a Portuguese merchant whom I expected to call on me. I put the money in my safe as I received it from you, and the merchant not turning up, I did not look at it again.'

'We can but inquire,' the manager said doubtfully. 'It is probable we have a note of the fifties, but unlikely in the case of the tens.'

But it chanced that the teller had taken the precaution to record the numbers of all the notes. These were given to French, who asked the manager to advise the Yard if any were discovered.

'That's satisfactory about the notes,' French commented when Mr Duke and he had reached the street. 'But you see what the key being there means? It means that the copy was made from the key which you carry. Someone must therefore had had it in his possession long enough to take a mould of it in wax. This, of course, is a very rapid operation; a couple of seconds would do the whole thing. A skilful man would hold the wax in the palm of his hand, "palmed" as the conjurers call it, and the key could be pressed into it in so natural a way that no unsuspecting person would be any the wiser. Now I want you to think again very carefully. If no one but Mr Gething handled the key, he *must* have taken the impression. There is no other way out. I would like you, then, to be sure that no one else ever did get his hands upon it, even for a moment. You see my point?'

'Of course I see it,' Mr Duke returned a trifle testily, 'but, unanswerable as it seems, I don't believe Gething ever did anything of the kind. It would seem the likely thing to you, Inspector, because you didn't know the man. But I've known him too long to doubt him. Someone else must have got hold of the key, but I confess I can't imagine who.'

'Someone at night, while you were asleep?'

Mr Duke shrugged his shoulders.

'I can only say, it is unlikely.'

'Well, consider the possibilities at all events. I must go back to headquarters.'

'And I to the Gethings,' Mr Duke returned. 'I hear the wife is very ill. The shock has completely broken her down. You'll let me know how things go on?'

'Certainly, sir. Immediately I have anything to report, you shall hear it.'

The police station was not far away, and soon French was bending over all that was mortal of Charles Gething. He was not concerned with the actual remains, except to take prints from the dead fingers, to compare with those found in the office. But he went through the contents of the pockets, among which he had hoped to gain some clue as to the nature of the business which had brought the dead man to the office. Unfortunately there was nothing to give the slightest indication.

The inquest had been fixed for five o'clock that evening, and French spent some time with the superintendent going over the evidence which was to be put forward by the police. Of the verdict, there could, of course, be no doubt.

Believing that by this time Mr Duke would have left the Gethings, French thought that he might himself call there. The more he could learn about the old man the better.

He hailed a taxi, and some fifteen minutes later reached Monkton Street, a narrow and rather depressing side street off the Fulham Road. The door of No. 37 was opened by a brown-haired woman of some five-and-thirty, with a pleasant and kindly, though somewhat worn expression. French took off his hat.

'Miss Gething?' he inquired.

'No, I am Mrs Gamage. But my sister is in, if you wish to see her.' She spoke with a sort of plaintive softness which French found rather attractive.

'I'm afraid I must trouble you both,' he answered with his kindly smile, as he introduced himself and stated his business.

Mrs Gamage stepped back into the narrow passage.

'Come in,' she invited. 'We are naturally anxious to help you. Besides, the police have been very kind. Nothing could have been kinder than that constable who came round last night with the news. Indeed everyone has been more than good. Mr Duke has just been round himself to inquire. A time like this shows what people are.'

'I was sorry to hear that Mrs Gething is so unwell,' French observed, and he followed his guide into the tiny front parlour. He was surprised to find the house far from comfortably furnished. Everything, indeed, bore the stamp of an almost desperate attempt to preserve decency and self-respect in the face of a grinding poverty. The threadbare carpet was worn into holes and had been neatly darned, and so had the upholstery of the two rather upright easy chairs. The leg of the third chair was broken and had been mended with nails and wire. Everything was shabby, though spotlessly clean and evidently looked after with the utmost care. Though the day was bitter, no spark of fire burned in the grate. Here, the inspector thought, was certainly a matter to be inquired into. If Gething was really as poor a man as this furniture seemed to indicate, it undoubtedly would have a bearing on the problem.

'My mother has been an invalid for many years,' Mrs Gamage answered, unconsciously supplying the explanation French wanted. 'She suffers from a diseased hip bone and will never be well. My poor father spent a small fortune on doctors and treatment for her, but I don't think any of them did her much good. Now this news has broken her down altogether. She is practically unconscious, and we fear the end at any time.'

'Allow me to express my sympathy,' French murmured, and his voice seemed to convey quite genuine sorrow. 'What you tell me makes me doubly regret having to force my unpleasant business on your notice. But I cannot help myself.'

'Of course I understand.' Mrs Gamage smiled gently. 'Ask what you want and I shall try to answer, and when you have finished with me I'll relieve Esther with mother and send her down.'

But there was not a great deal that Mrs Gamage could tell. Since her marriage some four years previously she had seen comparatively little of her father. That she idolised him was obvious, but the cares of her own establishment prevented her paying more than an occasional visit to her

36

old home. French therefore soon thanked her for her help, and asked her to send her sister down to him.

Esther Gething was evidently the younger of the two. She was like Mrs Gamage, but better looking. Indeed, she was pretty in a mild, unobstrusive way. She had the same brown eyes, but so steadfast and truthful that even French felt satisfied that she was one to be trusted. Her expression was equally kindly, but she gave the impression of greater competence than her sister. He could imagine how her parents leaned on her. A good woman, he thought, using an adjective he did not often apply to the sex, and the phrase, in its fullest significance, seemed only just adequate.

Under the inspector's skilful lead she described the somewhat humdrum existence which she and her parents had led for some years past. Her mother's illness seemed to have been the ruling factor in their lives, everything being subordinated to the sufferer's welfare, and the expenses in connection with it forming a heavy drain on the family exchequer. From Mr Duke's records, French had learned that the dead man's salary had been about £400 per annum, though quite recently it had been increased to £450, following a visit the merchant had paid to the house during a short illness of his head clerk. Mr Duke, Miss Gething said, had always acted as a considerate employer.

Asked if her father had continued in his usual health and spirits up to the end, she said no, that for some three weeks past he had seemed depressed and worried. On different occasions she had tried to find out the cause, but he had not enlightened her except to say that he had been having some trouble at the office. Once, however, he dropped a phrase which set her thinking, though she was unable to discover his meaning, and he had refused to explain. He had asked her did she believe that a man could ever be right in doing evil that good might come, and when she had answered that she could not tell, he had sighed and said, 'Pray God you may never be called on to decide.'

On the evening of his death it had been arranged that he would sit with Mrs Gething, in order to allow his daughter to attend a social connected with the choir of the church to which she belonged. But that evening he came home more worried and upset than she had ever seen him, and he had told her with many expressions of regret that some unexpected work which had just come in would require his presence that evening in the office, and that unless she was able to get someone else to look after her mother, she would have to give up her social. He had been too nervous and ill at ease to make a good meal, and had gone off about eight o'clock, saying he did not know at what hour he would be back. That was the last time she had seen him alive, and she had heard nothing of him until the policeman had come with his terrible news about half-past eleven.

Miss Gething was clearly at one with her sister in her admiration and affection for her father, and French recognised that she was as mystified as to his death as he was himself. Seeing that he could learn no more, he presently took his leave, with renewed expressions of sympathy for her trouble.

When he reached the Yard he found that enlarged photographs of the various finger prints he had discovered were ready, and he sat down with some eagerness to compare the impressions with those on his cards. He spent some time counting and measuring lines and whorls, and at last reached the following conclusions. All the finger marks on the safe, both inside and out, belonged either to Mr Duke or to Mr Gething, the majority being the latter's; the mark on the handle of the coal shovel was Mr Gething's, and the remaining prints were those of various members of the office staff. His hopes of help from this source were therefore dashed.

With a sigh he looked at his watch. There would be time before the inquest to make some inquiries as to the truth of Orchard's statement of his movements on the previous evening. Half an hour later he had found the man with whom the clerk had dined in Ilford, and he fully substantiated the other's story. Orchard was therefore definitely eliminated from the inquiry.

The proceedings before the Coroner were practically formal. Orchard, Mr Duke, and Constable Alcorn told their stories, and with very little further examination were dismissed. French and the local superintendent watched the case on behalf of the police, but did not interfere, and the next of kin of the deceased were not legally represented. After half an hour, the Coroner summed up, and the jury without retiring brought in the obvious verdict of wilful murder against some person or persons unknown.

That evening, when French had dined and had settled himself before the fire in his sitting room with a pipe between his lips and his notebook on the table at his elbow, he set himself to take mental stock of his position and get a clear grasp of his new problem.

In the first place, it was obvious that this Charles Gething had been murdered for the sake of the diamonds in Mr Duke's safe. It was certain from the position of the wound that it could not have been accidental, nor could it by any chance have been self-inflicted. Moreover, a planned robbery was indicated by the cutting of the duplicate key. But the stones were not on old Gething's body. It therefore followed that someone else had taken them, though whether Gething had abstracted them from the safe in the first instance was not clear.

So far French had no trouble in marshalling his facts, but when he attempted to go further he found himself in difficulties.

There was first of all Gething's poverty. Though his salary was not unreasonable for his position, the drain of his wife's illness had kept him continually struggling to make ends meet. French let his imagination dwell on the wearing nature of such a struggle. To obtain relief a man would risk a good deal. Then there was his knowledge of the wealth which lay within his reach, provided only that he made a spirited effort to obtain it. Had the man fallen before the temptation?

That he had had something on his mind for two or three weeks before his death was obvious, and it was equally clear that this was something secret. When Mr Duke inquired as to the cause of the trouble, Gething had mentioned family matters and his wife's health, but when his daughter had asked the same question he had said it was due to business worries. The old man had therefore carried his efforts at concealment to direct lying to one or other.

It seemed evident also that this worry or trouble had become intensified on the evening of his death. He had told his daughter that special business required his presence at the office. But Mr Duke knew of no such business, nor was any record of it obtainable.

But all these mysterious contradictions fell into line and

became comprehensible if some two or three weeks back Gething had decided to rob the safe, and his special agitation on the evening of his death was accounted for if that were the date he had selected to make the attempt.

On the other hand, several considerations did not support such a view. The first was the man's known character. He had worked for the firm for over twenty years, and after all that experience of him Mr Duke absolutely refused to believe in his guilt. His daughters also evidently had the warmest feelings towards him, and from what French had seen of the latter he felt that would have been impossible had Gething been a man of bad or weak character. Such other evidence as French had been able to obtain tended in the same direction.

Next, there was the open way in which Gething returned to the office. Had he intended to burgle the safe, would he not have kept the fact of his visit a secret? Yet he told the office boy he was returning when instructing him to keep up the fire in the inner office, and he also mentioned it to his daughter when discussing her proposed choir meeting.

Further, there was this matter of the fire in the private office. If Gething was going to rob the safe, what was the fire for? It was not merely that he had instructed the office boy to keep it up. He had himself afterwards put coal on, as was evidenced by his finger marks on the handle of the shovel. The robbing of the safe would have been a matter of minutes only. Did the episode of the fire not look as if Gething really was employed at some exceptional work, as he had stated to his daughter?

On the whole, French thought, the evidence for Gething's guilt was stronger than that against it, and he began to form a tentative theory somewhat as follows: That Gething, finding the conditions of his home life onerous beyond further endurance, and realising the unusually valuable deposit in the safe, had decided to help himself, probably to a quite small portion, knowing that the loss would fall, not on Mr Duke, but on the insurance company; that he had obtained an impression of the key from which he had had a duplicate made; that he had invented the business in the office as a safeguard should he be accidentally found there during the evening; that he *had* been found there, probably accidentally, by someone who, seeing the possibilities opening out in front of him, had been swept off his feet by the sudden temptation and had killed the old man and made off with the swag.

This theory seemed to meet at least most of the facts. French was not pleased with it, but it was the best he could produce, and he decided to adopt it as a working hypothesis. At the same time he kept an open mind, recognising that the discovery of some fresh fact might put a different complexion on the whole affair.

Next morning he put some obvious investigations in train. By astute indirect inquiries, he satisfied himself that neither Mr Gething nor any other worker in the Duke & Peabody office had the technical skill to have cut the key, and he put a man on to try and trace the professional who had done it. He issued a description of the stolen diamonds to the British and Dutch police, as well as to certain dealers from whom he hoped to obtain information of attempted sales. He saw that a general advice was sent to the banks as to the missing notes, and he searched, unsuccessfully, for any person who might have known of the treasure and who was unable satisfactorily to account for his movements on the night of the murder.

But as the days slipped by without bringing any news, French grew seriously uneasy and redoubled his efforts. He suspected everyone he could think of, including the typist, the office boy, and even Mr Duke himself, but still without result. The typist proved she was at home all the evening, Billy Newton was undoubtedly at a Boy Scouts' Rally, while guarded inquiries at the principal's club and home proved that his statement as to how he had passed his evening was correct in every particular. Stanley Harrington's movements he had already investigated, and though the young man's alibi could not be absolutely established he could find nothing to incriminate him.

Baffled in every direction, French began to lose heart, while his superiors asked more and more insistent and unpleasant questions.

4

Missing

About ten o'clock on the morning of the tenth day after the murder of Charles Gething, Inspector French sat in his room at New Scotland Yard wondering for the thousandth time if there was no clue in the affair which he had overlooked, no line of research which he had omitted to follow up.

He had seldom found himself up against so baffling a problem. Though from the nature of the case, as he told himself with exasperation, a solution should be easily reached, yet he could find nothing to go on. The clues he had obtained looked promising enough, but—they led nowhere. None of the stolen notes had reached the bank, nor had any of the diamonds come on the market; no one in whom he was interested had become suddenly rich, and all his possible suspects were able more or less satisfactorily to account for their time on the fatal evening.

French had just taken up his pen to write out a statement of what he had done, in the hope of discovering some omission, when his telephone rang. Absent-mindedly he took up the receiver.

'I want to speak to Inspector French,' he heard in a familiar voice. 'Say that Mr Duke of Duke & Peabody is on the 'phone.'

There was a suggestion of eagerness in the voice that instantly roused the inspector's interest.

'Inspector French speaking,' he answered promptly. 'Good-morning, Mr Duke. I hope you have some news for me?'

'I have some news,' the distant voice returned, 'but I don't know whether it bears on our quest. I have just had a letter from Schoofs, you remember, the manager of our Amsterdam branch, and from what he tells me it looks as if Vanderkemp had disappeared.'

'Disappeared?' French echoed. 'How? Since when?'

'I don't know exactly. I am having the files looked up to try and settle dates. It appears that he has been absent from the Amsterdam office for several days, and Schoofs thought he was over here. But we've not seen him. I don't understand the matter. Perhaps if you're not too busy you could come round and I'll show you Schoofs' letter.'

'I'll come at once.'

Half an hour later French was mounting the stairs of the Hatton Garden office. With a face wreathed in smiles, Billy Newton ushered him into the private office. Mr Duke seemed nervous and a trifle excited as he shook hands.

'The more I think over this affair, Inspector, the less I like it,' he began immediately. 'I do hope there is nothing wrong. I will tell you all I know, but before I show you Schoofs' letter I had better explain how it came to be written.'

He looked up interrogatively, then as French nodded, continued:

'As I think I already mentioned, Vanderkemp is my travelling agent. He attends sales and auctions in all the countries of Europe. He has carried through some very large deals for me, and I have every confidence both in his business acumen and in his integrity. I told you also that amongst others he had purchased and brought to London the greater part of the missing stones.'

'You told me that, sir.'

'Of late years, when Vanderkemp is not on the road, he has been working in the Amsterdam branch. Some three or four days before poor Gething's death he had returned from a tour through southern Germany where he had been buying jewels from some of the former nobility who had fallen on evil days since the revolution. Three days ago, on last Monday to be exact, I learnt that a very famous collection of jewels was shortly to be sold in Florence, and I wrote that evening to Schoofs telling him to send Vanderkemp to Italy to inspect and value the stones with a view to my purchasing some of them. This is Schoofs' reply which I received this morning. You see what he says: "I note your instructions re sending Vanderkemp to Florence, but he had not yet returned here from London, where I presumed he was staying with your knowledge and by your orders. When he arrives I shall send him on at once." What do you make of that, Inspector?'

'Vanderkemp did not come to London, then?'

'Not to my knowledge. He certainly did not come here.'

'I should like to know why Mr Schoofs thought he had, and also the date he was supposed to start.'

'We can learn that by wiring to Schoofs.'

Inspector French remained silent for a few moments. It seemed to him now that he had neglected this Dutch office.

It was at least another line of inquiry, and once which might easily bear fruitful results.

The staff there, Mr Duke had stated, consisted of four persons, the manager, a typist, and an office boy. There was also at times this traveller, Vanderkemp, the same Vanderkemp who was uncle to Stanley Harrington. It was more than likely that these persons knew of the collection of diamonds. The manager would certainly be in Mr Duke's confidence on the matter. Vanderkemp had actually purchased and brought to London a large number of the stones, which he had seen put into the safe, though, of course, it did not follow that he knew that they had been retained there. Besides, in the same way as in the London office, leakage of the information to outside acquaintances might easily occur. Inquiries in Amsterdam seemed to French to be indicated.

'I think I shouldn't wire,' he said at last. 'There is no use in starting scares unless we're sure something is wrong. Probably the thing is capable of the most ordinary explanation. But I'll tell you what I'll do. I'll slip across to Amsterdam and make a few inquiries. If anything is wrong I'll get to know.'

'Good. I'd be very pleased if you did that. I'll write Schoofs and tell him to help you in every way that he can.'

French shook his head.

'I shouldn't do that either, if you don't mind,' he declared. 'I'll just go over and have a look round. There is no need to mention it to anyone.'

Mr Duke demurred, pointing out that a note from him would enlist Mr Schoofs' help. But French maintained his ground, and the merchant agreed to carry out his wishes.

French crossed by the night service from Harwich, and

at half-past eight o'clock next day emerged from the Central Station into the delightful, old world capital. Though bent on sordid enough business, he could not but feel the quaint charm of the city as he drove to the Bible Hotel in the Damrak, and again as, after breakfast, he sauntered out to reconnoitre.

Messrs Duke & Peabody's office was close by in the Singelgracht, a semi-business street with a tree-lined canal down its centre, and crouching at one corner, a heavily-gabled church with a queer little wooden tower not unlike a monstrous candle extinguisher. French had opposed Mr Duke's offer to write to the manager introducing him, as he did not wish any of the Amsterdam staff to be aware beforehand of his visit. He had on many occasions obtained a vital hint from the start or sudden look of apprehension which an unexpected question had produced, and he was anxious not to neglect the possibility of a similar suggestion in this case. He therefore pushed open the swing door, and without giving a name, asked for the manager.

Mr Schoofs was a dapper little man with a pompous manner and an evident sense of his own value. He spoke excellent English, and greeted his caller politely as he motioned him to a chair. French lost no time in coming to the point.

'I have called, sir,' he began in a harsh tone, not at all in accord with his usual 'Soapy Joe' character, while he transfixed the other with a cold and inimical stare, 'with reference to the murder of Mr Gething. I am Inspector French of the Criminal Investigation Department of New Scotland Yard.'

But his little plot did not come off. Mr Schoofs merely raised his eyebrows, and with a slight shrug of his shoulders contrived to produce a subtle suggestion that he was surprised not with the matter, but with the manner, of his visitor's announcement.

'Ah yes!' he murmured easily. 'A sad business truly! And I understand there is no trace of the murderer and thief? It must be disquieting to Londoners to have deeds of violence committed with such impunity in their great city.'

French, realising that he had lost the first move, changed his tone.

'It is true, sir, that we have as yet made no arrest, but we are not without hope of doing so shortly. It was to gain some further information that I came over to see you.'

'I am quite at your disposal.'

'I needn't ask you if you can give me any directly helpful news, because in that case you would have already volunteered it. But it may be that you can throw light upon some side issue, of which you may not have realised the importance.'

'Such as?'

'Such, for example, as the names of persons who were aware of the existence of the diamonds in Mr Duke's safe. That is one of many lines.'

'Yes? And others?'

'Suppose we take that one first. Can you, as a matter of fact, tell me if the matter was known of over here?'

'I knew of it, if that is what you mean,' Mr Schoofs answered in a slightly dry tone. 'Mr Duke told me of his proposed deal, and asked me to look out for stones for him. Mr Vanderkemp also knew of it, as he bought a lot of the stones and took them to London. But I do not think anyone else knew.'

'What about your clerk and office boy?'

Mr Schoofs shook his head.

'It is impossible that either could have heard of it.'

French, though he had begun inauspiciously, continued the interrogation with his usual suavity. He asked several other questions, but without either learning anything of interest, or surprising Schoofs into showing embarrassment or suspicious symptoms. Then he turned to the real object of his visit.

'Now about your traveller, Mr Schoofs. What kind of man is Mr Vanderkemp?'

Under the genial and deferent manner which French was now exhibiting, Schoofs had thawed, and he really seemed anxious to give all the help he could. Vanderkemp, it appeared, was a considerable asset to the firm, though owing to his age—he was just over sixty—he was not able to do so much as formerly. Personally he was not very attractive; he drank a little too much, he gambled, and there were discreditable though unsubstantiated tales of his private life. Moreover, he was of morose temper and somewhat short manners, except when actually negotiating a deal, when he could be suave and polished enough. But he had been known to perform kind actions, for instance, he had been exceedingly good to his nephew Harrington. Neither Schoofs nor anyone else in the concern particularly liked him, but he had one invaluable gift, a profound knowledge of precious stones and an accuracy in valuing them which was almost uncanny. He had done well for the firm, and Mr Duke was glad to overlook his shortcomings in order to retain his services.

'I should like to have a chat with him. Is he in at present?'

'No, he went to London nearly a fortnight ago. He has not returned yet. But I'm expecting him every day, as I have instructions from Mr Duke to send him to Florence.'

French looked interested.

'He went to London?' he repeated. 'But I can assure you he never arrived there, or at least never reached Mr Duke's office. I have asked Mr Duke on several occasions about his staff, and he distinctly told me that he had not seen this Mr Vanderkemp since two or three weeks before the murder.'

'But that's most extraordinary,' Schoofs exclaimed. 'He certainly left here to go to London on—what day was it?—it was the very day poor Gething was murdered. He left by the day service via Rotterdam and Queenborough. At least, he was to do so, for I only saw him on the previous evening.'

'Well, he never arrived. Was it on business he was going?'

'Yes, Mr Duke wrote for him.'

'Mr Duke wrote for him?' French echoed, at last genuinely surprised. 'What? To cross that day?'

'To see him in the office on the following morning. I can show you the letter.' He touched a bell and gave the necessary instructions. 'There it is,' he continued, handing over the paper which the clerk brought in.

It was an octavo sheet of memorandum paper with the firm's name printed on the top, and bore the following typewritten letter:

'20th November.

'H. A. SCHOOFS, ESQ.

'I should be obliged if you would please ask Mr Vanderkemp to come over and see me here at 10.00 a.m. on Wednesday, 26th inst., as I wish him to undertake negotiations for a fresh purchase. He may have to go to Stockholm at short notice.'

The note was signed 'R. A. Duke,' with the attendant flourish with which French had grown familiar.

He sat staring at the sheet of paper, trying to fit this new discovery into the scheme of things. But it seemed to him an insoluble puzzle. Was Mr Duke not really the innocent, kindly old gentleman he had fancied, but rather a member, if not the author, of some deep-seated conspiracy? If he had written this note, why had he not mentioned the fact when Vanderkemp was being discussed? Why had he shown surprise when he received Schoofs' letter saying that the traveller had crossed to London? What was at the bottom of the whole affair?

An idea struck him, and he examined the letter more closely.

'Are you sure this is really Mr Duke's signature?' he asked slowly.

Mr Schoofs looked at him curiously.

'Why, yes,' he answered. 'At least, it never occurred to me to doubt it.'

'You might let me see some of his other letters.'

In a few seconds half a dozen were produced, and French began whistling below his breath as he sat comparing the signatures, using a lens which he took from his pocket. After he had examined each systematically, he laid them down on the table and sat back in his chair.

'That was stupid of me,' he announced. 'I should have learnt all I wanted without asking for these other letters. That signature is forged. See here, look at it for yourself.'

He passed the lens to Schoofs, who in his turn examined the name.

'You see, the lines of that writing are not smooth; they are a mass of tiny shakes and quivers. That means that they have not been written quickly and boldly; they have been slowly drawn or traced over pencil. Compare one of these other notes and you will see that while at a distance the signatures look identical, in reality they are quite different. No, Mr Duke never wrote that. I am afraid Mr Vanderkemp has been the victim of some trick.'

Schoofs was visibly excited. He hung on the other's words and nodded emphatically at his conclusions. Then he swore comprehensively in Dutch. 'Good heavens, Inspector!' he cried. 'You see the significance of all that?'

French glanced at him keenly.

'In what way?' he demanded.

'Why, here we have a murder and a robbery, and then we have this, occurring at the very same time . . . Well, does it not look suggestive?'

'You mean the two things are connected?'

'Well, what do you think?' Mr Schoofs replied with some impatience.

'It certainly does look like it,' French admitted slowly. Already his active brain was building up a theory, but he wanted to get the other's views. 'You are suggesting, I take it, that Vanderkemp may have been concerned in the crime?'

Schoofs shook his head decidedly.

'I am suggesting nothing of the kind,' he retorted. 'That's not my job. The thing merely struck me as peculiar.'

'No, no,' French answered smoothly, 'I have not expressed myself clearly. Neither of us are making any accusation. We are simply consulting together in a private, and, I hope, a friendly way, each anxious only to find out

53

the truth. Any suggestion may be helpful. If I make the suggestion that Mr Vanderkemp is the guilty man in order to enable us to discuss the possibility, it does not follow that either of us believe it to be true, still less that I should act on it.'

'I am aware of that, but I don't make any such suggestion.'

'Then I do,' French declared, 'simply as a basis for discussion. Let us suppose then, purely for argument's sake, that Mr Vanderkemp decides to make some of the firm's wealth his own. He is present when the stones are being put into the safe, and in some way when Mr Duke's back is turned, he takes an impression of the key. He crosses to London, either finds Gething in the office or is interrupted by him, murders the old man, takes the diamonds, and clears out. What do you think of that?'

'What about the letter?'

'Well, that surely fits in? Mr Vanderkemp must leave this office in some way which won't arouse your suspicion or cause you to ask questions of the London office. What better way than by forging the letter?'

Mr Schoofs swore for the second time. 'If he has done that,' he cried hotly, 'let him hang! I'll do everything I can, Inspector, to help you to find out, and that not only on general grounds, but for old Gething's sake, for whom I had a sincere regard.'

'I thought you would feel that way, sir. Now to return to details. I suppose you haven't the envelope that letter came in?'

'Never saw it,' Mr Schoofs replied. 'The clerk who opened it would destroy it.'

'Better have the clerk in, and we'll ask the question.'

Mr Schoofs made a sudden gesture.

'By jove!' he cried. 'It was Vanderkemp himself. He acts as head clerk when he is here.'

'Then we don't get any evidence there. Either the letter came through the post, in which case he destroyed the envelope in the usual way, or else he brought the letter to the office and slipped it in among the others.'

French picked up the letter again. Experience had taught him that typescript could be extremely characteristic, and he wondered if this in question could be made to yield up any of its secrets.

It certainly had peculiarities. The lens revealed a dent in the curve of the n, where the type had evidently struck something hard, and the tail of the g was slightly defective.

French next examined the genuine letters, and was interested to find their type showed the same irregularities. It was therefore certain that the forged letter had been typed in the London office.

He sat thinking deeply, unconsciously whistling his little tune through his closed teeth. There was another peculiarity about the forged note. The letters were a trifle indented, showing that the typewriter keys had been struck with rather more than the usual force. He turned the sheet over, and he saw that so much was this the case that the stops were punched almost through. Picking up the genuine letters, he looked for the same peculiarity, but the touch in these cases was much lighter and even the full stop barely showed through. This seemed to justify a further deduction—that the writer of the forged note was unskilled, probably an amateur, while that of the others was an expert. French felt he could safely assume that the forged note had been typed by some unauthorised person, using the machine in the London office.

But, so far as he could see, these deductions threw no light on the guilt or innocence of Vanderkemp. The letter might have come from some other person in London, or Vanderkemp might have typed it himself during one of his visits to the metropolis. More data was wanted before a conclusion could be reached.

Though from what he had seen of Schoofs, the inspector thought it unlikely that he was mixed up in what he was beginning to believe was a far-reaching conspiracy, he did not mention his discoveries to him, but continued trying to pump him for further information about the missing traveller. Vanderkemp, it seemed, was a tall man, or would have been if he held himself erect, but he had stooped shoulders and a slouching way of walking which detracted from his height. He was inclining to stoutness, and had dark hair and a sallow complexion. His chin was clean shaven, but he wore a heavy dark moustache. Glasses covered his shortsighted eyes.

French obtained some samples of his handwriting, but no photograph of him was available. In fact, Mr Schoofs did not seem able to supply any further information, nor did an interrogation of the typist and office boy, both of whom spoke a little English, produce any better results.

'Where did Mr Vanderkemp live?' French asked, when he thought he had exhausted the resources of the office.

It appeared that the traveller was unmarried, and Mr Schoofs did not know if he had any living relatives other than Harrington. He boarded with Mevrouw Bondix, in the Kinkerstraat, and thither the two men betook themselves, French begging the other's company in case he should be needed as interpreter. Mevrouw Bondix was a garrulous little old lady who had but little English, and upon whom Schoofs' questions acted as a push button does on an electric bell. She overwhelmed them with a flood of conversation of which French could understand not one word, and from which even the manager was hard put to it to extract the meaning. But the gist of the matter was that Vanderkemp had left her house at half-past eight on the night before the murder, with the expressed intention of taking the 9.00 train for London. Since then she had neither seen him nor heard from him.

'But,' French exclaimed, 'I thought you told me he had crossed by the daylight service on the day of the murder?'

'He said he would,' Schoofs answered with a somewhat puzzled air. 'He said so most distinctly. I remember it particularly because he pointed out that Mr Duke would probably ask him, after the interview, to start by the afternoon Continental train on his new journey, and he preferred to travel during the previous day so as to insure a good night's sleep in London. He said that in answer to a suggestion of mine that he would be in time enough if he went over on the night before his interview.'

'What time do these trains get in to London?'

'I don't know, but we can find out at the office.'

'I'd like to go to the Central Station next, if you don't mind coming along,' French declared, 'so we could look them up there. But before I go I want you to tell me if Mr Vanderkemp figures in any of these?' He pointed to a number of photographic groups which adorned the chimneypiece and walls.

It happened that the missing traveller appeared in one of the groups, and both Mr Schoofs and Mevrouw Bondix bore testimony to the excellence of the portrait.

'Then I'll take it,' French announced, as he slipped the card into his pocket.

The two men next went to the Central Station and looked up the trains. They found that the day service did not reach Victoria until 10.5 p.m. The significance of this was not lost upon French. Orchard stated he had reached the office in Hatton Garden at 10.15, and that it could not have been later was established by the evidence of Constable Alcorn. The body at that time was cold, so that the crime must have taken place some considerable time earlier. A man, therefore, who had crossed by the daylight service from Amsterdam could not possibly have had time to commit the murder. Had Vanderkemp lied deliberately to Schoofs when he told him he was using that daylight service? If so, was it in order to establish an alibi? Had he a secret appointment with Gething for an earlier hour on the fatal evening, and had he crossed the night before with the object of keeping it? French felt these were questions which required satisfactory answers, and he made a mental note not to rest until he had found them.

With his new friend's aid he began to interrogate the staff of the Central Station, in the hope of ascertaining whether or not the missing man had actually left by the train in question. But of this he could learn nothing. None of the employees appeared to know Vanderkemp's appearance, nor after that lapse of time could anyone recall having seen a passenger of his description.

That day and the next French spent in the charming old city, trying to learn what he could of the missing man's life and habits. He came across a number of persons who were acquainted with the traveller, but no one with whom he had been really intimate. None of these people could give him much information, nor did any of them seem to care whether or no Vanderkemp should ever be heard of again. From all he heard, French concluded that Vanderkemp's character was such as might be expected in the guilty man, but there was but little evidence of motive, and none at all of guilt.

He returned to London by the night service, and having ascertained that the steamer he crossed by was the same that had run on the date of Vanderkemp's assumed journey; he made exhaustive inquiries as to the latter from the staff on board, unfortunately with negative results.

Next day his efforts were equally fruitless. He spent most of it in discussing the situation with Mr Duke, and trying to make a list of the persons who could have had access to the typewriter, but nowhere could he get a gleam of light. The authorship of the letter remained as inscrutable a mystery as the murder of Gething.

Having circulated a description of Vanderkemp containing a copy of the photograph, French went home that night a worried and disconsolate man. But though he did not know it, further news was even at the moment on the way to him.

5

French Takes a Journey

Inspector French had not quite finished supper that evening when his telephone bell rang. He was wanted back at the Yard immediately. Some information about the case had come in.

Cheerful and hopeful, he set off and in a few minutes was once more seated in his office. There a note was awaiting him, which had been delivered by hand a short time previously. He eagerly tore it open, and read:

'City of London Banking Co.,
'Reading Branch, 11th December.

'SIR,—With reference to your inquiry re certain bank-notes, I beg to inform you that Bank of England ten-pound notes numbers A/V 173258 W and N/L 386427 P were paid into this Branch just before closing time today. Our teller fortunately noticed the numbers almost immediately, and he thinks, though is not positive, they were paid in by a Colonel FitzGeorge of this town, whose address is Oaklands, Windsor Road.

'I am sending this note by one of our clerks, who is going to town this afternoon.

> 'Yours faithfully,
> 'HERBERT HINCKSTON,
> '*Manager.*'

French received this information with a feeling of delight which speedily changed to misgiving. At first sight what could be more valuable to his quest than the discovery of some of the stolen notes? And yet when he considered that these had been passed in by an army man residing in Reading, the doubt immediately insinuated itself that here also might be a promising clue which would lead to nothing. Obviously, if this Colonel FitzGeorge had indeed paid in the notes, it did not at all follow that he was the thief, or even that he had obtained them from the thief. Before they reached the bank in Reading they might have passed through a dozen hands.

But, be this as it might, French's procedure was at least clear. A visit to Colonel FitzGeorge was undoubtedly his next step.

He picked up a Bradshaw. Yes, there would be time to go that night. A train left Paddington at 8.10 which would bring him to Reading before 9.00.

He ran down through the great building, and hailing a taxi, was driven to the terminus. He caught the train with a minute to spare, and shortly before nine he was in conversation with a taxi driver outside the Great Western Station in Reading.

'Yessir,' the man assured him, 'I know the 'ouse. Ten minutes drive out along the Windsor Road.'

The night was dark, and French could not take minute

stock of his surroundings, but he presently learnt from the sounds of his car's wheels that Oaklands was reached from the road by an appreciable drive coated with fine gravel, and the bulk of the house, looming large above him as he stood before the porch, indicated an owner well endowed with this world's goods. The impression was confirmed when in answer to his inquiry a venerable butler conducted him through a hall of imposing dimensions to a luxurious sitting-room. There the man left him, returning in a few minutes to say his master was in the library and would see Mr French.

Colonel FitzGeorge was a tall, white-haired man, with an erect carriage and excessively courteous manners. He bowed as French entered, and indicated a deep leather-lined arm-chair drawn up opposite his own before the blazing fire of pine logs.

'A chilly evening, Inspector,' he said pleasantly. 'Won't you sit down?'

French thanked him, and after apologising for the hour of his call, went on:

'My visit, sir, is in connection with certain bank notes which I am trying to trace. Some, time ago there was a robbery in the City in which a number of Bank of England notes were stolen. The owner fortunately was able to find out their numbers from his bank. When the matter was reported to us, we naturally asked the banks generally to keep a lookout for them. Nothing was heard of them until today, but this afternoon, just before closing time, two of them were paid into the Reading Branch of the City of London Bank. The teller, though not certain, believed that you had paid them in. You can see, therefore, the object of my call. It is to ask you if you can possibly help me to trace the thief by telling me where you received the notes. There were two, both for ten pounds, and the numbers were A/V 173258 W and N/L 386427 P.'

Colonel FitzGeorge looked interested.

'I certainly called at the bank this afternoon and lodged some money,' he answered. 'It was mostly in the form of dividend warrants, but there were a few notes. Now where did I get those? I should be able to tell you off-hand, but I'm not at all sure that I can. Let me think, please.'

For some moments silence reigned in the luxuriously-furnished room. French, always suspicious, surreptitiously watched his new acquaintance, but he had to admit that he could discern none of the customary signs of guilt. But he reminded himself that you never knew, and determined that unless he was completely satisfied by the coming reply, he would make an investigation into Colonel FitzGeorge's movements on the night of the murder.

'I *believe*,' said the Colonel suddenly, 'I know where I got those notes. I am not by any means certain, but I think I can tell you. Unless I am very much mistaken, it was from the manager of the Hotel Beau-Sejour in Chamonix.'

'Chamonix?' French repeated in surprise. This was by no means what he had expected to hear.

'Yes. I have been for the last six weeks in Switzerland and Savoy, and two days ago, on last Tuesday afternoon, to be exact, I left Chamonix. I caught the night train from Geneva, was in Paris next morning, and reached Charing Cross yesterday, Wednesday, afternoon. Today I went through my correspondence, and after lunch took in my dividends and some spare cash to lodge in the bank.'

'And the two ten-pound notes, sir?'

'The two ten-pound notes, as I say, I believe I received at

the Chamonix hotel. I found I had to return home sooner than I had intended, and as I was leaving the country I wanted to change back all but a small amount of my foreign money. It was convenient to do it at the hotel, and besides, you can't always be sure of getting enough change at Calais or on the boat. I asked the manager of the Beau-Sejour to give me English money for my francs, and he did so at once.'

'Why do you think these particular notes were handed over by him?'

'He paid me in ten-pound notes only. He gave me five of them—I changed fifty pounds' worth of francs altogether. It is true that I had some other English notes, and there were some at home here, but so far as I can remember, there were no tens among them—only fives and Treasury notes.'

With this, French had to be content. Though he asked many other questions he could learn nothing further to help him. But on the pretext that the notes might have been received at some other place, he obtained a note of the Colonel's itinerary while abroad. According to this, it appeared that on the night of Charles Gething's murder, the traveller had slept in the Bellevue Hotel at Kandersteg, prior to walking over the Gemmi Pass on the following day. This French noted as a point capable of being checked, should checking become desirable.

He had kept his taxi, and after a little trouble he found the address of the teller of the City of London Bank, and paid him a late call. But from him he learnt nothing new, except that the man seemed much more certain that Colonel FitzGeorge had really handed in the notes than the letter of his manager had led French to believe. He admitted that he was relying on memory alone, but said he had checked over his money just before the Colonel's visit, and he was positive the stolen notes were not then there.

Inspector French was in a distinctly pessimistic frame of mind as he sat in the corner of a smoking compartment of the last train from Reading to town, and next morning as he put the facts he had learnt before his chief, he was but slightly more sanguine. Two of the stolen notes had been discovered; that was really all that could be stated with certainty. That Colonel FitzGeorge had paid them into the bank was by no means sure, still less that he really had received them from a hotel manager in Chamonix. But even assuming the Colonel's recollection was accurate, it did not greatly help. It was unlikely that the manager could state from whom he in his turn had received those particular notes. Indeed, even were he able to do so, and by some miracle were French able to trace the giver, in all probability the latter also would turn out to be innocent, and the goal would be no nearer. The whole episode seemed to French, as he expressed it to his chief, a wash-out.

But the great man took a different view. He replied in the same words which French himself had used in another connection.

'You never know,' he declared. 'You miss this chance and you're down and out, so far as I can see. But if you go over and see the manager you don't know what you mayn't light on. If the thief stayed in that hotel, he must have registered. You might get something from that. Mind you, I agree that it's a thin chance, but a thin chance is better than none.'

'Then you think, sir, I ought to go to Chamonix?'

'Yes. It won't cost a great deal, and you may get something. Have you ever been there?'

'No, sir.'

'Well, you'll enjoy it. I'd give a good deal to take your place.'

'Oh, I shall enjoy it right enough, sir. But I'm not hopeful of the result.'

The chief gave a dry but kindly smile.

'French, you're not usually such a confounded pessimist. Get along, and hope for the best.'

French had looked up the positions of Chamonix and Kandersteg on the previous evening, and he had seen that by taking a comparatively slight detour it would be possible for him to visit the latter place on his way to the former. He decided, therefore, that he might as well set his mind at rest on the question of Colonel FitzGeorge's whereabouts on the night of the murder. He did not suspect the man, but it would be better to be sure.

But to do this, some further information was necessary. He must, if possible, obtain a photograph of the Colonel and a sample of his signature. It was not yet ten o'clock, and he thought it would be possible to get these and catch the afternoon train for the Continent.

By half-past eleven he was back in Reading. There he handed a taxi man a note which he had written during the journey, telling him to take it to Colonel FitzGeorge's, and to bring the answer back to him at the station. The note, he admitted to himself, was clumsy, but it was the best he could think of at the moment. In it he regretted troubling his new acquaintance so soon again, but he had most stupidly lost the memorandum he had taken of the name of the hotel in Chamonix at which the stolen notes were obtained, and would Colonel FitzGeorge be so kind as to let him have it again.

The note despatched, he turned to the second portion of his business. With his usual detailed observation, he had seen on the chimneypiece of the Colonel's library a photograph of the gentleman himself, and noted that it was the work of Messrs Gale & Hardwood, of Reading. An inquiry from the taxi driver had given him the address of the studio, and he now set off there in the hope of obtaining a copy.

In this he was unexpectedly successful. Messrs Gale & Hardwood had a print in one of their showcases, which in five minutes was transferred to the inspector's pocket, and he was back at the station before his taxi man turned up with the reply to his note.

In this also his luck was in. The man had found Colonel FitzGeorge just about to start for Reading. He handed French back his own note, across which was written in a firm, masculine hand: 'Beau-Sejour. B. L. FitzGeorge.'

Stowing the photograph and the note away in his pocket-book, French returned to town, and the same afternoon at 2.00 he left Victoria on his second trip to the Continent. He had been to France and Germany on a previous occasion, but never to Switzerland, and he was looking forward to getting a glimpse of some of the wonderful mountain scenery of that country.

He disembarked at Calais, passed through the customs, and took his seat in the Lötschberg-Simplon express with true British disapproval of all that he saw. But later the excellent dinner served while the train ran through the pleasant country between Abbeville and Amiens brought him to a more acquiescent mood, and over a good cigar and a cup of such coffee as he had seldom before tasted, he complacently watched day fade into night. About half-past six o'clock next morning he followed the example of his countless British predecessors, and climbed down on the long platform at Bale to drink his morning coffee. Then again on through scenery of growing interest, past Bern to Spiez, where he found the Lake of Thun really had the incredible colouring he had so often scoffed at, but secretly admired, in the Swiss posters he had seen in London. Finally, after crawling round the loops on the side of the Frütigen valley, the train stopped at Kandesteg, and bag in hand he descended to the platform. A porter with the name 'Bellevue' on his cap caught his eye, and a short drive brought him to the hotel.

After déjeuner he sought the manager, a suave functionary whose English accent was a trifle suggestive of New York. No, it was not the matter of his room. French regretted that on that occasion he could not remain overnight in the hotel—he hoped he would soon be free to return and to do so—but for the moment he was on business. He would take the manager into his confidence. He was a detective . . . in short, could the manager help him? That was the gentleman's photograph.

'But, of course! Yes,' the manager answered promptly on glancing at the portrait. 'It is the Colonel FitzGeorge, the English gentleman from London. He was here, let me see, two—three weeks ago. I will look up the register.'

Further inquiries elicted the information that the Colonel had stayed for three nights at the hotel, and had left early on the day after the murder with the intention of walking to Leukerbad over the Gemmi Pass.

His business at Kandersteg completed, French conscientiously looked up the next train to Chamonix. But he found he could not get through that day, and being tired from his journey, he decided to remain where he was until the next morning. He spent the afternoon lost in admiration of the charming valley, and that night slept to the murmur of a mountain stream which flowed beneath his window.

Next morning he took the southbound train, and having passed through the nine miles of the Loetschberg tunnel, he gazed with veritable awe into the dreary waste of the Loetschenthal and the great gulf of the Rhone Valley, marvelling as the train raced along the side of the stupendous cliff. He changed at Brigue, passed down the Rhone Valley, and changing again at Martigny, spent another four hours on what a fellow traveller with a nasal drawl described as 'the most elegant ride he'd struck,' through Vallorcine and Argentiere to Chamonix. On crossing the divide, the panorama which suddenly burst on his view of the vast mass of the Mont Blanc massif hanging in the sky above the valley, literally took away his breath, and he swore that his next holidays would certainly be spent in the overwhelming scenery of these tremendous mountains.

At Chamonix history tended to repeat itself. He reached his hotel, dined excellently, and then sought the manager. M. Marcel, like his *confrère* in Kandersteg, was courtesy personified, and listened carefully to French's statement. But when he realised the nature of the problem he was called upon to solve, he could but shake his head and shrug his shoulders.

'Alas, monsieur,' he wailed, 'but with the best will in the world, how can I? I change so many English notes . . . I recall giving those ten-pound notes to a gentleman from England, because it is comparatively seldom that I am asked to change French money into English, but I am constantly receiving English notes. No, I am sorry, but I could not tell you where those came from.'

Though French had scarcely hoped for any other reply, he was nevertheless disappointed. He showed Colonel FitzGeorge's photograph to the manager, who instantly recognised it as that of the Englishman for whom he had exchanged the notes. But he could give no further help.

This clue having petered out, French determined to call for the register and make a search therein in the hope of recognising the handwriting of some entry. But before he did so he asked about Vanderkemp. Had anyone of that name been a recent visitor?

The manager could not recall the name, but he had a thorough search made of the records. This also drew blank. French then handed him the photograph of Vanderkemp which he had obtained in Amsterdam, asking if he had ever seen the original.

With that the luck turned. M. Marcel beamed. 'But yes, monsieur,' he exclaimed, with a succession of nods, 'your friend was here for several days. He left about a fortnight ago. M. Harrison from one of your great Midland towns, is it not? He told me which, but I have forgotten.'

'That's the man,' cried French heartily, delighted beyond words at this new development. 'I have been following him round. Might I see his entry in the register?'

Again the records were brought into requisition, and as he looked French felt wholly triumphant. On comparing the 'J. Harrison, Huddersfield, England,' to which the manager pointed, with the samples of Vanderkemp's handwriting which he had obtained from Mr Schoofs, he saw that unquestionably they were written by the same hand.

So Vanderkemp was his man! After this there could be no further doubt of his guilt.

For a moment he remained silent, considering what this discovery meant. It was now evident that Vanderkemp, under the alias Harrison, had arrived at the Beau-Sejour Hotel about midday on the second day after the crime, and after staying a week, had departed for an unknown destination. But the matter did not end there. With a sudden, theatrical gesture the manager indicated that he had more to say.

'You have recalled something to my mind, monsieur,' he announced. 'That M. Harrison asked me to change notes for him. In fact, I remember the whole thing clearly. His bill came to between four and five hundred francs, and he paid with an English ten-pound note. With the exchange as it is at present, he should have had about 300 francs change. But I now remember he asked me at the same time to change a second ten-pound note. I did so, and gave him about 1000 francs. So it is possible, I do not say certain, but it is possible . . . He shrugged his shoulders and threw out his hands, as if to indicate that Fate and not he was responsible for the possibility, and looked inquiringly at his visitor.

Inspector French was exultant. This news seemed to him to complete his case. When in Amsterdam he had found cause to suspect Vanderkemp of the crime, and now here was corroborative evidence of the most convincing character. Rapidly he ran over in his mind the salient points of the case against the traveller.

Vanderkemp possessed all the special knowledge necessary to commit the crime. He knew of the collection of diamonds, and was familiar with the London office and the characters and habits of the workers there. As he was by no means well off, this knowledge would have consti- tuted a very real temptation. So much on general grounds.

Then as to details. A forged letter calling the man to London, or some similar device, would be a necessary feature of the case. But this letter existed; moreover Vanderkemp had access to the machine on which it had been typed. While telling Mr Schoofs that he was crossing by a certain train, which arrived in town after the murder had been committed, he had in reality gone by an earlier service, which would have brought him there in time to carry out the crime. Such evidence, though circumstantial, was pretty strong. But when was added to it the facts that Vanderkemp had disappeared without explanation from his firm, had arrived in Chamonix on the second day after the murder, had registered under a false name and address, and most important of all, had paid out two of the notes stolen from Mr Duke's safe, the case became overwhelming. It was impossible not to believe in his guilt; in fact, seldom had the inspector known so clear a case. When he had found and arrested Vanderkemp his work would be done.

But just in the flush of victory, his luck again turned. The man had left the Beau-Sejour a week previously, and the manager had no idea what direction he had taken. In vain French asked questions and made suggestions, hoping to say something which might recall the information to the other's mind. But the manager readily gave his help in interviewing the whole of the staff who had in any way come in contact with the wanted man. And here, thanks again to his persistent thoroughness, he obtained just the hint that was needed.

He had worked through the whole staff without result,

and he was about to give up, when it occurred to him that none of those to whom he had spoken had admitted having brought down Vanderkemp's luggage from his room on the day of his departure. French then asked directly who had done this, and further inquiries revealed the fact that in the absence of the usual man, an under porter, usually employed about the kitchen, had been called upon. This man stated he had noticed the label on Vanderkemp's suitcase. It was to a hotel in Barcelona. He could not recall the name of the hotel, but he was sure of the city.

When French had thanked the manager, distributed backsheesh among the staff, and with the help of the head porter worked out his journey from Chamonix to Barcelona, he felt his work in Savoy was done. He went exultantly to bed, and next morning left by an early train on his way to Spain.

6

The Hotel in Barcelona

To a comparative stay-at-home like Inspector French, who considered a run to Plymouth or Newcastle a long journey, the trailing of Jan Vanderkemp across south-west France opened up a conception of the size of the globe whereon he moved and had his being, which left him slightly awestruck. The journey from Savoy to Spain seemed endless, the distances incredible, the expanse of country between himself and home illimitable. Hour after hour he sat in the train, while elms and oaks gave place to cypresses and olives, apples to vines, and corn to maize, and it was not until daylight had gone on the evening of the second day that the train rolled into the Estacion de Francia in Barcelona.

The porter at the Beau-Sejour at Chamonix had written down the names of two or three hotels at which he thought English would be spoken, and passing out of the station, French showed the paper to a taxi driver. The man at first ogled it distrustfully, then with a smile of comprehension he emitted a rapid flood of some unknown language, opened the taxi door, bowed his fare in, and rapidly cranking his engine, set off into the night. French was conscious of being whirled down a great avenue wider than any he had yet seen, brilliantly lighted, and with rows of palms down the centre; they turned through a vast square with what looked like a commemorative column in the middle, then up a slightly narrower, tree-lined boulevard, where presently the vehicle swung into the curb and French found himself at his destination—the Hôtel d'Orient.

To his extreme relief, the head porter spoke English. He got him to settle with the taxi man, and soon he began to forget the fatigues of the journey with the help of a luxurious bath and dinner.

He decided that he had done enough for one day, and presently, soothed by a cigar, he went out into the great street in front of the hotel, with its rows of trees and brilliant arc lamps. He did not know then that this gently-sloping boulevard was one of the famous streets of the world—the Rambla, known as is Piccadilly in London, the Champs Élysées in Paris, or Fifth Avenue in New York. For an hour he roamed, then, tired out, he returned to the Orient, and a few minutes later was sunk in dreamless slumber.

Early next morning he was seated with the manager, who also spoke English. But neither the manager nor any of his staff could help him, and French recognised that so far as the Orient was concerned he had drawn blank. He therefore set to work on the other hotels, taking the larger first, the Colon, in the Plaza de Cataluna, the Cuatro Naciones, and such like. Then he went on to the smaller establishments, and at the fourth he paused suddenly, thrilled by an unexpected sight.

The hotel was in a side street off the Paseo de Colon, the great boulevard through which he had been driven on the previous evening. The entrance door led into a kind of lounge in which were seated half a dozen people, evidently waiting for déjeuner. With one exception these were obviously Spaniards, but that exception, French felt he could swear, was the original of the photograph.

In spite of such a meeting being what he was hoping for, the inspector was taken aback. But his hesitation was momentary. Passing immediately on to the little office at the back of the lounge, he said in English:

'Can I have lunch, please? Will it soon be ready?'

A dark-eyed, dark-haired girl came forward, smiling but shaking her head regretfully, and murmuring what was evidently that she couldn't understand.

'You don't speak English, miss?' the detective went on, speaking loudly and very clearly. 'I want to know can I have lunch, and if it will soon be ready?'

As the girl still shook her head, French turned back into the lounge.

'Excuse me,' he addressed the company generally, 'but might I ask if any of you gentlemen speak English? I can't make this young lady understand.'

The little ruse succeeded. The man resembling Vanderkemp rose.

'I speak English,' he answered. 'What is it you want?'

'Lunch,' French returned, 'and to know if it will soon be ready.'

'I can answer that for you,' the other declared, after he had explained the situation to the girl. 'Lunch will be ready in exactly five minutes, and visitors are usually welcome.'

'Thank you.' French spoke in a leisurely, conversational

way. 'I am staying at the Orient, where one or two of them speak English, but business brought me to this part of the town, and I did not want to go all that way back to lunch. A confounded nuisance this language business! It makes you feel pretty helpless when you want to talk to people.'

'That's true,' the stranger admitted. 'In most of the larger hotels they speak French and English, but at practically none of the smaller. In this one, for example, one waiter has a few words of French only. No English or Italian or German. Some of the staff don't even speak Spanish.'

French was interested in spite of the larger question which was occupying his mind.

'Not Spanish?' he repeated. 'How do you mean? What do they speak?'

'Catalan. This is Catalonia, you know, and both the race and the language is different from the rest of Spain. They are more go-ahead and enterprising than the people farther south.'

'That sounds a bit like Ireland,' French remarked. 'I've been both in Belfast and in the south, and the same thing seems to hold good. Though Dublin is a fine city, and no mistake.'

They continued discussing peoples and languages and the northerly concentration of energy to be found in most countries, until the hands of the clock pointed to noon and lunch time. Then French caught what he had been angling for. The stranger asked him to share his table.

The inspector continued to make himself agreeable, and after they had finished invited the other to have coffee and a cigar with him in a deserted corner of the lounge. Then thinking his companion was by this time off his guard, he introduced a new subject after a lull in the conversation.

'It's strange the different businesses people are engaged on,' he remarked ruminatively, as he poured himself out a second cup of coffee. 'Now, I wouldn't mind betting a ten-pound note you wouldn't guess what I am, and what my business here is.'

The other laughed.

'I confess I was wondering,' he admitted. 'I am afraid I should lose my money. I won't guess.'

'Well, I'll tell you, though our business is not a thing we speak of as a rule. I am a detective inspector from Scotland Yard.'

As he spoke French watched the other's face. If this were the man of whom he was in search, he could swear he would make him exhibit some emotion.

But so far he did not succeed. His new acquaintance merely laughed again.

'Then I should have lost. I admit I never thought of that.'

French continued to observe, and he went on with more seriousness in his manner.

'Yes, and I'm on rather important business, too. Man wanted for murder and robbery in the City. A bad affair enough. He murdered the confidential clerk of a diamond merchant in Hatton Garden and rifled the safe and got off with I don't know how many thousand pounds' worth of stuff.'

At the commencement of French's reply the stranger had listened with but little more than a conventional interest, but at the mention of a diamond merchant in Hatton Garden he figuratively sat up and began to take notice.

'Hatton Garden?' he repeated. 'That's an extraordinary coincidence. Why, I belong to a firm of diamond merchants in Hatton Garden. I know them all. Who was the man?'

Inspector French was puzzled. Either Vanderkemp—for

there could no longer be any doubt of his identity—was innocent, or he was an almost incredibly good actor. Anxious to observe the man further, he fenced a little in his reply.

'Is it possible you haven't heard?' he asked in apparent surprise. 'How long is it since you have heard from home?'

'Haven't had a line of any kind since I left, and that's nearly three weeks ago; on the night of the 25th of last month to be exact.'

'The 25th! Well, that's a coincidence, too. That's the very night poor old Mr Gething was killed.'

Vanderkemp stiffened suddenly and his hands closed on the arms of his chair.

'What?' he cried. 'Not Charles Gething of Messrs Duke & Peabody?'

French, now keenly observing him without any attempt at concealment, nodded.

'That's the man. You knew him then?'

'Of course I knew him. Why, it's my own firm. Good God, to think of poor old Gething! And you say the safe was rifled? You don't tell me Mr Duke's collection of stones is gone?'

'All of it, and money as well. The murderer made a clean sweep.'

Vanderkemp whistled and then swore.

'Tell me about it.'

French was more than ever puzzled. The traveller's manner, his evident emotion, his questions—all seemed those of an innocent man. He felt doubts arising in his mind; possibly there might be an explanation . . . He did not at once reply, as he turned over in his mind how he could best surprise the other into an admission of the truth.

But Vanderkemp also was evidently thinking, and suddenly an expression of deeper concern showed on his face. He made as if to speak, then hesitated and a wary look appeared in his eyes. He cleared his throat, then in a changed voice asked, 'At what time did it happen?'

French leaned forward swiftly and fixed his eyes on his companion as he said in a low, tense tone, 'That's what I want to ask you, Mr Vanderkemp.'

The man started. He did not answer, and the wary look in his eyes changed into definite anxiety, which deepened as the moments passed. At last he spoke.

'It had just dawned on me from what you said, Inspector, that our meeting here was not such a coincidence as I at first imagined. I see that you suspect me of the crime. What has happened I don't know, what you have against me I don't know either, but I can tell at once that I am not only absolutely innocent, but until you told me just now I was ignorant that a crime had been committed. I will tell you my whole story and answer any questions you may like to ask, whether you believe me or not.'

French nodded. Certainly, if guilty, this man was a consummate actor. There was at least the chance that he might be innocent, and he answered accordingly.

'I don't accuse you of anything, Mr Vanderkemp. But there are certain suspicious circumstances which require an explanation. You may be able to account for all of them—I hope you will. At the same time it is fair to warn you that, failing an explanation, your arrest is not impossible, and in that case anything that you may say now may be used against you in evidence.'

Vanderkemp was by this time extremely ill at ease. His face had paled and had already taken on a somewhat drawn and haggard expression. For a while he remained silent, buried in thought, then with a sudden gesture as of throwing further caution to the winds, he began to speak.

'I'll tell you what I know, Inspector,' he said earnestly. 'Whether, if you are going to arrest me, I am wise or foolish, I don't know. But I can at least assure you that it is the literal truth.'

He looked at the inspector, who nodded approval.

'Of course I can't advise you, Mr Vanderkemp,' he remarked, 'but all the same I believe you are doing the wise thing.'

'I am in a difficulty,' Vanderkemp went on, 'as I don't know how much of the circumstances you are familiar with. It would therefore be better if you would ask me questions.'

'I shall do so, but first I should like your own statement. I am aware of your name and position in the firm. Also that Mr Schoofs received a letter on the 21st of last month, asking him to send you to London to undertake an important commission in Sweden. Also that you left your lodgings in the Kinkerstraat at 8.30 on the evening of the 24th. I have since learned certain other facts as to your subsequent movements, which I need not mention at the moment. What I want you now to do is to let me have a detailed account of your experiences from the moment of your leaving your lodgings until the present time.'

'I will do so.' Vanderkemp spoke eagerly, as if now anxious to get through with the matter. 'But there is one thing which comes earlier in point of time which I must mention. You have probably heard of it from Mr Duke, but I shall tell you anyway. I mean about my further instructions as to my London visit—the private instructions. You have seen a copy of them?'

French, always cautious, was not giving away information. He wondered to what the other was referring, but merely said, 'Assume I have not, Mr Vanderkemp. It is obvious that I must check your statement by the information in my possession.'

'Well, then, though you probably know it already, I may tell you I received additional instructions about my visit. Mr Duke wrote me a private letter, addressed to my lodgings, in which he told me—but I have it here, and you can see it for yourself.'

He took an envelope from his pocketbook and passed it across. It contained a note almost identical in appearance with the forged one which Mr Schoofs had received. It was typewritten on a sheet of the firm's cheaper memorandum paper, with the same kind of type and the same coloured ribbon. Examination with the lens showed the same defects in the n and the g, the signature was obviously forged, and the back of the sheet was marked from a heavy touch. Evidently both letters had been written by the same person, and on the Hatton Garden machine. The note read:

'DEAR VANDERKEMP,—Further to my note to Mr Schoofs re your call here on Wednesday morning, 26th inst., the business on which I wish to see you has turned out to be more urgent that I at first believed, and I shall therefore have to ask you to advance the hour of your interview, and also to leave London for Paris—not Stockholm—immediately after it. I shall return to the office after dinner on Tuesday evening,

25th inst., and shall be glad if you will call there at 8.30 p.m., when I shall give you your instructions. This will enable you to catch the 9.30 p.m. for Paris, via Southampton and Havre.

'I wish to impress on you that as the business in question is exceptionally confidential, you will oblige my by keeping your change of plans to yourself.

'Yours truly,

'R. A. DUKE.'

Inspector French was keenly interested, but he recognised with exasperation how inconclusive the letter was as evidence. Either it had been sent to Vanderkemp as he stated, in which case he might be innocent, or the man had written it himself, in which case he certainly was guilty. It was true that in this instance an envelope was forthcoming which bore a London E.C. postmark and the correct date, but here again there's no proof that this was really the covering in which the letter had come. These points passed through the inspector's mind, but he banished them as matters to be thought out later, and turned once more to his companion.

'I shall keep this, if you don't mind,' he declared. 'Please proceed.'

'I carried out the instructions in the letter,' Vanderkemp resumed. 'The change of hours necessitated my leaving Amsterdam by the night train on the 24th, and I spent the following day at my hotel in London, and in doing a matinee. At 8.30, with my luggage, I reached Hatton Garden. I found the outer office was in darkness, but a light shone out of the doorway of the inner office. Mr Gething was there alone. He told me to come in and shut

83

the door, and I did so, and sat down in the clients' arm-chair. Mr Gething was seated at Mr Duke's desk, which was open.'

'Was the safe open?'

'No, nor was it opened while I was there. Mr Gething told me that Mr Duke had intended to be present to give me my instructions in person, but at the last moment he had been prevented coming down, and that he had asked him, Mr Gething, to do it instead. It seemed that Mr Duke had got information from a confidential agent at Constantinople that a member of the old Russian aristoc-racy had escaped with his family jewels from the clutches of the Bolsheviks, and that he now wished to dispose of the whole collection for what it would bring. He was at one time Duke Sergius of one of the Ural provinces—I have the name in my book upstairs—but was now passing himself off as a Pole under the name Francisko Loth. The collection was one of extraordinary excellence, and Mr Duke believed it could be purchased for a third, or even less, of its real value. He had approached the duke through the agent, and had offered to deal. The trouble, however, was that the Soviet Government had learned of the duke's escape, and were displaying immense energy in the hope of recapturing him. Their agents were scouring the whole of Europe, and Loth was in mortal terror, for discovery meant certain death. Mr Gething told me straight also, that should I succeed in purchasing, my life would not be worth a tinker's curse until I had handed over the stuff. He said that, recognising this, Mr Duke considered that my commission should be substantially increased, and he asked me was I willing to take on the job.'

'And you agreed?'

'Well, what do you think? Of course I agreed. I asked for further details, and he let me have them. For both my own safety and Loth's, I was to take extraordinary precautions. My name is pretty well known in dealers' circles over Europe, and therefore would be known to the Soviet emissaries, so I was to take another. I was to become John Harrison, of Huddersfield, a tinplate manufacturer. I was not to write to the office direct, but to send my reports, if any were necessary, to Mr Herbert Lyons, a friend of Mr Duke's, who lived not far from him at Hampstead. If I had to write, I was to be most careful to phrase my letter so that were I suspected and my correspondence tampered with, it would not give the affair away. Instructions to me would be sent to Harrison and written on plain notepaper, and would be worded in a similar careful way. Mr Gething gave me a code by which I could wire the amount agreed on, when the money would be sent me by special messenger; that is, if we could come to terms.'

Vanderkemp paused and glanced at the inspector, but the latter not speaking, he continued:

'Loth was hidden in Constantinople, but was trying to come west. He was not sure whether he could do so best by land or sea. If he could get out of Turkey by land, he would work his way up the Danube to Austria and Switzerland, and would stop eventually at the Beau-Sejour Hotel in Chamonix. If that proved impossible, he would try to leave by sea, and would travel by one of the Navigazione Generale Italiana boats to Genoa, and thence to Barcelona, where he would put up at the Gomez Hotel, that is, this one. He had let Mr Duke know through his Constantinople friend that if he didn't turn up at Chamonix by the 4th, it would mean either that the Bolsheviks had caught him, or that he was making for Barcelona. My instructions, therefore, were to go to Chamonix, put up at the Beau-Sejour, and look out until the 4th for a tall, white-complexioned, dark-haired man named Francisko Loth. If by that time he had not turned up, I was to move on here. I was to wait here for a fortnight, at the end of which time, if I had still heard nothing of him, I was to go on to Constantinople, look up Mr Duke's agent, and try for news of Loth's fate.'

'And you carried out the instructions?'

'Yes. I went to Chamonix, and stayed there for a week. Seeing no one who could possibly be the man, I came on here, and have been waiting here ever since. Tomorrow I proposed to leave for Constantinople.'

French threw away the butt of his cigar and selected another.

'Such a trip could not be accomplished without money,' he said slowly. 'How were you equipped in that way?'

'Mr Gething handed me a hundred pounds in ten-pound notes. I changed two in Chamonix and I have the remaining eight in my pocket.'

'You might let me see them.'

Vanderkemp readily complied, and the inspector found, as he expected, that the eight notes were among those stolen from the safe. He resumed his interrogation.

'You say you reached the office in Hatton Garden about half-past eight?'

'Yes, and left about nine. My business occupied only half an hour.'

'And you saw no one except Mr Gething?'

'No one.'

French, having offered his possible future prisoner

another cigar, sat silent, thinking deeply. He had no doubt that the story of the escaped Russian was a fabrication from beginning to end. Besides being an unlikely tale in itself, it broke down on the point of its authorship. Vanderkemp's statement was that Gething had been told the story by Mr Duke, and that Mr Duke would have been present to tell it to him, Vanderkemp, in person, were he not prevented by some unexpected cause. This also was an obvious fabrication, but the reason of its insertion into the tale was clear enough. Without it, the story would have no authority. The use of Mr Duke's name was an essential part of any such scheme, just as the forging of Mr Duke's signature had been necessary for the letters of instruction to Schoofs and Vanderkemp.

But though French felt sure enough of his ground so far, on trying to take a further step he was held up by the same difficulty with which he had been faced in considering the forged letters. Was Gething guilty, and had he invented this elaborate plan to throw suspicion on to Vanderkemp, or was Vanderkemp the criminal, and the story his scheme for accounting for his actions since the murder? That was a real difficulty, and French sat wondering if there was no test he could apply, no way in which he could reach certainty, no trap which the victim would be unable to avoid?

For some time he could think of none, but presently an idea occurred to him which he thought might be worth while following up. Some information might be gained through the typewriting of the two forged letters. Could Vanderkemp type, and if so, was his work done with a light or heavy touch? He turned to his companion.

'I wish you would write me a short statement of your

movements in London on the night of the crime, stating the times at which you arrived at and left the various places you visited. I should prefer it typed—that is, if you can type. Can you?'

Vanderkemp smiled wanly.

'I think so,' he answered. 'I type and write shorthand in four languages. But I've no machine here.'

'Borrow one from the office,' French suggested, as he expressed his admiration of the other's prowess.

It took a personal visit to the office, but Vanderkemp, anxious to defer to the inspector's whims, managed to overcome the scruples of the languorous, dark-eyed beauty who reigned therein, and returned triumphant with the machine. Ten minutes later French had his time-table.

Instantly he saw that Vanderkemp typed as an expert—with a light, sure touch that produced a perfect impression, but did not dint the paper. It was a point in the man's favour. By no means conclusive, it was still by no means negligible.

Inspector French was puzzled. His experience told him that in this world the ordinary, natural and obvious thing happened. A man who secretly visited the scene of a crime at about the hour at which the crime was known to be committed, and who then left the country on a mysterious and improbable mission, the reality of which was denied by its alleged author, a man, further, who had in his pocket banknotes stolen from the scene of the crime, such a man in ordinary, prosaic, everyday life was the criminal. Such, French thought, was common sense, and common sense, he considered, was right ninety-nine times out of a hundred.

But there was always the hundredth chance. Improbabilities and coincidences *did* occasionally happen. He would have given a good deal at that moment to know if this case was the exception that proves the rule.

He saw clearly that his second explanation, if somewhat more far-fetched, was still quite possibly true. It certainly might be that Vanderkemp had been duped, that he had been sent on this wild goose chase by the murderer, with the object of drawing on himself just that suspicion which he had attracted, and thus allowing the real scent to cool. A good many of the facts tended in that direction, the forged letters, the keeping of the alleged deal from Schoofs, the fact that no Russian nobleman had turned up at either of the rendezvous named, the travelling under a false name, the warning against communications with the office, and last, but not least, Vanderkemp's manner during the interview, all these undoubtedly supported the view that the traveller had been used to lay a gigantic false clue.

If so, it was a fiendish trap to set for the unfortunate dupe. French thought he could see how it was intended to pan out. Vanderkemp, while on these mysterious journeys—certainly when he reached Mr Duke's agent in Constantinople—would learn of the murder, and he would at once see how he had been victimised. The more he learned of the details, the more he would realise how completely he was in the toils. He would recognise that if he went home and told his story he would not have a dog's chance of clearing himself, and he would turn his apparent flight into a real one, and so permanently fasten upon himself a tacit admission of guilt. It was an ingenious scheme, and if it really were the explanation of these mysterious happenings, it gave an indication of the character and mentality of the man who had devised it.

French was by no means decided as to the truth of the

matter, but on the whole he thought that though he undoubtedly had evidence to justify him in applying for the arrest and extradition of the traveller, he would prefer to avoid this step if possible. If the man tried to give him the slip, the local police would get him in no time. Accordingly he turned once more to Vanderkemp.

'Mr Vanderkemp,' he began, 'I am strongly inclined to believe your story. But as a man of the world you will readily see that it must be more completely examined before it can be fully accepted. Now the question is, Are you willing to come back with me to London and give me your assistance towards finding out the truth? I can make you no promise that you will not be arrested on reaching British ground, but I can promise you that you will be fairly dealt with and get every chance and assistance to prove your innocence.'

Vanderkemp did not hesitate in his reply.

'I will go,' he said promptly. 'I am aware that you can have me arrested here, if you want to, by applying to the Spanish authorities, so I have no choice. But I think I should go in any case. I have done nothing contrary to the law, and I have done nothing to be ashamed of. I cannot now rest until my innocence is admitted.'

French nodded gravely.

'Once again, sir, I think you are doing the wise thing. Let us go tonight by the Paris express. In the meantime come with me to the post office and help me to send a wire to the Yard.'

Two mornings later they reached London. Mr Duke was naturally amazed at his subordinate's story, and on hearing the evidence, gave it as his opinion that Vanderkemp was the dupe of some person or persons unknown. What was more to the point, Chief Inspector Mitchell, French's immediate superior, took the same view, and Vanderkemp, therefore, was not arrested, though he was shadowed night and day. French undertook an investigation into his life and circumstances, which showed that these had been painted in somewhat darker colours than appeared justifiable, but which revealed no evidence about the crime. Furthermore, none of the jewels could be traced to him, nor any of the stolen notes other than those he had spoken of.

Once more the days began to slip past without bringing to light any fresh fact, and as time passed French grew more worried and despondent, and his superior officers more querulous. And then something occurred to turn his attention to a completely different side of the case, and send him off with fresh hope and energy on a new clue.

7

Concerning a Wedding

When Inspector French felt really up against it in the conduct of a case, it was his invariable habit to recount the circumstances in the fullest detail to his wife. She, poor woman, haled from the mysterious household employments in which her soul delighted, would resignedly fetch her sewing and sit placidly in the corner of the Chesterfield while her lord and master strode up and down the room stating his premises, arguing therefrom with ruthless logic and not a few gestures, sifting his facts, grouping them, restating them . . . Sometimes she interjected a remark, sometimes she didn't; usually she warned him to be careful not to knock over the small table beside the piano, and invariably she wished he would walk on the less worn parts of the carpet. But she listened to what he said, and occasionally expressed an opinion, or, as he called it, 'took a notion.' And more than once it had happened that these notions had thrown quite a new light on the point at issue, a light which in at least two cases had indicated the line of research which had eventually cleared up the mystery.

On the second evening after his return from Spain, the inspector was regaling her with a by no means brief *résumé* of the Hatton Garden crime. She had listened more carefully than usual, and presently he found she had taken a notion.

'I don't believe that poor old man was out to do anything wrong,' she declared. 'It's a shame for you to try to take away his character now he's dead.'

French, stopping his pacing of the room, faced round.

'But I'm not trying to take away his character, Emily dear,' he protested, nettled by this unexpected attack in the rear. 'I'm only saying that he's the only person we know of who could have got an impression of the key. If so, it surely follows he was out to rob the safe.'

'Well, I believe you're wrong,' the lady affirmed, continuing with a logic as relentless as his own, 'because if he was out to rob the safe, he wasn't the sort of man that you described, and if he was the sort of man that you described, why, then, he wasn't out to rob the safe. That's what I think about it.'

French was a trifle staggered. The difficulty he had recognised from the beginning, but he had not considered it serious. Now, put to him in the downright, uncompromising language in which his wife usually clothed her thoughts, it suddenly seemed to him overwhelming. What she said was true. There was here a discrepancy. If Gething really bore the character he was given by all who had known him, he was not a thief.

He ceased his restless movement, and sitting down at the table, he opened his notebook and began to look up what he had actually learned about the dead man. And the more he did so, the more he came to believe that his wife was right. Unless all this cloud of witnesses were surprisingly mistaken, Gething was innocent.

His mind reverted to the other horn of the dilemma. If Gething were innocent, who took the impression of the key? It was not obtained from that in the bank, therefore it was copied from that in Mr Duke's possession. Who had done it?

No one at the office, at least not unless Mr Duke was greatly mistaken. And he did not believe, the principal could be mistaken on such a point. The breaking through of his regular custom in a matter of such importance would almost certainly be noted and remembered. No, French felt that he might rely on Mr Duke's statement so far.

But with regard to his assertion that no one in his house could have tampered with the key, the inspector saw that he was on more shaky ground. In the nature of the case, the diamond merchant would be less alert in dealing with the members of his own household than with his business acquaintances. Believing he was surrounded by friends, he would subconsciously be more ready to asume his precautions adequate. Was Mr Duke's belief that no one would touch the key not the real basis of his statement that no one had done so?

It seemed to French that here was a possibility that he had overlooked, and it was in the nature of the man that the moment he reached such a conclusion he began to consider a way of retrieving his error.

At first he thought of taking Mr Duke into his confidence and asking him to assist him in some subterfuge by which he could enter the house. But presently he saw that it would be better if the old gentleman knew nothing of his plan, lest he might inadvertently warn a possible criminal.

For the same reason—that Mr Duke might get to know of it—he decided he would be wiser not to undertake the business in person. But he knew the man for the job—a certain detective-sergeant named Patrick Nolan. This man was something of a Don Juan in his way, and had a positive genius for extracting confidences from the fair sex. If he could scrape acquaintance with the maids of the establishment, it would not be long before he knew all they had to tell.

Accordingly next morning he sent for Sergeant Nolan and explained his idea, and Nolan, who, where his superiors were concerned, was a man of few words, said, 'Yes, sir,' and withdrew.

The following day he returned with his first report. It seemed that, changing into the garb of a better-class mechanic and taking a small kit of tools with him, he had called at Mr Duke's in the character of an electrician who had been sent to overhaul the light fittings.

Miss Duke happened to be out, and the rather pretty housemaid who opened the door, charmed with the newcomer's manner, admitted him without hesitation. He had gone all over the house, paying particular attention to Mr Duke's bedroom. In the middle of the day he had asked and been granted leave to heat his can of soup at the kitchen fire, and to such purpose had he used the opportunities thus gained that before he left he had prevailed on the pretty housemaid to go with him to supper and the pictures on her next evening out. 'Once I get a drop of spirits into her I'll get all she knows,' he concluded, 'though I doubt if it'll be much.'

'That's all right so far as it goes,' French admitted, 'but what have you actually found out?'

'Well, there's first of all the family. It's a small one; there's only the father and the daughter, Miss Sylvia. The mother's alive, but she has been in a lunatic asylum for years, quite incurable, they said. Miss Sylvia is a nice-looking young lady and well liked, by what Rachael says—that's the housemaid. Then there's the servants; this Rachael, and another girl, Annie, and Sarah, the cook, and there's a shover they call Manley. I didn't see him, but the girls seem all right—not the kind that would be after the keys of jewel safes anyway.'

'What's the house like?'

'It's a middling big house, and the furniture'll have been good when it was bought, though it's getting a trifle shabby now. Mr Duke's bedroom is at the end of the left wing, and Miss Duke's is in the front of the house, so anybody could go through Mr Duke's room without being seen. Anybody could get a mould of that key if he left it in his room, say, while he was having his bath.'

'Did you find out any possibilities; any tradesmen in, like yourself, or anyone staying in the house?'

The sergeant shook his head.

'I did not, sir,' he admitted. 'I thought I had maybe done enough for one day. I didn't want to be after starting them wondering about me. But I'll get that out of Rachael tomorrow night.'

'Better see that Manley, the chauffeur—or no, I shall see him myself. You stick to what you're at. Anything else?'

'No, sir, I think not. What the girls talked most about was Miss Sylvia's engagement. It seems she was engaged to some friend in the City and they were to have been married at the end of the month, and now they've had some bust up and the whole thing's postponed, if not off altogether.'

'That so? They didn't tell you the reason?'

'They did not, sir. But I can likely find out from Rachael if you want to know.'

'I don't suppose I do,' French returned, 'but you might as well find out what you can—on spec. You know who the young man is?'

'No, sir. They didn't say.'

French looked up his notebook.

'I seem to know a deal more about it than you do,' he grumbled. 'He is a clerk in Mr Duke's office, name of Harrington—Stanley Harrington. I interviewed him with the others in the office on the day after the murder, and he told me about the engagement. It seemed to be going strong then. When did they postpone it?'

'They didn't say that either, sir.'

'Well, find that out, too. That'll do for the present.'

That evening French, in the guise of an out-of-work mechanic, took up his stand near Mr Duke's house, and presently saw the old gentleman arrive back from business in his car. An hour later he followed the chauffeur from the garage to a house in a small street off Esther Road. There French hung about for perhaps another hour, when he had the satisfaction of seeing the quarry emerge again, pass down the street, and disappear into the Rose and Thistle bar. This was just what the inspector had hoped for, and after a few minutes he followed him in.

To scrape acquaintance was easy enough. French, as a motor mechanic out of work, was provided with a ready introduction to any chauffeur, and over a couple of glasses of beer he learned first of the chances of jobs in the district, and secondly, by skilful pumping, many details of his new companion's work and of the Duke menage. But he heard nothing that seemed in the slightest degree suspicious or interesting. The man himself, moreover, seemed of an honest, harmless type, and much too stupid to be concerned personally in enterprises with keys of safes.

For a day the inquiry hung fire, and then Sergeant Nolan brought in a report which turned the inspector's thoughts into still another channel. Nolan had, it appeared, taken the pretty housemaid, Rachael, first to the pictures and then to supper at a popular restaurant. The girl had what the sergeant called 'the gift of the gab,' and it had only been necessary for him judiciously to supply an occasional topic, to have a continuous stream of more or less relevant information poured into his receptive ears.

First he had tried to ascertain whether anyone had recently had access to Mr Duke's dressing-room during the night or early morning, and he soon learned that, prior to his own visit, no tradesmen had been in the house for many months. Moreover, the only visitor who had stayed overnight for a considerable time was Mr Stanley Harrington, Miss Duke's *fiancé*. The two young people had been feverishly engaged in rehearsals for a play given by a local amateur dramatic society, and for the four nights previous to the entertainment Miss Duke had refused to allow her swain to waste time in going to and from his rooms, and had insisted on his putting up with them. This occurred about a month before the murder, and Harrington had slept in a room just opposite to Mr Duke's. It was obvious, therefore, that had the key been left in the dressing-room at any time, Harrington could easily have taken the necessary impression.

Nolan then went on to tell what he had found out as to the postponed wedding, and in this French felt he had food for thought. It appeared that the trouble, whatever it was, had come suddenly, and it had taken place on the day after the murder. On the evening of the crime, so Rachael had said, Mr Duke was not at home for dinner, but Mr Harrington had turned up. He and Miss Duke had dined together, and then everything was *couleur de rose*. They had gone out together after dinner. About ten, Miss Duke had returned and had gone straight to bed. Almost certainly, therefore, she had not known that night of Mr Duke's call to the office. Next morning she had breakfasted with her father, and had presumably then learned of the tragedy. But not five minutes after breakfast began she had slipped out of the room and had made a telephone call, and directly Mr Duke had left the house she had put on her things and followed him. She had been absent for about twenty minutes, and had then gone direct to her bedroom, where, on the plea of a headache, she had spent the day. When Rachael had had occasion to enter, she found her lying down, but the girl had heard her hour after hour pacing the room, and in her opinion, her mistress's indisposition was more mental than physical. About four o'clock that afternoon Mr Harrington had called. Miss Duke saw him in her own sitting-room, and during the interview some terrible quarrel must have taken place. Mr Harrington left in about half an hour, and Rachael, who had opened the door to let him out, said that he looked as if he had received his death warrant. His face wore an expression of the most acute consternation and misery, and he seemed like a man in a dream, stupefied by some terrible calamity. He usually spoke pleasantly to the girl when leaving, but on this occasion he did not appear to notice her presence, but stumbled blindly out of the house and crept off like a broken man. Later the same evening she had seen Miss Duke, and she noticed that her eyes were red and swollen from crying. Since then, the young lady had changed out of all knowing. She had become silent, melancholy, and depressed. She had grown thin and old looking, and was eating nothing, and, Rachael had opined, if something were not done, they would soon see her in a decline.

Inspector French was not a little intrigued by all this information. That there was a connection between the murder of Charles Gething and the postponed wedding he could scarcely believe, and yet some of the facts seemed almost to point in that direction.

If Miss Duke had first learned of the tragedy from her father at breakfast, was this knowledge the cause of her telephone call? To whom was the call made? What had she done during her twenty-minute absence from the house? What had taken place at the interview between Miss Duke and Harrington, and, most important of all, why had the wedding been postponed? French felt that he could not rest until he had obtained answers to all these questions, and it seemed to him that the only way he could do so would be to trace the girl's movements in detail during the whole period in question.

For a long time he continued sitting at his desk as he considered ways and means. At last he telephoned once more for Sergeant Nolan.

'Look here,' he began, when the man presented himself, 'I want you to get something more out of that girl. When can you see her again?'

'Sunday, sir,' said the charmer. 'I left an opening for meeting her for fear it would maybe be wanted.'

'And this is Friday. Well, I suppose I shall have to wait. Better see her on Sunday and find out these things in this order. First, in what vehicle Miss Duke drove to her friend's girls' club on the night of the crime; secondly, what vehicle she came back in, and thirdly, whether she received any note or message between the time she returned that night and Mr Harrington's call next day, other than what she might have learned during her telephone call and absence from the house after breakfast. Got that?'

Nolan, signifying that he had, left the room, and French turned his attention to his routine work, which had got sadly behind.

On the following Monday morning, Sergeant Nolan made his report. He had taken his fair quarry up the river on Sunday afternoon, and there he had got his information.

Miss Duke and Mr Harrington had left in Mr Duke's car shortly before eight. Manley, the chauffeur, had mentioned to Rachael that his young mistress had told him he need not wait for her, as she expected that Mr Duke would want him later in the evening to take him home from his club. She had returned about ten in a taxi, and had come in quickly and gone to her room. So far as Rachael knew, she had received no caller, note or other message from then until Mr Harrington arrived next day, other than those excepted in the question.

French was anxious to keep secret the fact that he was looking into Miss Duke's doings, and he was therefore unwilling to question Manley on the matter. He had learned from Harrington the address of the girls' club, and he thought inquiries there might give him his information. Accordingly an hour later saw him standing before a somewhat dilapidated church school-house in a narrow street of drab and depressing houses in the Shadwell district. The school was closed, but inquiries next door produced the information that the caretaker lived in No. 47.

He betook himself to No. 47, and there found a pale, tired-looking young woman with a baby in her arms, who, when he asked for a few moments' conversation, invited him into an untidy and not overclean kitchen. She told him, in reply to his questions, that the club was run by a number of ladies, headed by a Miss Amy Lestrange. It was open each evening, but she, the speaker, was not present, her duty being only to keep the rooms clean. But her husband, the caretaker, was there off and on every evening. He might have been there when the young lady in question arrived, she did not know. But he worked in the factory near by, and would be in for his dinner in half an hour, if the gentleman liked to wait.

French said he would call back presently, and strolled out through the depressing neighbourhood. In forty-five minutes he was back at No. 47, where the caretaker had just arrived. French told him to go on with his dinner, and sat beside him as he ate. The man, evidently hoping the affair would have its financial side, was anxious to tell everything he knew.

It seemed that he had been present at the club on the evening in question, and when French had described his young couple, he remembered their arrival. It was not usual for so fine a motor to penetrate the fastnesses of that dismal region, and its appearance had fixed the matter in his memory. The gentleman had got out first and asked him if this was the Curtis Street Club, and had then assisted his companion to alight. The lady had called to the chauffeur that he need not either wait or return for her. She had then gone into the club, leaving the gentleman standing on the pavement. About half-past nine a taxi had driven up, and the same gentleman had got out and sent him, the caretaker, in to say that Mr Harrington was waiting for Miss Duke. The young lady had presently come down with Miss Lestrange, the head of the club. The three had talked for a few minutes, and then the strangers had got into the taxi and driven off.

'She's a fine girl, Miss Duke,' French observed, as he offered the caretaker a fill from his pouch. 'I never have seen her anything but smiling and pleasant all the years I've known her.'

'That's right,' the man returned, gloatingly loading his pipe. 'She's a peach and no mistake.'

French nodded in a satisfied way.

'I should have laid a quid on it,' he declared, 'that she would have been as smiling and pleasant going away as when she came. She always is.'

'Well, you'd ha' pulled it off. But, lor, guv'nor, it's easy for lydies as wot 'as lots o' money to be pleasant. W'y shouldn't they be?'

French rose.

'Ah, well, I expect they've their troubles like the rest of us,' he said, slipping half a crown into the man's eager hand.

If the caretaker was correct and Miss Duke was in good spirits on leaving the club, it followed that the upset, whatever it had been, had not up to then taken place. The next step, therefore, was obviously to find the taxi in which the two young people had driven to Hampstead, so as to learn whether anything unusual had occurred during the journey.

He returned to the Yard, and sending for some members of his staff, explained the point at issue. But, as he would have been the first to admit, it was more by luck than good guidance that on the very first day of the inquiry he gained his information. Taximan James Tomkins had driven the young couple on the evening in question, and by five o'clock he was at the Yard awaiting French's pleasure.

8

Sylvia and Harrington

Taximan Tomkins was a wizened-looking man with a surly manner and the air of having a constant grievance, but he was evidently overawed by the situation in which he found himself, and seemed anxious to do his best to answer the inspector's questions clearly.

He remembered the evening in question. He had been hailed by a gentleman near Liverpool Street, and told to drive to the Curtis Street Girls' Club. There, after some delay, they had picked up a young lady.

'What address did you get?' French asked.

'I don't just remember,' the man said slowly, scratching his head. 'Somewhere in Hampstead it was, but I'm blest if I could tell you where.'

'The Cedars, Hampstead, perhaps?'

'That's right, guv'nor. That was it.'

'And the two started off together?'

'Yes, the other young lydie just saw them off.'

'Now tell me, did they meet anyone else on the way home?'

'Not while they were in the keb, they didn't.'

'Or buy a paper, or stop for any purpose whatever?'

'They stopped and got out for a 'arf a mo', but I can't say if it was to buy a paper.'

'Oh, they stopped, did they? Where was that?'

'In Holborn, just past the end of Hatton Garden.'

'What?' cried French, surprised out of his usual calm superiority. 'Tell me about that.'

The driver was stupid and suspicious, but in time the details came out. The most direct route led along Holborn, and he had taken it, but when he reached the point in question the young man had hailed him through the speaking tube. 'Hold on a minute, driver,' he had called. 'Look sharp, please.' He had pulled over to the kerb, but almost before he had come to a stand the young man had jumped out and had hurried across the street. The lady had then alighted, had told Tomkins to wait, and had followed him. Tomkins had at first feared he was going to lose his money, but after a couple of minutes they had both returned and the girl had got in. She had bidden good-night to her friend, and he, Tomkins, had driven her off, leaving the man standing on the pavement. On arrival at Hampstead, the lady had paid him and entered the house. As far as the driver had noticed, neither of the young people was excited or upset.

This information gave French cause for thought. On obtaining Harrington's statement on the morning after the murder, he had imagined the young man was keeping something back. And now he found that he had been right. The young fellow had not mentioned the fact that he had been within a few yards of the scene of the crime at the time at which it had taken place. He had stated that he had seen Sylvia home, and now it appeared he had not done so, but had accompanied her only half-way. French reminded himself with satisfaction that his instinct on such a point was seldom far astray.

Furthermore, this news confirmed his growing suspicion that Miss Duke also knew something about the affair. It seemed too far-fetched a coincidence that this unexpected stop near the scene of the crime, the mental upset of both herself and Harrington, and the postponing of the wedding, were unconnected with the tragedy. What the connection might be he could not imagine, but he could not but believe it existed.

Determined to put the matter to the test without further delay, he drove to the Hatton Garden office and asked for Harrington. The young fellow received him politely, though French thought he could sense an air of strain in his manner. After the briefest greeting he came directly to the point.

'Mr Harrington,' he began, 'I want to ask you one question. In our conversation on the morning after the crime you told me you had seen Miss Duke home on the previous night. Why did you state this when you had only seen her as far as Hatton Garden.'

The young man paled somewhat. He did not seem taken aback, rather he gave French the impression of feeling that he was now face to face with a crisis he had long expected. He answered without hesitation and with an evident attempt at dignity.

'I quite admit that I left Miss Duke near the end of Hatton Garden, but I don't admit that that was in any way inconsistent with what I told you. Certainly I had no intention of deceiving you.'

'I don't appreciate your point, Mr Harrington,' French

said sternly. 'There is a very considerable difference between seeing Miss Duke home and not doing so.'

The young man flushed.

'I got a cab, drove to the club to meet Miss Duke, picked her up, and accompanied her a considerable part of the way home. I consider I was perfectly justified in saying I saw her home.'

'Then our ideas of the meanings of words are strangely different. I shall be glad if you will now tell me why you both alighted from your taxi near this street, and why you then allowed Miss Duke to proceed alone.'

This time Harrington seemed taken aback, but in a moment he pulled himself together, and he answered coherently enough:

'Certainly, there is no secret or mystery about it. As we were driving along, Miss Duke suddenly pointed to a tall girl in one of those glossy blue waterproofs, and told me to stop the cab, as she wished to speak to her. I shouted to the driver, and when he drew in to the kerb I jumped out and ran after the girl. Unfortunately she had disappeared, and though I searched round I could not find her. When I came back I found that Miss Duke had also alighted. I explained that I had missed her friend, but she only said, "Never mind, it can't be helped." She got into the cab again, and I was about to follow, but she said No, that there was no use in taking me farther out of my way, and that she would go home alone.'

'Did you know the girl?'

'No, Miss Duke did not tell me who she was.'

'You might describe her.'

'I really could not, except that she was tall and wearing the blue waterproof and carrying an umbrella. You see, it

108

was dark, and I only got a glimpse of her by the street lamps. She was swinging along quickly towards Oxford Street.'

'What did you do after Miss Duke drove off?'

'I went home, as I have already told you.'

And that was all Inspector French could get out of him. In spite of all his questions, the young man stuck absolutely to his story.

It was obvious to French that he must next get Miss Duke's statement, and with this in view he drove out to the The Cedars. He asked Harrington to accompany him, so as to prevent his telephoning to the young lady to put her on her guard, and on reaching the house he bade him good-day with a somewhat sardonic smile.

Miss Duke was at home, and presently joined him in the breakfast-room to which he had been shown.

She was a comely maiden, slightly given to plumpness, perhaps, but pretty and kindly and wholesome looking, a sight indeed to warm a man's heart. But she looked pale and worried, and French felt that her experience, whatever it was, had hit her hard.

'I am sorry to trouble you, Miss Duke, but I am inquiring into the recent crime at your father's office, and I find I require to ask you a few questions.'

As he spoke he watched her sharply, and he was intrigued to notice a flash of apprehension leap into her clear eyes.

'Won't you sit down?' she invited, with a somewhat strained smile.

He seated himself deliberately, continuing:

'My questions, I am afraid, are personal and impertinent, but I have no option but to ask them. I will go on to them at once, without further preamble. The first is, What was it that upset you so greatly on the day after the crime?'

She looked at him in evident surprise, and, he imagined, in some relief also.

'Why, how can you ask?' she exclaimed. 'Don't you think news like that was enough to upset anyone? You see, I had known poor Mr Gething all my life, and he had always been kind to me. I sincerely liked and respected him, and to learn suddenly that he had been murdered in that cold-blooded way, why, it was awful—*awful*. It certainly upset me, and I don't see how it could have done anything else.'

French nodded.

'Quite so, Miss Duke, I fully appreciate that. But I venture to suggest that there was something more in your mind than the tragic death of your old acquaintance; something of more pressing and more personal interest. Come now, Miss Duke, tell me what it was.'

The flash of apprehension returned to her eyes, and then once again the look of relief.

'You mean the loss of the diamonds,' she answered calmly. 'I deplored that, of course, particularly on my father's account. But it was Mr Gething's death that really, as you call it, upset me. The diamonds we could do without, but we could not give the poor old man back his life.'

'I did not mean the loss of the diamonds, Miss Duke. I meant something more personal than that. I'm afraid you must tell me about it.'

There was now no mistaking the girl's uneasiness, and French grew more and more hopeful that he was on the track of something vital. But she was not giving anything away.

'You must be mistaken,' she said in a lower tone. 'It was the news of the murder, and that alone, which upset me.'

French shook his head.

'I would rather not take that answer from you. Please reconsider it. Can you tell me nothing else?'

'Nothing. That is all I have to say.'

'Very well. I trust it may not be necessary to reopen the matter. Now I want you to tell me why you postponed your wedding with Mr Harrington.'

Miss Duke flushed deeply.

'I will tell you nothing of the sort, Mr Inspector!' she declared with some show of anger. 'What right have you to ask me such a question? That is a matter between Mr Harrington and myself alone.'

'I hope you are right, Miss Duke, but I fear there is a chance that you may be mistaken. Do you absolutely decline to answer me?'

'Of course I do! No girl would answer such a question. It is an impertinence to ask it.'

'In that case,' French said grimly, 'I shall not press the matter—for the present. Let me turn to another subject. I want you next to tell me why you stopped at Hatton Garden on your way home from the Curtis Street Girls' Club on the night of the crime.'

For a moment the girl seemed too much surprised to reply, then she answered with a show of indignation: 'Really, Mr French, this is too much! May I ask if you suspect me of the crime?'

'Not of committing it,' French returned gravely, 'but,' he leaned forward and gazed keenly into her eyes, 'I do suspect you of knowing something about it. Could you not, Miss Duke, if you chose, put me on the track of the criminal?'

111

'Oh, no, no, no!' the girl cried piteously, motioning with her hands as if to banish so terrible a thought from her purview. 'How can you suggest such a thing? It is shameful and horrible!'

'Of course, Miss Duke, I can't make you answer me if you don't want to. But I put it to you that it is worth your while thinking twice before you attempt to keep back information. Remember that if I am not satisfied, you may be asked these same questions in court, and then you will have to answer them whether you like it or not. Now I ask you once again, Why did you leave your taxi at Hatton Garden?'

'I think it is perfectly horrible of you to make all these insinuations against me without any grounds whatever,' she answered a little tremulously. 'There is no secret about why I stopped the taxi, and I have never made any mystery about it. Why it should have any importance I can't imagine.' She paused, then with a little gesture as if throwing discretion to the winds, continued: 'The fact is that as we were driving home I suddenly saw a girl in the street whom I particularly wished to meet. I stopped the cab and sent Mr Harrington after her, but he missed her.'

'Who was she?'

'I don't know; that is why I was so anxious to see her. I suppose you want the whole story?' She tossed her head and went on without waiting for him to reply. 'Last summer I was coming up to town from Tonbridge, where I had been staying, and this girl and I had a carriage to ourselves. We began to talk, and became quite friendly. When they came to collect the tickets I found I had lost mine. The man wanted to take my name, but the girl insisted on lending me the money to pay my fare. I wrote down her name and address on a scrap of paper so that I could return the money to her, but when I reached home I found I had lost the paper, and I stupidly had not committed the address to memory. I could not send her the money, and I don't know what she must have thought of me. You can understand, therefore, my anxiety to meet her when I saw her from the cab.'

'But why did you pay your fare a second time? You must have known that all you had to do was to give your name and address to the ticket collector.'

'I suppose I did,' she admitted, 'but I preferred to pay rather than have the trouble of explanations and probably letters to the head office.'

Inspector French was chagrined. Instinctively he doubted the story, but Miss Duke had answered his question in a reasonable way, and if she stuck to the tale, he did not see how he could break her down. After this lapse of time it would be quite impossible to obtain confirmation or otherwise of the details, especially as Miss Duke's hypothetical fellow-traveller could not be produced. He pointedly made no comment on the statement as he resumed his investigation.

'To whom did you telephone after breakfast on the morning after the murder?'

That Miss Duke was amazed at the extent of the inspector's knowledge was evident, but she answered immediately.

'To Mr Harrington.'

'To say what?'

'If I must repeat my private conversations to my future husband, it was to ask him to meet me at once as I had something to say to him.'

'What was the nature of the communication?'

Miss Duke flushed again.

'Really,' she exclaimed, 'I protest against this. What possible connection can our private affairs have with your business?'

'It is your own fault, Miss Duke. You are not telling me the whole truth, and I am therefore suspicious. I want to find out what you are keeping back, and I may tell you that I am going to do so. What did you want to see Mr Harrington about so urgently?'

The girl seemed terribly distressed.

'If you will have it, it was about the postponement of the wedding,' she said in a low voice. You understand, we had been discussing the matter on the night before, when no conclusion had been come to. But on sleeping on it I had made up my mind in favour of the postponement, and I wanted to tell Mr Harrington at once.'

'But why was it so urgent? Could you not have waited until later in the day?'

'I felt I couldn't wait. It was so important to us both.'

'And you refuse to give the reason of the postponement?'

'I do. You have no right to ask it.'

'You did meet Mr Harrington that morning?'

'Yes.'

'Where?'

'At the entrance to the Finchley Road tube station.'

'Why did you not tell him to call on you instead of yourself going out?'

'In order as far as possible to prevent him from being late at the office.'

French suddenly remembered that Harrington had entered the office during his visit there on the morning after the crime, and had apologised to Mr Duke for his late arrival. It had not struck French at the time, but now he recalled that when Mr Duke had spoken to him of the tragedy he had stated he had heard of it already. Where? French now wondered. Was it merely from the morning paper, or *was it from Miss Duke?* Or, still more pressing question, had they both known of it on the previous night?

Suddenly a possible theory flashed into his mind, and he sat for a few moments in silence, considering it. Suppose that on the stop near Hatton Garden, Harrington had mentioned that he wanted for some purpose to call at the office, or suppose Miss Duke had asked him to do so, and that he had left her for that purpose. Next morning at breakfast she hears from her father of the murder, and is at once panic stricken about Harrington. She sees that if he admits his visit he may be suspected of the crime, and she sends for him before he reaches the office in order to warn him. Or could it be that, knowing of this hypothetical visit, Miss Duke had herself suspected Harrington, and had sent for him at the earliest possible moment to hear his explanation? French was not satisfied with these suggestions, but he felt more than ever certain these two young people had conspired to hide vital information.

He left the house profoundly dissatisfied, and returning to Hatton Garden, had another interview with Harrington. He pressed the young man as hard as he could, taxing him directly with having been present in the office on the fatal night. This Harrington strenuously denied, and French could get nothing further out of him. He went again into the man's movements on the night of the crime, but without getting any further light thrown thereon. Harrington said he had walked to his rooms after parting from Miss Duke, but no direct evidence was forthcoming as to the truth or falsehood of his statement.

Suddenly another theory leaped into the detective's mind, but after careful thought he felt he must reject it. If Vanderkemp were guilty, the whole of these mysterious happenings would be cleared up. Harrington was under a deep debt of gratitude to his uncle, and appeared attached to him. Whether Miss Duke shared, or was endeavouring to share, his feelings, French did not know, but it was certainly possible. Suppose he and Miss Duke, driving home from the East End, had seen Vanderkemp at the end of Hatton Garden. Suppose, moreover, something in the man's appearance had attracted their attention, something furtive or evil, something unlike his usual expression. This, coupled with the fact that the traveller was supposed to be in Amsterdam, might easily have impelled Harrington to stop the cab to have a word with his uncle. But by the time he had reached the pavement, Vanderkemp had disappeared. The incident would have been dismissed by both as trivial, until next morning at breakfast, when Miss Duke learned of the murder, its significance would become apparent. She might not believe the traveller guilty, but she would recognise that the circumstances required some explanation. Immediately the paramount importance of communicating with Harrington would appear, lest he might incautiously mention that he had seen his uncle virtually on the scene of the murder. She would instantly telephone in the hope of catching her lover before he left his rooms. She could not give her message over the telephone, so she would arrange the meeting. She would instruct Harrington to return to her as soon as possible, so as to hear what had taken place at the office. He would therefore call in the afternoon, and at the interview they would decide that in the uncertainty of the situation, the wedding should be postponed. The supposed flight of Vanderkemp would confirm their suspicions, and would account for the perturbed state of mind which both exhibited.

The theory was so fascinating that next day French once more interviewed Harrington and Miss Duke and put the question directly to them, Had they seen Vanderkemp? But both denied having done so, and baffled and irritated, he wrathfully watched another promising clue petering out before him. He had the two young people shadowed, and spent a considerable time in investigating their past life, but without result.

So the days began to draw out into weeks, and the solution of the mystery seemed as far off as ever.

9

Mrs Root of Pittsburg

One morning about six weeks after the murder in Hatton Garden, Inspector French was summoned to the presence of his chief.

'Look here, French,' he was greeted, 'you've been at that Gething case long enough. I can't have any more time wasted on it. What are you doing now?'

French, his usual cheery confidence sadly deflated, hesitatingly admitted that at the moment he was not doing very much, embellishing this in the course of a somewhat painful conversation with the further information that he was doing nothing whatever, and that he was severally up against it and down and out.

'I thought so,' the chief declared. 'In that case you'll have time to go and see Williams & Davies, of Cockspur Street, the money-lenders. I have just had a 'phone from them, and they say that some diamonds recently came into their possession which they are told resemble those stolen from Duke & Peabody. You might look into the matter.'

It was a rejuvenated French that fifteen minutes later

118

ascended the stairs of Straker House, Cockspur Street, to the office of Messrs Williams & Davies. Gone was the lassitude and the dejection and the weary brooding look, and instead there was once again the old cheery optimism, the smiling self-confidence, the springy step. He pushed open a swing door, and with an air of fatherly benevolence demanded of a diminutive office boy if Mr Williams was in.

The senior partner was disengaged, and two minutes later French was ushered into a small, rather dark office, in which sat a tall, well-groomed man with graying hair, and a precise, somewhat pedantic manner.

'They 'phoned me from the Yard that you were coming across, Inspector,' he announced, when French had introduced himself. 'I can only say I hope I have not brought you on a wild goose chase. But the affair should certainly be looked into.'

'I have not heard the circumstances yet, sir,' French reminded him. 'I shall naturally be glad if you can give me some helpful information.'

'I did not care to give details over the 'phone,' Mr Williams explained. 'You can never tell who overhears you. I once heard a girl declining what was evidently a proposal of marriage. The circumstances in this case are very simple. About six weeks ago a lady, giving her name as Mrs Chauncey S. Root, and evidently an American, called and asked if she could see one of the principals of my firm. She was shown in to me, and she explained that she was the wife of a Mr Chauncey S. Root, a rich steel manufacturer of Pittsburg. She had just crossed by the *Olympic* for a holiday in Europe, reaching London on the previous evening. She said a series of misfortunes had brought her

119

into a somewhat awkward predicament, and she wondered if I could do anything to assist her. In the first place she had been foolish enough to get into a gambling set on the way over, and had lost, as she expressed it, "the hell of a lot of money." She spoke in a very racy and American way, but she gave me the impression of being thoroughly competent and efficient. Her losses ran into several hundred pounds—she did not tell me the exact amount—but all her ready money was gone and in addition she had given several I.O.U.'s. This, however, she would not have thought twice about, as she had letters of credit for many times the amount, had it not been that a further calamity befell her in Southampton. There, in the crush on the quays, the small despatch case in which she kept her ready money and papers had been snatched from her, and she was left practically penniless, as well as without her letters of credit and her passport or other means of identification. She had, of course, reported the matter to the police authorities, but they had rather shaken their heads over it, though promising to do everything possible. She had had, indeed, to borrow a twenty-pound note from one of her travelling acquaintances to get her to London, and now she was practically without money at all. She wished, therefore, to borrow £3000, which would enable her to pay her gambling debts and to carry on in London until fresh letters of credit could be sent. Fortunately, she had with her a collection of unmounted diamonds, which she intended to have set by London jewellers, of whose skill she had heard great accounts. These diamonds she proposed to deposit as security, and she would agree to pay whatever rate of interest was customary. She asked me if my firm would be prepared to lend the money on these terms.'

'Why did she not cable to her husband?'

'I asked her that, and she explained that she did not wish to tell Mr Root, as he had an inveterate dislike to gambling, and they had had several disagreements about her betting proclivities. In fact, relations had been seriously strained until she had promised amendment, and a confession might easily lead to a serious breach. She could not, either, attribute the loss to the theft, as it ran to so great a figure that she could not possibly be carrying the amount in her despatch case. She said she would prefer to borrow the money until she could write to her man of business to realise some of her own stocks.

'I said that her proposition, as such, was acceptable, as we frequently took stones and jewellery as security for loans, but that as she was a stranger to us, before we could do business we should obviously require some evidence of her *bona fides*. She replied that that was all right, that she quite recognised that owing to the loss of her papers and particularly of her passport something of the kind would be necessary. She said we could make what inquiries we liked, provided only we were quick about them, for she wanted the money as soon as possible. She asked how long we should take, and when I said twenty-four hours, she admitted that was reasonable. She suggested that if we did business we should take the stones to be valued to one of the best-known London jewellers. I agreed to this, and rang up Mr Stronge, of Hurst & Stronge, of Bond Street, to ask him if he would undertake the valuation. He is, as you probably know, one of the most famous experts in the world. He consented, and I settled with him the amount of his fee. Finally it was arranged that, provided our inquiries were satisfactory, I should meet Mrs Root at

121

Hurst & Stronge's at half-past ten on the following morning, she with the stones and I with my cheque book. I was to pay her five-sixths of the value of the diamonds. She said she expected to pay back the loan in about four weeks, and suitable terms of interest were arranged.'

Mr Williams paused and glanced at his companion, as though to assure himself that his story was receiving the attention he evidently felt it deserved. But French's air of thrilled interest left him no room for doubt, and he continued:

'I made my inquiries, and all appeared satisfactory. I called up Mrs Root at the Savoy, told her I was prepared to deal, and at the hour named met her at Hurst & Stronge's. Mr Stronge took us to his private room, and there Mrs Root produced a bag of stones, mostly diamonds, though there were a few emeralds and a large ruby, all unmounted. There were sixteen stones ranging in value from £40 to £400, but averaging about £200 or £220. Mr Stronge valued them very carefully, and after a long wait we got his opinion. The whole were worth about £3300, and in accordance with our bargain I proposed to hand Mrs Root a cheque for £2750. She admitted the correctness of this, but said she wanted the £3000, and after some conversation I agreed to meet her wishes and filled the cheque for the latter sum. She then objected that no bank would pay her without inquiring as to her identity, which would mean another delay, and asked me if I would go with her to the bank to certify that she was the person for whom I intended the money. I agreed to this, and we went to the Piccadilly branch of the London and Counties Bank. There we saw the manager, and there I left her. I returned here and lodged the stones in my safe.'

'The manager took your identification, I suppose?'

'Oh, yes. I know him personally and there was no difficulty. That ended the matter as far as I was concerned, and for four weeks I thought no more of it. But as the fifth and sixth week passed and the lady made no sign, I began to wonder. I telephoned to the Savoy, but it appeared she had left on the day of our deal. I assumed, however, that she was on the Continent, and no suspicion that all was not right occurred to me.'

'Then what roused your suspicion?'

'I am coming to that,' Mr Williams answered in a slightly frigid tone. 'This morning I happened to show the stones—without saying how they came into my possession, of course—to a personal friend of my own, a diamond merchant named Sproule, who had called with me on other business. When he saw them he grew very much excited, and asked me where I had got them from. I pressed him for an explanation, and he said they fitted the description circulated of those stolen from Messrs Duke & Peabody. He was emphatic that I should inform the firm, but I thought it better to ring you up instead.'

'Very wise, sir,' French approved. 'That was certainly your proper course. Now, I take it the first thing we have to do is to see if your friend, Mr Sproule, is correct in his supposition. I have a list of the missing stones in my pocket, but I don't know that I'm expert enough to identify them. I think we'll have Mr Duke over. May I use your 'phone?'

Mr Duke was naturally eager to learn details of the new development, and in less than half an hour he joined the others in Mr Williams's office. French explained the situation, ending up, 'Now we want you, Mr Duke, to tell us if these were among the stones you lost.'

The diamond merchant, obviously much excited, began at once to make his examination. He inspected the stones minutely through a lens, weighed them on a delicate balance he had brought, and put them to other tests which greatly interested his companions. As he put each down he gave his judgment. One after another were identified. All were among those stolen from him. They were the sixteen smallest and least valuable stones of the collection.

The fact was learned by the three men with very different emotions. Mr Duke's gain was Mr Williams's loss, and resulting satisfaction and consternation showed on their respective faces, while French's countenance wore an expression of the liveliest delight, not unmixed with mystification.

'Good heavens!' Mr Williams cried, his voice trembling with agitation and excitement. 'Then I've been swindled! Swindled out of three thousand pounds!' He glared at the inspector as if he were at fault. 'I suppose,' he continued, 'that if this gentleman establishes his claim, the loss will fall on me? God knows, I can ill afford it.'

'We shall hope not, sir,' French said sympathetically. 'We shall hope that with luck you'll recover your money. But we must not waste any more time. I shall start by going to the bank to see if all the money has been withdrawn. I'd be obliged, Mr Williams, if you would come also. I'll keep you advised, Mr Duke, how things go on, and of course you'll get back your stones after the usual formalities have been carried out.'

Mr Williams had recovered his composure, and, the gems having been locked in his safe, the three men left the office and descended to the street. There French said good-day to Mr Duke, who somewhat reluctantly took his leave, the other two continuing to the bank After a few moments' wait they were shown into the manager's room.

'I am afraid, Mr Scarlett, I have had a serious misfortune,' Mr Williams began, almost before they were seated. 'I have just learned that I have been swindled out of £3000. This is Inspector French of Scotland Yard, and we both want your help in the matter.'

Mr Scarlett, a well-groomed, middle-aged gentleman of fashionable appearance and suave manners, looked suitably concerned. He shook hands with French, and expressed his commiseration with his client's loss in a few easy words, declaring also his desire to be of service.

'Do you remember,' Mr Williams went on eagerly, 'my coming to see you one morning about six weeks ago with a lady whom I introduced as Mrs Root, of Pittsburg, U.S.A.? She held my cheque for £3000, and I came to introduce her to you.'

The manager recalled the incident.

'That money was a loan, for which she deposited with me a number of diamonds. The diamonds were valued by Mr Stronge of Hurst & Stronge's, and I gave her less than their value. I thought I had taken all reasonable precautions, but now,' Mr Williams made a faint gesture of despair, 'now it seems that they were stolen.'

'Stolen?' Mr Scarlett repeated in a shocked voice. 'My dear sir! Allow me to say how extremely sorry I am to have to tell you that I fear your discovery has come too late. Your cheque had been paid practically in full.'

Mr Williams gave a little groan, though he had evidently been expecting the bad news. He would have spoken, but French broke in with, 'Is that so, sir? That is really what we came to ask. Now I want you please to give me as detailed an account of the whole business as you can.'

'I will do so, of course,' Mr Scarlett returned, 'but I fear my story will not help you much.' He raised his desk telephone. 'Ask Mr Plenteous to come here,' he directed, and when a young, fair-haired man had entered he resumed, 'This is Mr Plenteous who carried out the details of the transaction. As Mr Williams has said, he and the lady called on me,' he turned over the leaves of a diary, 'about midday on Thursday, 26th November. He introduced the lady as a Mrs Chauncey S. Root, of Pittsburg, and stated he had called to certify that she was the person referred to in a cheque he had made out. She produced a cheque for £3000, and Mr Williams identified it as his. She thanked him and he withdrew. She then said that she wished to open a temporary account, and that she would like cash for £1500, and to lodge the remainder. I sent for Mr Plenteous, and asked him to arrange the matter, and he showed the lady out to his counter. Next day the balance was withdrawn except for a few shillings, which I believe we still hold. Is not that correct, Plenteous?'

'Yes, sir,' the fair-haired young man answered, 'quite correct. I can turn you up the exact balance in a moment.'

'Presently, thank you, Mr Plenteous,' French interposed. 'In the meantime perhaps you would tell us what took place between you and the lady after you left this office.'

After a glance at his chief, the clerk answered:

'Mrs Root handed me the cheque for £3000, and said she wished to lodge half. I filled the customary forms, took her signature, and gave her a passbook, all in the usual way. Then she told me she would like the other £1500 cashed in notes of small value. She said she was a stranger

126

to London, but that already she had discovered the difficulty of changing Bank of England notes. Being short of ready money, she had proferred a twenty-pound note in a shop. It was refused, and on asking for change in a bank which happened to be next door, the cashier politely informed her he was not permitted to change notes for strangers. She had, indeed, to go back to her hotel before she could get it done. She said she therefore wanted nothing larger than ten pounds, and at her further request I counted her out a hundred tens and a hundred fives. She stowed them away in a despatch case she was carrying. I pointed out that that was not a very safe way to carry so large a sum, but she laughed and said she guessed it was all right, that no one would know she had money in it. She said good-day and went out, and that was the last I saw of her.'

'You noticed nothing in any way suspicious about her manner or actions?'

'Nothing whatever.'

'You say the lodgment was subsequently withdrawn? You might tell me about that.'

'It was withdrawn in the sense that cheques were issued for almost the whole amount. The lady did not herself call again, nor was the account closed. There is still a small balance.'

French nodded.

'Yes, I understood you to say so. Could you let me see the ledger, and also the cheques that were issued?'

In a few seconds the clerk returned with a ponderous tome, which he opened at the name Mrs Helen Sadie Root. The account possessed but few items. On the debit side there was but the single entry of £1500, but on the other

127

side there were six entries, varying from £210 10s. to £295, and totalling £1495 7s. 9d. Six cancelled cheques corresponded with the entries. As French examined these, he was interested to see that all were made out on fashionable London jewellers.

'Can you lend me these?' he asked, pointing to the cheques.

The clerk hesitated, but Mr Scarlett intervened.

'Certainly,' he answered readily, 'but you will have to give us a receipt for our auditors.'

This was soon arranged, and after French had asked a few more questions, he and Mr Williams left the bank.

'Now,' he said briskly, before his companion could frame a remark, 'I am going round to these six jewellers, but first I want some further information from you. Shall we go back to your office?'

Mr Williams assented eagerly. He had lost his air of detached precision, and, like a somewhat spoiled child, plied the other with questions as to his probable chances of success. French answered in his usual cheery, optimistic way, and it was not until they were once more seated in Mr Williams's sanctum that he dropped his air of fatherly benevolence and became once more the shrewd and competent officer of Scotland Yard.

'In the first place,' he began, as he took out his notebook, 'I want *your* description of the lady. I gather she was a good-looking woman, attractive both in appearance and manner. Did you find her so?'

Mr Williams hesitated.

'Well, yes, I did,' he admitted, somewhat apologetically, as French thought. 'She certainly had a way with her— something different from my usual clients. From her manner I never should have suspected she was other than all right.'

'Most women crooks are attractive looking,' French declared smoothly. 'It's part of their stock in trade. Just let me have as detailed a description of her as you can.'

It seemed she was of middle height, and dark, very dark as to hair and eyelashes, but less so as to eyes. They were rather a golden shade of brown. She had a somewhat retroussé nose, and a tiny mouth set in an oval face, with a complexion of extreme, but healthy, pallor. She wore her hair low over her ears, and her smile revealed an unexpected dimple. Mr Williams had remarked these details so thoroughly that French smiled inwardly, as he solemnly noted them in his book. The money-lender had not particularly observed what she was wearing, but this did not matter as Mr Scarlett had, and a detailed description of her dress was already entered up.

'Tell me next, please, Mr Williams, what identification the lady gave of herself, and what inquiries you made to test her statement. She had lost her passport?'

'Yes, I told you how, or rather I told you what she said about it. She gave me her card, and showed me the envelopes of several letters addressed to her at Pittsburg. She also showed me some photographs of groups in which she appeared which had been taken on board the *Olympic*, as well as a dinner menu dated for the third day out. She explained that her return ticket had been stolen with the passport, so that she could not let me see it.'

'Not very conclusive, I'm afraid,' French commented. 'All that evidence might have been faked.'

'I quite see that, and saw it at the time,' declared the

money-lender. 'But I did not rest there. I applied to Dashford's, you know, the private inquiry people. I asked them to cable their agents in Pittsburg for a description of Mrs Root, and to know if she had left for England on the *Olympic*. There is the reply.'

He took a paper from a file and handed it across. It was headed, 'J. T. Dashford & Co., Private Inquiry Agents,' and read:

'DEAR SIR,

'MRS CHAUNCEY S. ROOT.

'In reply to your inquiry of yesterday, we beg to inform you that we have cabled our agents in Pittsburg on the matter in question, and have received the following reply:

'"Chauncey S. Root, partner local steel firm, wealthy, wife handsome, height middle, hair dark, complexion pale, face oval, mouth small, manner bright and attractive. Left for Europe by *Olympic*. Family O.K.'

'We trust this information will meet your requirements.

'Yours faithfully,
'J. T. DASHFORD & CO.,
'M.S.'

French whistled thoughtfully.

'That seems right enough,' he said slowly. 'I know something about Dashford's people, and they are reliable enough about a thing like this. It's beginning to look like impersonation.'

'Ah,' Mr Williams ejaculated. 'Impersonation! I hadn't thought of that.' He paused in his turn, then continued, 'But yet I don't see how it could be. I didn't stop with an application to Dashford's. I rang up the White Star offices, and they told me there that Mrs Root had actually made the journey. I also rang up the Savoy, and they told me there that she had arrived at the hour she had told me, with trunks bearing *Olympic* labels. Finally, to make the matter, as I thought, sure, I 'phoned the Southampton police and found out from them that the story of the stolen despatch case was true. It had happened just as Mrs Root described. When I got all this information I felt absolutely satisfied.'

'I'm not surprised at that, sir,' French admitted. 'It would have satisfied most people. You see, it's quite different with us now, because our suspicions have been aroused. There was nothing in the circumstances of this lady's call to make you doubt her story. I quite sympathise with you, though I'm afraid that doesn't help the situation much . . . But you see now, of course, that none of the information you collected is really conclusive. I have no doubt that there is a Mrs Chauncey S. Root of Pittsburg who travelled to Europe in the *Olympic*, and that, generally speaking, she resembles your friend, but I very gravely doubt that she was the lady who negotiated the loan. You see, the real identifications, the passport, the return ticket, on which her name would be inscribed, were missing. Moreover, she refused to allow Mr Root to be consulted. No, I think we may take it that the woman who came here was not Mrs

Root. But, on the other hand, she must either have been acquainted with Mrs Root personally or have known a thundering lot about her. How does that strike you, sir?'

'It sounds right, it certainly sounds right, Inspector. I fear it must be as you say. But if so, what chance is there of getting back my money?'

French shook his head.

'I'm afraid the prospects are not very rosy,' he admitted. 'But you never know. We'll try to get our hands on the woman, of course, and we may find she has not spent the money. Now, sir, if there is nothing more than you can tell me, I think I shall get along to the Savoy and to those shops where she paid the cheques.'

Inspector French walked slowly down Cockspur Street, his brain bemused by this unexpected development. The impersonation of Mrs Root was easy—or, at least, comparatively easy—to understand. He could see that it would present no serious difficulties to a resourceful woman, though the application to the Southampton police was certainly staggering. But what he could not form the slightest idea of was how this woman could possibly have got hold of Mr Duke's diamonds. The impersonation must have actually been arranged *before* the robbery took place, and if this were so, it pointed to a much more far-reaching crime than he had had any conception of. And there must have been more than one in it, too—unless this mysterious woman had actually committed the murder, which he found hard to believe. He smiled with satisfaction as he thought of the vistas of possible information which were opening out before him, and by which he might hope to retrieve the loss of prestige which he had suffered.

Suddenly he thought of Miss Duke. Was there a connection between her and this mysterious woman? Was Mrs Root the woman in the waterproof? Was she Miss Duke herself? Here were far-reaching questions. As he considered them, he saw that his work for the next few days was cut out for him.

10

Some Pairs of Blankets

During Inspector French's brief lunch hour he continued turning over in his mind the immediate problem which Mr Williams's story had raised for him, namely, at what point he had best attack his new inquiry.

The facts postulated a good deal of obvious detailed investigation, and he felt he should carry this through in his usual systematic way before attempting to evolve a comprehensive theory of the crime. He had first to learn what he could of the mysterious Mrs Root, and in this connection he foresaw inquiries at Pittsburg, from the White Star people, from the Southampton police, at the Savoy, and at the various firms of jewellers to whom the cheques had been made out. He had, if possible, to find the lady, or her impersonator. These things accomplished, he could turn his attention to an attempt to connect the person found with Miss Duke, or at all events with Mr Duke's jewels, and subsequently with the murder of Charles Gething.

By the time his meal was ended he had decided that he

would commence operations at the Savoy, and ten minutes later he turned into the courtyard, and making his way to the office, inquired for the manager.

In due course he explained his business to the great man, but the latter shook his head when he heard what was required of him, and asked French for suggestions as to how he could help.

'First I should like to see the register,' French explained.

'That, at least, is easily done.'

The manager led the way to the office and introduced French to the radiant young woman who presided at the reception counter. Then turning over the pages of the register, he presently exclaimed, 'That looks like it, Inspector, I fancy.'

The entry read: 'Nov. 24. Mrs Chauncey S. Root, Pittsburg, U.S.A. 137.'

French drew out the cheques he had obtained from Mr Scarlett and carefully compared the signatures. 'That's it,' he declared. 'There's not a doubt those are in the same handwriting. Now the question is, Can this young lady remember the woman?'

The clerk hesitated.

'We had a lot of Americans in that day,' she said slowly, as she ran her eyes down the list of names. 'It is not easy to keep track of them all. And this is six weeks ago.' She paused again, then shook her head. 'I'm afraid I can't just place her.'

'It was the day the *Olympic* got to Southampton,' French prompted. 'There would no doubt have been a number of people off the steamer special.' He glanced once more at the book. 'See, here is a crowd of Americans all together. New York, Boston, New York, New York, Philadelphia, and so on. That represents the special. But—' He paused and ran his finger down the column. 'Now, this is really rather interesting. Mrs Root's name is not among them. Here it is, down near the end of the list. That means that she came in late in the evening, doesn't it? Does that help you at all, Miss Pearson?' He waited, but the girl not replying, he continued, 'Or the room? Does No. 137 bring anything to your mind?'

The girl shook her pretty head.

'Turn up the account, Miss Pearson,' the manager suggested.

The girl produced another huge book, and all three went through the items. Mrs Root, it appeared, had paid for the rooms—No. 137 was a suite consisting of one bedroom, bathroom and sitting-room—for the three nights, the 24th, 25th, and 26th of November. She had had seven meals in the hotel, dinner on the night of arrival, and breakfast, lunch, and dinner on the next two days. All these meals she had had served in her private room.

'Avoiding publicity,' French thought, continuing aloud, 'Then she didn't breakfast on the morning she left?'

At his remark Miss Pearson gave an exclamation.

'I remember her now,' she cried. 'It was your saying that brought her to my mind. No, she didn't breakfast the morning you mean because she left on the previous night. I remember the whole circumstances now. She came in on the night'—she glanced at the register—' of the 24th— pretty late—it was between seven and eight, I should think—and asked for a suite for three or four weeks. She was dark-haired and pale complexioned and very American in her speech. I fixed her up with No. 137, and she said she wanted dinner sent up to her room. Two evenings later, shortly before eight o'clock, she came back to the office and said she had had an urgent wire from Paris, and that she had to go over that night. She hoped to be back in about a week, but she would not keep the rooms on, as she was not certain of her plans. I made out the bill, and what brings the thing back to my mind is that I had to charge her for that night in accordance with our rule. She didn't seem to mind, the way some people do in such a case. She left then, and I never saw her since.'

This being all the pretty clerk could tell him, French asked next to see the chambermaid who had attended No. 137 on the night in question.

From this woman he at first learned nothing. For a quarter of an hour he prompted fruitlessly, then, just as in the case of the clerk, a chance word brought a ray of light. Asked if she could remember having seen luggage with *Olympic* labels and the name Mrs Root, she suddenly admitted that she could. Her attention had been attracted by the name Root, as she had been reading in the papers of a distinguished American of the same name, and she had wondered if the owner of the luggage was any connection. She remembered the luggage distinctly. There were two big, new-looking American trunks, labelled on steamer labels, Mrs Something Root. Yes, she thought it was Chauncey. Something like that anyway, some queer, foreign name that only an American would bear. But though she remembered the luggage, the chambermaid could not recall anything about the lady herself.

After fruitlessly interrogating several other of the hotel servants, French retreated into a deserted corner of the lounge and set himself to think the thing out. And presently it occurred to him that the trunks might represent a clue. Did their removal not involve a taxi, and if so, could he find it?

He went back to the head porter to make inquiries. Vehicles were usually obtained from the rank in the street adjoining. Of course it frequently happened that a driver looking for a fare would pass at the critical moment and be employed, but seven out of ten were obtained from the rank.

French left the hotel, and, sauntering down to the cab rank, engaged the driver of the leading car in conversation. All the taxis on the rank, the man stated, were the property of one firm, Metropolitan Transport, Ltd. The men returned the runs they made on their daily journals, and French could, if he chose to apply to the office in Victoria Street, learn all there was to be known about it.

French did choose, and a quarter of an hour later was in conversation with the manager. But that gentleman was dubious that he could supply the desired information. It was true they kept a pretty complete record of the runs made and these had to balance with the readings of the meters and with the money handed in, but obviously no note was made of the names or descriptions of the fares. He could find out if a car had gone from the Savoy to Victoria about 7.45 p.m. on the night of the 26th November, but he could not say who might have travelled in it.

'If you could let me have a note of the cars which left the hotel between 7.40 and 8.10, irrespective of their destinations, I should be obliged,' French declared. 'I could see all the drivers, and possibly someone of them might remember the woman.'

'I can give you that,' the manager assented, 'but it will take a little time to get out.' He rang for a clerk and gave the necessary instruction, then leaned back in his chair and went on conversationally, 'What's the trouble? Is it indiscreet to ask?'

French smiled benevolently.

'Certainly not,' he assured the other. 'I'll tell you the whole thing. We believe that the lady I'm after is a crook—a diamond thief. She gave out that she was the wife of a wealthy American steel magnate, but we believe she's no more that than you are. She left the hotel that night with two trunks and some small luggage, to go to Paris by the 8.20 from Victoria, and has vanished. I'm trying now to trace her.'

The manager seemed interested.

'Well,' he said, 'that's a useful hint you have given just now. Our drivers record the luggage, that is, outside luggage for which there is a charge. It'll narrow the thing down a bit if we've only to count vehicles with two packages outside.'

'That's a point,' French admitted, 'and a good one. But I only know that there were two large trunks besides hand luggage. There might have been more than two packages outside.'

'It's not likely. If there was only one lady she would have taken the hand stuff in with her. Ah, here's the list.'

From the tabulated sheet handed to the manager, it appeared that between the hours of 7.40 and 8.10 on the night in question, no less than twenty-eight taxis had left the Savoy. Of these, twenty had gone to theatres. Of the remaining eight, two had gone to Euston, one to King's Cross, one to Hampstead, one to Kensington, and three to Victoria.

'There you are,' said the manager, pointing to the second

to Victoria. 'See under extras, "Two packages." That's what you want.'

It looked as if the manager was right. The first of the three vehicles to Victoria had no outside luggage, and the third was for a party of five. No. 2 had left at 7.55 with one passenger and two outside packages.

'It's promising enough,' French admitted. 'If you could tell me where to find the driver of that car I should be much obliged.'

'John Straker.' The manager picked up his desk telephone. 'Where is John Straker at present?' he called, and in a moment to French, 'He's out at work. He's on the stand beside the Savoy, and if you go there now, and don't mind waiting, you'll see him. I'll give you a note to him. It will make him more ready to talk. He's a peculiar-looking man, clean-shaven, with a thin white face and hooked nose and very black eyes; you'll recognise him at once. Better take his time-book also. It may bring the trip back to his memory.'

French, having thanked the manager, returned to the cab rank. As he walked down it glancing at the drivers, a taxi drove up and took its place, at the tail of the line. Its driver answered the description, and when he had switched off his engine and seemed at liberty, French accosted him and explained his business.

For some seconds the man pondered, scratching his head and turning over the leaves of his timebook. At last he looked at French.

'I remember the trip,' he said. 'It's a strange thing, but that was the only trip I made to Victoria that week. It's a place we're at pretty often, as you'll understand. But I remember going that night. It was with a lady, and she

140

had two big boxes; I remember them because they were rather big for the space on the car. But I got them fixed up all right.'

'Where did you go to?'

'I believe the main line departure side of Victoria, though I'm not just certain.'

'Good!' said French heartily. 'Now, could you describe the lady?'

This, however, was beyond the driver's powers. He had not noticed her specially, nor could he describe the porter who had taken the luggage. But French had not expected that, indeed, he was surprised and delighted at having got so much.

The rest of that day and most of the next he spent at Victoria, interviewing porters, inspectors, ticket collectors, and any other officials he could find, who might by chance have seen the quarry. But nowhere had he any luck. The unknown remained unknown.

As he continued turning the matter over in his mind, a further possible clue in connection with the trunks occurred to him. They were large; they could not be taken in the carriage. It was nearly certain, therefore, that they must have been registered through. Were there records, he wondered, of such registration?

He went to the registration office and saw the clerk in charge. Yes, there were records; they were kept for a while and then destroyed. He could with a little trouble turn up those for the Newhaven boat train on the 26th November, and he would certainly do so to oblige the inspector.

But the records, when at last they were produced, revealed neither the name of Mrs Root nor the fact that anyone had registered two large trunks by that train.

French discussed the possibility of those in question having been taken unregistered. It seemed that this was possible, but most unlikely. In any case, had it been done, the clerk believed the Customs people would have noted it. But it would take some time to find out.

'Don't trouble about it,' French told him; 'at least, not in the meantime.'

Suppose this woman crook was impersonating Mrs Root, as he believed she was, would she not, as soon as she had disposed of the diamonds, seek to vanish and to resume her real personality? If so, did this not involve getting rid of the trunks? Did she really require them, or had they served their purpose when they reached Victoria?

As a forlorn hope, he decided he would act on this idea. Suppose she wanted to get rid of them, how would she do it?

There were several ways, but he felt satisfied that the easiest and best would be simply to leave them in the left luggage office. A considerable time would elapse before any question would arise about them, and it would then probably only take the form of their being opened by the railway company, and their contents sold for what they would bring.

He went round to the left luggage office and propounded his inquiry. And immediately he received a pleasant surprise. The clerk to whom he was referred smiled, and turning over some papers, pointed to an item. It read, 'Two large American trunks: White Star labels, S.S. *Olympic*. Mrs Chauncey S. Root, passenger to Southampton.'

'Bit of luck for you, sir,' the clerk remarked. 'I was looking over the list only today, and I noticed the item.

Boxes were left in on 26th of last month, and have not been claimed.'

'I want to open them and perhaps take them to the Yard.'

The necessary authority was soon obtained, and French followed the clerk to a huge room stored with luggage of all descriptions. Calling the porter in charge, they were conducted to a corner in which stood two large boxes, and French, looking at the labels, found they were those of which he was in search.

'Pull those out, George,' the clerk directed, 'so as this gentleman can open them, and let him take them away if he wants to. That all you want, sir?'

French, left to himself, began by satisfying himself that the handwriting on the labels was the same as that of the cheques. Then, taking a bunch of skeleton keys from his pockets, he set to work on the locks. In a few moments both stood open.

For a space he stood staring down in amazement at their contents. They were full of blankets! Just new, thin blankets of a poor cheap quality. They were fairly tightly packed, and completely filled the trunks.

He took out the blankets, and opening each out, shook it to make sure that no small article was concealed in the folds. But there was nothing.

Nor was there any smooth surface within the empty trunks upon which finger impressions might have been left. They were lined with canvas, fine as to quality, but still too rough to carry prints.

Inspector French felt more puzzled and baffled than ever. What, under the sun, were the blankets for? And where was the woman who had carried them about?

He was certainly no further on as to finding her. Whether she had crossed to France, or travelled to some other point on the Southern system, or had simply walked out of the station and been swallowed up in the wilderness of London, she was just as completely lost to him as ever. Hard luck that so unexpected a lift as the finding of the trunks should have led to so little.

But there was one thing it had led to. It settled the question of the impersonation. On no other hypothesis could the abandonment of the trunks be explained.

A point of which he had already thought recurred to him. If the unknown had impersonated Mrs Root she either knew her or knew a great deal about her. The chances, therefore, were that Mrs Root knew the unknown. It also seemed pretty certain that Mrs X, as he began to call the unknown in his mind, had really crossed in the *Olympic*. How else would she obtain the labels and the dinner menu? Granted these two probabilities, it almost certainly followed that the real Mrs Root and Mrs X had met on board. If so, would it not be worth while interviewing Mrs Root in the hope that she might by the method of elimination suggest the names of one or more persons who might have carried out the trick, and thus provide French with another point of attack.

Thinking it would be worth while to investigate the matter, he returned to the Yard and sent a cable to the Pittsburg police asking them to obtain Mrs Root's present address.

He glanced at his watch. It was not yet five o'clock, and he saw that he would have time to make another call before going off duty. Fifteen minutes later he pushed open

144

the door of Dashford's Inquiry Agency in Suffolk Street, off the Strand.

'Mr Parker in?' he demanded of the bright young lady who came to the counter, continuing in response to her request for his name, 'Inspector French from the Yard, but Mr Parker's an old friend and I'll just go right in.'

The girl eyed him doubtfully as he passed through the counter, and, crossing the office, tapped at a door in the farther wall. Without waiting for a reply, he pushed the door open and passed within, shutting it behind him.

Writing at a desk in the centre of the room was an enormously stout man. He did not look up, but grunted impatiently 'Well?'

'Well yourself,' French grunted, mimicking the other's tone.

The fat man looked up, then a smile dawned on his rubicund countenance, and he got heavily to his feet and held out a huge hand. 'Why, Joe, old son, I'm glad to see you. It's a long time since you blew in. Bring the chair round to the fire and let's hear the news.'

French did as he was told, as he answered, 'All's well, Tom? Busy?'

'Not too busy for a chat with you. How's the Yard?'

'The Yard's going strong; same old six and eightpence. I often think you did wisely to chuck it up and start in here. More your own boss, eh?'

The fat man shook his head.

'I don't know,' he said slowly, handing a tobacco pouch to his visitor. 'I don't know. More your own boss, perhaps, but more worry. If you don't get jobs here, you don't get your pay, and no pension at the end except the interest on

145

what you save up. I've thought of that pension many a time since I left.'

'Rubbish!' French exclaimed genially as he filled his pipe. 'You're too young to be talking of pensions. I was here looking for you about a week ago, but you were in Scotland.'

'Yes, I was at that Munro case. Acting for old Munro. I think he'll pull it off.'

'I dare say.' The talk drifted on, then French turned it to the object of his call.

'I'm on a case that you people have had a finger in. I wish you'd tell me what you can about it. It's that business of Mrs Root of Pittsburg that Williams & Davies of Cockspur Street put you on to six weeks ago. They wanted you to find out what she was like, and if she crossed by the *Olympic*.'

'Huh,' said the fat man. 'Well, we told 'em. I handled it myself.'

'Did they tell you why they wanted to know?'

'Nope. Only asked the question.'

'That's where they made the mistake. A woman called on Williams, saying she was Mrs Root and had crossed by the *Olympic*. She said she had lost her despatch case with her passport and tickets and money, and she wanted a loan of £3000 on the security of—diamonds she had in her trunk.'

'Well? Was it not right?'

'It was perfectly right so far. Williams was satisfied from what you told him that she was the woman, and he lent the money.'

French paused, smiling, and his friend swore.

'Confound it, man! Can't you get on? Were the stones paste?'

'Not at all. They took them to Stronge, of Hurst & Stronge's, and he valued them. They were perfectly all right, worth £3300 odd, *but*'—French paused and became very impressive—' they were all stolen from Duke & Peabody the night before!'

The fat man was visibly impressed. He stared fixedly at French, as he might had that philosopher turned into Mrs Root before his eyes. Then heavily he smote his thigh.

'Je—hoshaphat!' he observed slowly. 'The night before! Some crook that! Tell me.'

'That's about all there is to tell,' French declared. 'The woman arrived at the Savoy about eight o'clock the night before, ostensibly from the *Olympic,* and she left next night and has vanished. No clue so far. I traced her to Victoria and there lost the trail.'

The fat man thought profoundly.

'Well, if Williams & Davies want to blame us for it, they can look elsewhere,' he presently announced. 'They asked us a question, and we gave them a correct and immediate reply.'

'I know that,' French agreed. 'Williams asked you the wrong question. Mrs Root was impersonated; at least, that's my theory. But what I wanted to know from you was how you got your information. Between ourselves, are you satisfied about it?'

The fat man shook his fist good-humouredly.

'Now, young man,' he advised, 'don't you get fresh with me. But I'll tell you,' he went on, suddenly grave. 'It was through Pinkerton's. We have an arrangement with them. I cabled their New York depot and they got the information.'

'I knew it would be all right,' French answered, 'but I was curious to know how you worked.'

The two men chatted for some time, then French said he must go. Half an hour later he reached his house, and with a sigh of relief at the thought of his slippers and his arm-chair, let himself in.

11

A Deal in Jewellery

Inspector French's cheery self-confidence was never so strongly marked as when his mind was free from misgiving as to his course of action in the immediate future. When something was obviously waiting to be done he invariably went straight in and did it, shrinking neither from difficulty nor unpleasantness, provided only he could carry through his task to a successful conclusion. It was only when he did not see his way clear that he became depressed, and then he grew surly as a bear with a sore head, and his subordinates kept at as great a distance from him as their several activities would permit.

On the morning following his conversation with the stout representative of the inquiry agency, he was in great form, signifying that not only were his plans for the day satisfactorily in being, but that no doubt of their super-excellence clouded his mind. He had decided first to call on the jewellers to whom Mrs X had paid the cheques, after which, if these visits indicated no fresh line of attack, he would prosecute inquiries at the White Star company's office. By that time a reply from Pittsburg should have arrived.

When he had made his usual report at the Yard, he took out the cheques and made a note of the places to be visited. The first two were in Piccadilly, and he began his quest by taking a bus thither.

By one o'clock he had been round the whole six, and as he sat lunching in a small French restaurant off Cranbourne Street, he thought over what he had learned. In each shop, after more or less delay, he had found the salesman who had served Mrs X. All six men remembered her, and her proceedings with each seemed to have been the same. In each case she had asked for a piece of jewellery for a dear friend who was going to be married—something plain, but good; a diamond ring or a jewelled bangle or some costly trifle which would please a young girl's fancy. In each shop her purchases came to somewhere between two and three hundred pounds, and in each case she had proffered a cheque. She had volunteered to wait while a messenger was sent to the bank, as she had admitted that she couldn't expect the shop people to take her cheque when they didn't know her. The salesmen had all protested that this was unnecessary, and had politely kept her talking while they took the precaution. Finally, a telephone from the bank having reassured them, they had handed her her purchase and bowed her out. None of them had either noticed or suspected anything unusual in the transactions, and all were satisfied everything about them was O.K.

French was considerably puzzled by the whole business, but under the stimulus of a cup of coffee, a possible theory flashed into his mind.

Was it not probable that this purchase of costly but

commonplace articles of jewellery at six different shops was simply a part of the plan to transform Mr Duke's sixteen stones into money? As he thought over it, French thought he could dimly grasp that plan as a whole. First, the minds of Mr Williams and of Mr Hurst were prepared for what was coming by a previous visit. It was impossible that any suspicion could attach to that first visit, as when it was paid the robbery had not taken place. And now French saw that, but for the accident of the clerk, Orchard, visiting the office, these two gentlemen would not have known anything about the robbery when the second call was made, a distinctly clever achievement from the criminal's point of view. However, be that as it might, Mrs X's bluff carried her through, and she exchanged her stones, or rather Mr Duke's, for Mr Williams's cheque. But she was evidently afraid to cash the whole of the cheque, and French saw her point, namely, that the opening of an account and the lodging of £1500 was an astute move, calculated to prevent the suspicion that might possibly be caused by the cashing of £3000 in small notes. But this safeguard left her with the necessity of devising a plan for cashing her deposit, and here, in the purchase of the jewellery, French saw the plan. *Would she not sell what she had just bought?* If she could do so, there was the whole £3000 changed into untraceable notes.

Of course there would be a loss at every step of the operation. There was first of all a loss in disposing of the jewels. Mr Stronge had valued them at £3300, and she had received only £3000 from Mr Williams. She would lose even more heavily if she really had sold the jewellery she bought in Piccadilly and Regent Street, and she had lost a small deposit which she had left in her bank. But in spite of this, her scheme was well worth while. By it she would obtain perhaps seventy to eighty per cent, of the value of the stones, whereas if she had dealt with one of the recognised fences she would not have received more than from fifteen to twenty per cent. Moreover, her plan was safe. Up to the present she had succeeded in concealing her identity, but application to a fence would have left her either in his power to blackmail, or in that of the intermediary she employed to reach him. No, the plan was clear enough and good enough, too, and in spite of all French's optimism there remained at the back of his mind the sinking fear that she might yet pull it off.

But if this theory were true, it followed that if he could trace these sales he would be furnished with another jumping-off place or places from which to resume his quest of the elusive Mrs X. His next problem therefore became, Had Mrs X sold the trinkets, and if so, could he trace the sales?

He went back to the six jewellers, and obtained a detailed description of the articles bought. Then he returned to the Yard, and with the help of a directory and his knowledge of the City, drew up a list of dealers who might be expected to handle such business. Half a dozen plain clothes men were then impressed into the service, with orders to call on these persons and find out if any of the articles in question had fallen into their hands.

Inspector French had just completed these arrangements when a cable was handed to him. It was in reply to his of the previous night, and read:

'Mrs Chauncey S. Root, Hotel Bellegarde, Mürren, till end of month.'

Mürren? That was in Switzerland, wasn't it? He sent for an atlas and a Continental Bradshaw, and looked it up. Yes, it was in Switzerland; moreover, it was close to where he had already been, past that lake with the marvellous colouring—the Lake of Thun, and so to Interlaken and the far-famed Bernese Oberland, places which he had long desired to visit. It was with more than a little eagerness that he once more ran over his reasons for wanting to see Mrs Root, and then, satisfied, went to his chief's room. The great man listened and was convinced, and French, jubilant, went to prepare for his departure on the following evening.

On his way to the Yard next morning, he called at the White Star offices and got a copy of the *Olympic's* passenger list of the trip in question. The ship, they told him, was in New York, but would be sailing in another three days. She would therefore be due in Southampton on the following Wednesday week.

He learned also that specimens of the handwriting of each traveller were available. Forms were filled and declarations signed both in connection with the purchase of the ticket and with the passing of the luggage through the customs. If French was anxious to examine these, he could do so by applying to their Southampton office or to the customs authorities in the same city.

French decided that if his interview with Mrs Root led to nothing, he would follow this advice, and he resolved that in this case he would go to Southampton when the *Olympic* was in, so as to interview the ship's staff as well.

When he returned to the Yard, he found that some information had already come in about the jewellery. One of his six plain clothes men had had a stroke of luck. At his very first call, Robsons' of Oxford Street, he had found

a ring which answered the description of one of the
purchased articles, and which had been bought from a
lady on the afternoon of the day after that on which
Mrs X had opened her bank account. He had taken the
ring to Messrs Lewes & Tottenham, who had made the
sale in question, and they identified it as that sold to Mrs
X and paid for by a Mrs Root's cheque. Robson had paid
£190 for it, while Messrs Lewes & Tottenham had charged
£225, so the lady had lost rather badly over the transaction. She had taken her money in notes of small value,
the numbers of which had not been observed.

The assistant at Robsons' who had served Mrs X could
not recall her appearance; in fact, it was only when
confronted with the records of the purchase that he remembered the matter at all. But he was satisfied the client was
an American lady, and he thought she was neither very
old nor very young, nor in any way remarkable looking.

Inspector French was delighted with his news. It proved
to him beyond possibility of doubt that his theory was
correct. The purchase of these jewels was simply part of
the plan to turn the stolen diamonds into money in a form
which could not be traced. Further, it showed that he had
also been right in assuming the lady had not gone to France
on the evening she drove to Victoria; on the following day
she was still in London.

But so far as he could see, the discovery brought him
no nearer to finding the mysterious woman. The dealer's
assistant could not describe her, nor had she left any traces
which could be followed up. In fact, here was another
promising clue which bade fair to vanish in smoke, and
as he thought over the possibility, some measure of chagrin
began to dull the keenness of his delight.

During the forenoon another of the plain clothes men struck oil, and by lunch time a third transaction had come to light. Unfortunately, both of these cases was as unproductive as the original discovery. None of the shop people could remember who had sold the trinket. French went himself to each shop, but his most persistent efforts failed to extract any further information.

That night he left for Mürren. In due time he reached Berne, and changing trains, travelled down past Spiez, under the great conical hill of Niesen, along the shores of the Lake of Thun and into Interlaken. There he slept the night, and next morning took the narrow gauge line that led south into the heart of the giants of the Bernese Oberland. He felt overpowered by the towering chain of mountains, the Matterhorn, the Eiger, the Mönch, the Jungfrau, and as they wound their way up the narrow valley he felt as if the overwhelming masses were closing down on him from either side. Reaching Lauterbrunnen, he went up by the funiculaire to the Mürren plateau, and continued his way by the electric tramway to the famous resort. There, as he walked to the Bellegarde, he gazed fascinated across the valley at the mighty buttresses of the Jungfrau, one summit of dazzling white succeeding another, up and up and up into the clear, thin blue of the sky. It took more to bring him to earth than a fellow-traveller's gratified suggestion that at last they would be able to get a decent drink after all that travelling through the snow. He and his new friend went to the bar of the Bellegarde and had two of Scotch, and gradually the magic of the mountains faded, and the interview with Mrs Root began to reassume its former importance.

An examination of the register revealed the name,

Mrs Chauncey S. Root, Pittsburg, U.S.A., same as at the Savoy, but here it was written in quite a different hand. The real Mrs Root this time, French thought, as he turned away from the office.

He decided to wait until after lunch before tackling the lady, but he got the head waiter to point her out as she entered the restaurant. She undoubtedly answered the description given by the American detectives as well as by Mr Williams, but on looking at her he recognised more than ever the vague and unsatisfactory nature of that description. It was one that would apply to hundreds of women.

In the lounge after lunch he spoke to her. He apologised for intruding, explained who he was, and begged that she would give him an interview, and, if possible, some information.

'Why certainly,' she agreed. 'We'll go right to my sitting-room,' and French told himself that from nowhere on earth save the United States of America could that voice have come.

'You are Mrs Chauncey S. Root?' he began, when they were settled in the private room of the best suite the hotel contained. 'I should be glad if, before we begin to talk, you would be good enough to let me see your passport. I shall explain why later.'

'I guess you'd better tell me first,' she returned, leaning back in her arm-chair and lighting a cigarette.

French smiled.

'As you will, madam. The fact is that two ladies, each calling herself Mrs Chauncey S. Root, of Pittsburg, U.S.A., crossed by the *Olympic* to Southampton. I have been sent from Scotland Yard to find out which is the real one.'

The lady looked incredulous.

'Say, now, what started you on to that yarn? I crossed by the *Olympic,* but there was no one else of that name aboard.'

'Nevertheless a Mrs Chauncey S. Root, who had just crossed by the *Olympic,* turned up at the Savoy Hotel on the day the ship reached Liverpool, and put through a fraud on a man in London to the tune of £3000. I know, madam, it was not you, but I have to get some proof of it that will convince my superiors.'

With little ejaculations of interest and astonishment the lady arose, and unlocking a despatch case, took from it a book.

'You can have that passport right now,' she declared. 'You have interested me quite a lot. Start right in and tell me the story.'

French examined the document, and as he did so his last doubt vanished. The lady before him was Mrs Root. Mrs X remained—Mrs X.

Asking her to keep the story to herself, he told her in considerable detail all that he knew of Mr Williams's mysterious visitor, continuing:

'Now, Mrs Root, you will see where I want your help. Someone has impersonated you, someone who more than probably crossed with you from New York. I want you to think whom it might have been. Here's a copy of the passenger list. Please take your time, and go over the people you met on the trip. Eliminate those you are sure of, and put a mark opposite the others. You follow what I mean?'

'I follow you all right, but it isn't as easy as you seem to think. I couldn't remember all the people I came across between New York and London.'

'I suppose not. But, after all, the thing isn't so big as

that. Only a very few of the women would fill the bill. First, she must be roughly of your height and your figure— not very like, of course, but approximately. You need not mind her colouring, for she could make that up—except her eyes; her eyes are a light golden brown. Can you remember anyone with eyes like that?'

The lady shook her head, and French went on:

'Then she must be a clever woman; clever and coura- geous and determined, and something of an actress also. She must be all those things to have carried such a deal off successfully.'

French paused to allow his words to sink in, then continued once more:

'And she knows quite a lot about you. Not only has she observed your appearance, but she would obviously try to find out all she could about you, so that she might answer questions she might be asked. Do none of these points bring anyone to your mind? Please, Mrs Root, try to help me. If you cannot give me some ideas I may as well confess I don't know where to turn next.'

'Well, I'll do what I can, but I don't see any light so far.' She crossed the room and once more hunted through the despatch case. 'Here are some pictures I took with my kodak. Maybe they'll suggest someone.'

There were two dozen or more photographs of groups of passengers, taken on board the liner. Mrs Root began with systematic precision to go through them. As she pointed to each individual she repeated to the inspector what she knew about her.

'Mrs Jelfs—guess she wouldn't do—too fat. Miss— Miss—I just don't recall that young woman's name. But she's too tall anyway; half a head taller'n me. Next is

Haidee Squance, daughter of Old Man Squance of Consolidated Oil. I've known her since I've known anything. Then this one is—say now, who is this one? I've got it; a little girl called Dinsmore: Irish, I think. She's no good either—eyes of the lightest blue I ever saw. Next is Mrs Purce,' and so on for five-and-twenty minutes by the electric clock on the mantelpiece.

French was highly delighted with the efficient way in which his hostess had tackled the job, but when all was said and done the result was disappointingly small. Eight persons in the photographs had been marked as possibles, of whom Mrs Root remembered the names of five. Of these five, one, a Mrs Ward, whom Mrs Root had met for the first time on board, seemed the most likely for several reasons. She was about Mrs Root's height, though stouter, had, Mrs Root believed, light brown eyes, and had been friendly, and, Mrs Root now remembered, just a trifle inquisitive. But she was ruled out by her nationality. That she really was English, as she claimed, Mrs Root had no doubt whatever. French showed her the cheques, but she could not recall ever having seen the handwriting in which they were filled out.

But she did give him one hint that he felt might prove valuable. She said that the stewardess who had looked after her cabin was a peculiarly intelligent and observant woman. Mrs Root had been surprised on different occasions by the intimate knowledge of herself and her fellow travellers which this stewardess exhibited. She did not exactly accuse her of spying, but she thought she would be more likely to answer French's inquiries than anyone else he could find. She did not remember the woman's name, but she was rather striking looking, with dark eyes, a young face, and perfectly white hair, and he would have no difficulty in identifying her.

Mrs Root was extremely interested in the whole affair, and begged the inspector to keep her posted as to developments. This he promised to do, as he took his leave.

He had now more reason than ever for visiting Southampton when the *Olympic* was next in, and he set out on the following morning on his return journey, reaching London on the Tuesday afternoon.

At the Yard he found that three more of the transactions of the mysterious lady had come to light, but unfortunately in each case without supplying any clue which might lead to her identification. These discoveries accounted for some £1200 worth of the jewellery Mrs X had bought, and for this she had received £1090, making a loss on the transaction of only about nine per cent.

He took an early opportunity of visiting Mr Williams, to ask him if he could identify his mysterious caller in Mrs Root's group. But the moneylender was not illuminative. He did not reply for some time, turning the cards over as if uncertain, but finally he pointed to Mrs Ward's figure.

'That's like the lady,' he said doubtfully, 'but I confess I am not sure of her. If it is she, it is an uncommonly bad photograph.' He continued staring at the picture. 'You know,' he went on slowly, 'I've seen that woman before; that woman that you say is Mrs Ward. I've certainly seen her somewhere. It's a curious thing, but I had the same impression when my visitor called here with the diamonds; I thought vaguely that I had seen her before. But I wasn't so sure as I am about this Mrs Ward. Somewhere, at some time, I've seen her. I wish to heaven I could remember where.'

'I wish to heaven you could,' French agreed in somewhat aggrieved tones. 'It would make things a lot easier for me.'

'If I can't remember to help find my £3000, it's not likely I shall be able to do it to ease your job,' the other declared dryly. 'I can't place her. I've thought and thought, and it's no good. Someone I've seen in a train or a restaurant most likely. I don't think it's anyone I've ever met.'

French next called at the Piccadilly branch of the London and Counties Bank, and saw Mr Scarlett and the clerk, Plenteous. Both these gentlemen hesitatingly selected Mrs Ward's photograph as being like that of their mysterious client, though neither believed it was she. As in the case of Mr Williams, the manager thought the lady's features were familiar, though he was sure he had never met her before. With this, French had to be content.

He spent his afternoon in driving round the shops and agents with whom the elusive Mrs X had dealt. Of the eleven assistants who had served her, seven thought she was like Mrs Ward, and four could not recall her appearance.

All this testimony was very unsatisfactory to French, but he thought the balance of probability was in favour of Mrs Ward being the woman he sought, and more hopeful than he had been for some time, he travelled down to Southampton on the Wednesday evening, so as to be there for the arrival of the *Olympic* on the following day.

12

The Elusive Mrs X

Inspector French put up at a small hotel near the town station, and next morning was early at the White Star offices. There he learned that the *Olympic* was even at that moment coming in, and he went down to the quays and watched the berthing of the monster vessel. It was an impressive experience to see her creep up to her place, manœuvre into position, and make fast. Then from her gangways began to stream the travellers who, for the better part of a week, had journeyed aboard her. Some were hurrying, already intent on business or anxious to catch trains, others leisurely awaiting taxis and motor-cars, some smilingly greeting friends or waving farewells to voyage acquaintances, all drifting gradually away, their places taken by others—and still others . . . French began to think the exodus would never cease, but at last the crowd diminished, and he pushed his way on board and began a search for the purser. Urgent work in connection with the arrival prevented that busy official from attending to him at once, but he sent a steward to show French to his cabin, and presently joined him there.

'Sorry for keeping you waiting, Inspector,' he apologised. 'You want some information about our home trip in late November?'

'Yes,' French answered, and he explained his business and produced Mrs Root's marked photographs, concluding, 'I want to find out the names and addresses of these eight women, and as much information as possible about them.'

'I'm afraid I could scarcely give you that,' the purser answered. 'The records of each trip go ashore at the end of the trip, and I have only those of this present run. But some of the staff might remember the names of the ladies, and if so, you could get their addresses at the office ashore.'

'That would do excellently. I have a copy of the passenger list here, if it would be of any use.'

'Yes, it would be a reminder. Let me see now if I can help you myself, and if not, I think I can put you in the way of getting to know.' He began to scrutinise the photographs.

'That's Mrs Root,' French indicated, moving round and looking over the other's shoulder. 'She gave me the names of five, but I should like to check her recollection. The other three she couldn't remember.'

The purser nodded as he turned the pictures over. 'That's a Mrs Forbes,' he pointed, 'and I rather think that is a Miss Grayson or Graves or some name like that. I remember most of these other faces, but not the people's names.'

'Mrs Forbes and Miss Grayson are correct according to Mrs Root.'

The purser laid down the photographs with the air of quiet decision which seemed characteristic.

'I'm afraid that's my limit.' He touched a bell. 'Ask Mrs Hope to come here,' he ordered, continuing to French, 'Mrs Hope is the chief stewardess. You can go round with her, and I expect she'll get you what you want all right.'

Mrs Hope was an efficient-looking woman, who quickly grasped what was required of her. She asked French to accompany her to her sanctum, and there looked over the photographs. She was herself able to identify six of the portraits, and on calling on some of her underlings, the names of the remaining two were speedily forthcoming.

French was glad to find that Mrs Root's recollection of the names of her fellow travellers had been correct as far as it had gone, and as he left the great vessel he devoutly hoped that she might have been correct also in her belief that Mrs X was among the eight women she had indicated. If so, he was well on his way to identify that elusive lady.

He returned to the White Star office and explained that he wanted to know the Christian names, addresses, and other available particulars of the eight women whose names were marked on the passenger list which he handed in, as well as to see a specimen of the handwriting of each.

He realised that the only conclusive test was the hand-writing. If one of the eight women wrote the hand of the Mrs X cheques, he had reached his goal. If not, he determined to go through the declarations of every woman who had crossed on the trip in question in the hope of finding what he sought.

The clerk who had been instructed to attend to him brought out a mass of papers. 'I wonder,' he said apologetically, 'if you would mind looking through these yourself? It is our busy day, and I've an awful lot to get through. You see, it's quite simple. These are the embarkation declarations for the trip, and you can turn up anyone you want quite easily. They are arranged in alphabetical order in the different classes. They'll give you what you want to know straight off.'

'Right you are,' French declared, delighted thus to get a free hand. 'Don't you bother about me. I'll peg away, and come and ask you if I get into trouble.'

He 'pegged away,' looking up the declaration of each of the eight women, noting the name, address, nationality, and other particulars, and then comparing the handwriting with the signatures on the Mrs X cheques.

He was not a handwriting expert, but he knew enough about the science to recognise the characteristics which remain unchanged when the writing is disguised. He was, therefore, very patient and thorough in his search, never passing a signature because it looked unlike the model at first sight, but testing each by the rules he had learned, and satisfying himself that it really had been written by a different hand.

He went on without incident until he reached the eighth name on his list. But when he turned to the declaration of Mrs Ward, the lady whom Mrs Root had thought the most likely of the lot, he gave a sudden little chuckle of delight. There was the hand of the cheques, the same hand unquestionably, and written without any attempt at disguise! There it was! Mrs Elizabeth Ward, aged 39, British subject, etc., etc., of Oaklands, Thirsk Road, York. He had reached his goal!

But immediately he was assailed by misgivings. Mrs Root had thought of Mrs Ward, but had ruled her out because of her nationality. Mrs Ward, she had said, was English, while all the people who had seen Mrs X, seventeen or eighteen persons at least, had agreed she was an American. He would have assumed that Mrs Root had made a mistake, but for the fact that the declaration said English also. French was puzzled, and he decided that he would go back to the ship and ascertain the views of the staff on the point.

But they all supported Mrs Root. Mrs Ward was English; undoubtedly and unquestionably English. The stewards and the stewardesses had some experience on the point, and they guessed they knew. Also he came across the doctor, who, it appeared, had spoken on several occasions to Mrs Ward, and he was equally positive.

It chanced that as he was leaving the ship he encountered the woman to whom Mrs Root had advised him to apply, the striking-looking stewardess with dark eyes and white hair, and he stopped and spoke to her.

Unfortunately, she could not tell him very much. She remembered Mrs Ward, both by name and appearance, though she had not attended to her. But it chanced, never-theless, that her attention had been specially directed to her because of a certain incident which had taken place towards the end of the voyage. Passing down the corridor while lunch was being served, she had seen the door of one of the cabins in her own charge open slightly, and a lady appear and glance quickly round, as if to see if she was unobserved. The cabin was occupied by a Mrs Root, an American, but the lady was this Mrs Ward. Something stealthy and furtive in her appearance had excited the stewardess's suspicion, and she had drawn back into another cabin to await developments. Mrs Ward, evidently satisfied that she was unnoticed, had turned to the dining saloon and taken her place. The stewardess had kept her eye on her, and after the meal she had seen her go up to Mrs Root and speak to her, as if reporting the result of her mission. This action had lulled the stewardess's suspicion, but she had returned to Mrs Root's cabin and had had a look round to see if anything had been disturbed. So far as she could see, nothing had, nor had Mrs Root made any complaint about her things having been interfered with.

If further confirmation of his suspicions were needed, French felt that this episode supplied it. Doubtless Mrs Ward was amassing information as to the other's clothes and belongings to assist her in her impersonation. Perhaps also she was photographing envelopes or other documents of which to prepare forgeries in case of need.

There still remained the difficulty of her nationality. Obviously it is easy to mimic the accent and manner of a foreigner, but French found it hard to believe that such mimicry could be so perfect as to deceive a large number of persons, many of whom were experts on that particular point. This, however, was only a small part of the general problem, and did not affect his next business, to find Mrs Elizabeth Ward, Thirsk Road, York.

He went ashore, and, turning into a telegraph office, sent a wire to the chief of police at York, asking him if a lady of that name lived at the address in question and, if so, to wire was she at home.

His next business was at police headquarters, and thither he was directing his steps when a thought struck him, and he turned aside to the sheds in which the transatlantic luggage is examined. Several of the customs officers were still there, and he went up and spoke to one of them.

'Now,' the young fellow answered in surprise, 'it's a darned queer thing that you came to me about that. Quite a coincidence, that is. I know the man who went through those trunks. He told me about it at the time. It seemed a darned silly thing that anyone should want to brings trunks of blankets from America. If you come along I'll find him for you. And so the lady's wanted, is she? Say, Jack!' he called a colleague, another clean, efficient young fellow of the same type, 'here's someone wants you. He wants to know about those trunks of blankets you were telling me about two or three trips of the *Olympic* back. A darned queer coincidence that he should come to me about them. That's what I call it!'

'Yes, you've made a lucky shot, haven't you?' the second man said to French. 'I remember the trunks and the lady they belonged to, because I couldn't understand why anyone should want to bring trunks of blankets across the Atlantic. I've never known anyone do it before.'

'You didn't make any remark about them,' French asked.

'No, but she did. She said she reckoned I hadn't often seen trunks of blankets brought over from America. You see, I was a bit suspicious at first, and was examining the things pretty carefully. I said that was so, and she said she was taking back a small but valuable collection of porcelain ornaments, which she would pack in the blankets, and that when she had to bring the trunks anyway, she thought she might as well bring the packing as well and so save buying new. I thought the whole business a bit off, but there was nothing dutiable in the case, and it wasn't my job to interfere. Is there anything wrong about it?'

'I don't know,' French told him. 'I think the woman was a crook, but I'm not on to the blanket stunt yet. By the way, is she in one of those groups?'

The young man identified Mrs Ward without hesitation, and French, finding he had learned all that the customs men could tell him, resumed his way to the police station.

He wondered what this blanket business really did mean. Then as he walked slowly along with head bent forward and eyes vacantly scanning the pavement, a possible explanation occurred to him. These trunks, apparently, were required solely as properties to assist in the fraud. Mrs Root, the wife of a Pittsburg magnate, would scarcely arrive at the Savoy from America without American trunks. But when Mrs Root came to disappear, the trunks would become an embarrassment. They would have to be got rid of, and, as a matter of fact, they were got rid of. They must therefore contain nothing of the lady's, no personal possession which might act as a clue to its owner. But they must contain something. Empty trunks would be too light, and might be observed by the chambermaid, and comments might be occasioned among the hotel staff which might reach the management, and which would become important if Mr Williams rang up to make his inquiries. But blankets would exactly fill the bill; indeed, French could think of nothing more suitable for the purpose. They would give the trunks a moderate weight, they would not supply a clue to Mrs Ward, and they would be cheap, while their presence could be accounted for sufficiently reasonably to the customs officers. Yes, French thought, it was a probable enough explanation.

Arrived at the police station, he sent in his name with a request to see the officer in charge.

Superintendent Hayes had been stationed in London before he got his present appointment, and had come across French on more than one occasion. He therefore greeted the inspector cordially, found him a comfortable chair, and supplied him with an excellent cigar.

'From Trinidad,' he explained. 'I get them direct from a man I know out there. And what's the best news of you?'

They discussed old times for some minutes, then French turned to the business in hand.

'It's an interesting case,' he said as he gave the other the details, continuing, 'The woman must be a pretty cool hand. She could easily invent that tale about losing her passport, for old Williams's edification, but under the circumstances her coming to you about it was a bit class.'

'She had a nerve; yes,' the superintendent admitted. 'But, you see, it was necessary. She must have known that the absence of the passport would strike Williams as suspicious, and it was necessary for her to remove that suspicion. She couldn't very well get a bag of that kind stolen without informing the police, so she had to inform them. She would see how easily Williams could check her statement, as indeed he did. No, I don't see how she could have avoided coming to us. It was an obvious precaution.'

'I quite agree with all you say,' French returned, 'but it argues a cool customer for all that; not only, so to speak, putting her head into the lion's mouth, but at the same time calling his attention to it's being there. Anyway, I've got to find her, and I wish you'd let me have details about her. I've got some from the *Olympic* people, but I want to pick up everything I can.'

The superintendent telephoned to someone to 'send up Sergeant McAfee,' and when a tall, cadaverous man entered, he introduced him as the man who had dealt with the business in question.

'Sergeant McAfee has just been transferred to us from Liverpool,' he explained. 'Sit down, McAfee. Inspector French wants to know some details about that woman who lost her handbag coming off the *Olympic* some seven weeks ago. I think you handled the thing. Do you remember a Mrs Root of Pittsburg?'

'I mind her rightly, sir,' the man answered in what French

believed was a Belfast accent. 'But it wasn't coming off the *Olympic* she lost it. It was later on that same day, though it was on the quays right enough.'

'Tell us all you can about it.'

The sergeant pulled out his notebook. 'I have it in me other book,' he announced. 'If ye'll excuse me, I'll get it.'

In a moment he returned, sat down, and turning over the dog's-eared pages of a well-worn book, began as if reciting evidence in court:

'On the 24th November last at about 3.00 p.m., I was passing through the crowd on the outer quays when I heard a woman cry out. "Thief, thief," she shouted, and she ran up and caught me by the arm. She was middling tall and thinnish, her face pale and her hair dark. She spoke in an American voice, and seemed upset or excited. She said to me, breathless like, "Say, officer," she said, "I've just had my despatch case stolen." I asked her where, and how, and what was in it. She said right there where we were standing, and not three seconds before. She was carrying it in her hand, and it was snatched out of it. She turned round and saw a man juke away in the crowd. She shouted and made after him, but he was away before she could get near. I asked her what the case was like, and she said a small square brown morocco leather one with gold fittings. I went and told the two men on duty close by, and we kept a watch on the exits, but we never saw a sign of it.' Sergeant McAfee shook his head gloomily as he concluded. 'She hadn't any call to be carrying a gold fitted case in that crowd anyway.'

'That's a fact, Sergeant,' the superintendent agreed. 'And you never came on any trace of it?'

'No, sir. I brought her up to the station, and took her

name and all particulars. There's the report.' He unfolded
a paper and laid it on the superintendent's desk.

In the document was a detailed description of the lady,
of the alleged despatch case and its contents, and of the
means that had been taken to try to trace it. The pawn-
brokers had been advised and a special watch kept on
fences and other usual channels for the disposal of stolen
goods.

When French had digested these particulars, he brought
out once more his photographs and handed them to the
sergeant.

'Look at those, Sergeant, and tell me if you see the
woman among them.'

Slowly the sergeant turned them over, gazing at them in
precisely the same puzzled way as had done Mr Williams,
Mr Scarlett, and the other London men to whom they had
been shown. And with the same doubt and hesitation he
presently fixed on Mrs Ward.

'That would be to be her,' he declared slowly, 'that is, if
she's there at all. It isn't a good likeness, but I believe it's
her all the same.'

'You wouldn't swear to her?'

'I'd hardly. But I believe it's her for all that.'

French nodded. The sergeant's statement, agreeing as it
did with those of Messrs Williams, Scarlett and Co., seemed
capable of but one explanation. Mrs X was Mrs Ward all
right, but before meeting these men she had made herself
up to impersonate Mrs Root. They saw a likeness to Mrs
Ward because it really was she, but they were doubtful
because she was disguised.

The inspector leaned forward and tapped the photograph.

'Put it this way, Sergeant,' he suggested. 'Here is a picture of the lady as she really is. When you saw her she was made up to look like another woman. How's that, do you think?'

In Sergeant's McAfee's lacklustre eye there shone a sudden gleam. 'That's just what it is, sir,' he answered with an approach to something almost like interest in his manner. 'That's it and no mistake. She's like the photograph by her features, but not by her make-up.' He nodded his head several times in appreciation.

'Very good.' Inspector French invariably liked as many strings to his bow as he could get. 'Now I want some hint from you that will help me trace her.'

But this was just what Sergeant McAfee could not supply. The woman had given two addresses, the Savoy in London and Mrs Root's home in Pittsburg. There was no help in either, and no other information was forthcoming.

He lunched with his friend the superintendent, afterwards withdrawing to the lounge of his hotel to have a quiet smoke and to think things over.

While he sat there, a page appeared with a telegram. It was a reply from the police at York and read:

'Your wire. No one of that name or address known.'

French swore disgustedly. He had, of course, realised that the name might be false, but yet he had hoped against hope that he might really have reached the end of at least this portion of his quest. But here he was, as far from the truth as ever! He would now have to make a fresh start to trace this elusive lady—he used another adjective in his mind—and he couldn't see that he was any better equipped for the search now than when he had started out from Mr Williams's office. It was a confoundedly exasperating case—just bristling with promising clues which one after another petered out as he came to follow them up. Being on it was like trying to cross a stream on stepping-stones which invariably gave way when he came to place his weight on them. It was an annoying thought also that that would scarcely be the view his chief would take of the matter. The chief had not been over-complimentary already in his comments on his handling of the case, and French felt that he would view this new check in anything but a sympathetic spirit.

However, grousing about it wouldn't lead anywhere, and with an effort he switched his thoughts back to his problem. As he thought it over a further point occurred to him.

Since his first visit to the Savoy he had wondered why the lady had turned up there so much later than the other passengers from, the *Olympic,* and now he saw the reason. The episode of the handbag had taken place some four hours after the vessel's arrival, long after the special boat train had left. Mrs X—for she was still Mrs X—must therefore have travelled up by an afternoon train, probably the 5.26 or 6.22 p.m. from the West Station, which got in at 6.58 and 8.20 respectively. Now, why this delay? What had she done during these four hours?

The answer was not far to seek. Was it not to give her time and opportunity to assume her disguise? He felt it must be so.

The lady was her natural self—other than in name—on board the *Olympic*, and having no opportunity to alter her appearance, she had passed through the customs in the same character. Hence the ship's staff and the customs officer had instantly recognised her photograph. But it was obvious that her impersonation of Mrs Root must begin before she interviewed the Southampton police, and that accounted for the hesitation of Sergeant McAfee and the people in London in identifying her. She had therefore made herself up between passing through the customs at, say, eleven o'clock, and calling on the sergeant at three. Where was she during those four hours?

He put himself in her place. Confronted with her problem, what would he have done?

Gone to a hotel, unquestionably. Taken a room in which to assume the disguise. Had Mrs X engaged a bedroom in one of the Southampton hotels for that afternoon?

As he thought over the thing, further probabilities occurred to him. The lady would go up to her bedroom as one person and come down as another. Therefore, surely, the larger the hotel, the less chance of the transformation being observed. One of a crowd, she would go to the reception office and engage a room for a few hours' rest, and pay for it then and there. Then, having accomplished the make-up, she would slip out, unobserved in the stream of passers-by. Yes, French felt sure he was on the right track, and, with a fresh accession of energy, he jumped to his feet, knocked out his pipe, and left the building.

He called first at the South Western and made his inquiries. But here he drew blank. At the Dolphin he had no better luck, but at the Polygon he found what he wanted. After examining the records, the reception clerk there was able to recall the transaction. About midday an American lady had come in, and saying she wanted a few hours' rest before catching the 5.26 to London, had engaged a bedroom on a quiet floor until that hour. She had registered, and French, on looking up the book, was delighted to find once more the handwriting of the lady of the cheques. It was true that on this occasion she figured as Mrs Silas R. Clamm, of Hill Drive, Boston, Mass.; but knowing what he knew of her habits, French would have been surprised to have found a name he had seen before.

At first he was delighted at so striking a confirmation of his theory, but as he pursued his inquiries his satisfaction vanished, and once more depression and exasperation swept over him. For the reception clerk could not remember anything more than the mere fact of the letting of the room, and no one else in the building remembered the woman at all. With his usual pertinacity, he questioned all who might have come in contact with her, but from none of them did he receive the slightest help. That Mrs X had made herself up at the hotel for her impersonation stunt was clear, but unfortunately it was equally clear that she had vanished from the building without leaving any trace.

The worst of the whole business was that he didn't see what more he could do. The special clues upon which he had been building had failed him, and he felt there was now nothing for it but to fall back on the general one of the photographs. One of the portraits was excellently clear as to details, and he decided he would have an enlargement made of Mrs X, and circulate it among the police in the hope that some member at some time might recognise the lady. Not a very hopeful method certainly, but all he had left.

He took an evening train from the West Station, and a couple of hours afterwards reached his home, a thoroughly tired and disgruntled man.

13

Mrs French Takes a Notion

By the time Inspector French had finished supper and lit up a pipe of the special mixture he affected, he felt in considerably better form. He determined that instead of going early to bed, as he had intended while in the train, he would try to induce the long-suffering Mrs French to listen to a statement of his problem, in the hope that light thereon would be vouchsafed to her, in which in due course he would participate.

Accordingly, when she had finished with the supper things he begged her to come and share his difficulties, and when she had taken her place in her accustomed arm-chair and had commenced her placid knitting, he took up the tale of his woes.

Slowly and in the fullest detail he told her all he had done from the time he was sent to Messrs Williams & Davies, when he first heard of the mysterious Mrs X, up to his series of visits of that day, concluding by expressing his belief that Mrs X and Mrs Ward were one and the same person, and explaining the difficulty he found himself up against in tracing her. She heard him without comment, and when he had finished asked what he proposed to do next.

'Why, that's just it,' he exclaimed a trifle impatiently. 'That's the whole thing. If I was clear about that there would be no difficulty. What would you advise?'

She shook her head, and bending forward seemed to concentrate her whole attention on her knitting. This, French knew, did not indicate lack of interest in his story. It was just her way. He therefore waited more or less hopefully, and when after a few minutes she began to question him, his hopes were strengthened.

'You say that Mrs Root and those steamer people thought the woman was English?'

'That's so.'

'There were quite a lot of them thought she was English?'

'Why, yes,' French agreed. 'There was Mrs Root and the doctor and the purser and her dinner steward and at least four stewardesses. They were all quite satisfied. And the other passengers and attendants must have been satisfied too, or the thing would have been talked about. But I don't see exactly what you're getting at.'

Mrs French was not to be turned aside from her catechism.

'Well, do *you* think she was English?' she persisted.

French hesitated. Did he? He really was not sure. The evidence seemed strong, and yet it was just as strong, or stronger, for her being an American. Mr Williams, for example, was—

'You don't know,' Mrs French broke in. 'Well, now, see here. Mr Williams said she was American?'

'That's it,' her husband rejoined. 'He said—'

'And that bank manager and his clerk, they thought she was American?'

'Yes, but—'

'And the shops she bought and sold the jewellery at, and the Savoy, and the Southampton police, they all thought she was American?'

'Yes, but we don't—'

'Well, that ought surely to give you something.'

'That they were sisters? I thought of that, but the hand-writing shows that they weren't.'

'Of course I don't mean sisters. Think again.'

French sat up sharply.

'What do you mean, Emily? I don't follow what you're after.'

His wife ignored the interruption.

'And there's another thing you might have thought of,' she continued. 'That Williams man thought he had seen the woman before. What age is he?'

French was becoming utterly puzzled.

'What age?' he repeated helplessly. 'I don't know. About sixty, I should think.'

'Just so,' said his wife. 'And that other man, that Scarlett, he thought he had seen her before. What age is he?'

The inspector moved nervously.

'Really, Emily,' he protested, 'I wish you'd explain what you're getting at. I don't take your meaning in the least.'

'You would if you'd use your head,' his wife snapped. 'What age is that Scarlett?'

'About the same as the other—fifty-five or sixty. But what has that got to do—'

'But the young fellow, that bank clerk; he didn't remember her?'

'No, but—'

'Well, there you are—silly! What would a woman be who could make up like another woman, and put on an English or American talk, and be remembered by old Londoners? Why, a child could guess that, Watson!'

When Mrs French called her husband by the name of the companion of the great Holmes, it signified two things, first, that she was in what he always referred to as 'a good twist,' and secondly, that she felt pleasantly superior, having seen something—or thinking she had—which he had missed. He was therefore always delighted when a conversation reached this stage, believing that something helpful was about to materialise.

But on this occasion he grasped her meaning as soon as she had spoken. Of course! How in all the earthly world had he missed the point? The woman was an actress; a former London actress! That would explain the whole thing. And if so, he would soon find her. Actors' club secretaries and attendants, theatrical agents, stagedoor keepers, the editors of society papers—scores of people would have known her, and he would have an easy task to learn her name and her history.

He jumped up and kissed his wife. 'By jove, Emily! You're a fair wonder,' he cried warmly, and she, still placidly knitting, unsuccessfully attempted to hide the affection and admiration she felt for him by a trite remark anent the folly of an old fool.

Next morning, French, with a new and thoroughly satisfactory programme before him, sallied forth at quite the top of his form. He had made a list of theatrical agencies at which he intended first to apply, after which, if luck had up to then eluded him, he would go round the theatres and have a word with the stagedoor keepers, finally applying to the older actor-managers and producers and anyone else from whom he thought he might gain information.

But his quest turned out to be even simpler than he had dared to hope. The superior young ladies of the first three agencies at which he called shook their pretty heads over the photograph and could throw no light on his problem. But at the fourth, the girl made a suggestion at which French leaped.

'No,' she said, 'I don't know anyone like that, but if she's left the stage some time I wouldn't; I've only been here about two years. And I don't know anyone who could help you; this place has not been open very long. But I'll tell you,' she went on, brightening up. 'Mr Rohmer is inside. If anyone in London would know, he should. If you catch him coming out you could ask him.'

Mr Horace Rohmer! The prince of producers! French knew his name well, though he had never met him. He thanked the girl and sat down to wait.

Presently she called to him, 'He's just going,' and French, stepping forward, saw a short, stout, rather Jewish-looking gentleman moving to the stairs. He hastened, after him, and, introducing himself, produced his photograph and asked his question.

The famous producer glanced at the card and smiled.

'Oh, Lor' yes,' he announced, 'I know her. But these people wouldn't.' He indicated the agency and its personnel with a backward nod. 'She was before their time. Why, that's the great Cissie Winter; at least, she had the makings of being great at one time. She was first lady in Panton's company a dozen years ago or more. I remember her in

Oh, Johnny!, *The Duchess*, *The Office Girl*, and that lot—good enough plays in their day, but out of date now. I hope she's not in trouble?'

'It's a matter of stolen diamonds,' French answered, 'but I'm not suggesting she is guilty. We want some explanations, that's all.'

'I should be sorry to hear there was anything wrong,' Mr Rohmer declared. 'I thought a lot of her at one time, though she did go off and make a muck of things.'

'How was that, sir?'

'Some man. Went off to live with some man, a married man, and well on to being elderly. At least, that was the story at the time. I'm not straight-laced, and I shouldn't have minded that if she had only kept up her stage work. But she didn't. She just dropped out of sight. And she might have risen to anything. A promising young woman lost. Sickening, I call it.'

'I suppose you could give me no hint as to how I might trace her?'

The producer shrugged his shoulders.

'Not the slightest, I'm afraid. I didn't even know that she was alive.'

'What theatres did she play in?'

'Several, but it was in the Comedy she did her best work.'

'I'll try there.'

'You can try, but don't build too much on it. Theatrical staffs change quickly and have short memories. If you've no luck there you should go to Jacques—you know, Richard Jacques the producer. If my memory serves me, he put out those plays I mentioned. If not, he can tell you who did.'

French was overjoyed. This was indeed a stroke of luck. He had proved his theory—he was already beginning to overlook the part his wife had played in it—he had done a neat piece of deduction, and it had been justified. He had now obtained information which must lead him infallibly to his goal. His next business must be at the Comedy, where, if his luck held, he might obtain information which would put him straight on the woman's track.

As he turned away from the agency, French felt a touch on his shoulder. It was Mr Duke, and the old gentleman greeted him warmly and asked of his progress.

'I'm just going in here for some coffee,' he went on, indicating the somewhat old-fashioned and retiring restaurant before which they stood. 'Come and have a cup with me. It's ages since I saw you or heard what you were doing.'

French was full of his discovery, and eagerly seized the chance of a victim to whom to unfold the tale of his prowess. Accordingly, when they were seated in a quiet nook he began with gusto to relate his exploits. He told of his visit to Mürren, and of the photographs given to him by Mrs Root, of his tracing the movements of the elusive lady in Southampton, of his deduction that she was an actress, and finally of his great stroke in learning her identity.

Mr Duke, who had been following the recital with a thrilled interest that satisfied even French's egotism, remembered the lady's name, though he could not recall anything else about her.

'This will be good news for Vanderkemp,' he declared. 'I must tell him at once. Though you have taken off your surveillance, he feels that he has never really been cleared of suspicion. This discovery of yours will go far to satisfy him. Yes, and what then?'

He settled himself again to listen, but when he realised that French had finished his tale and was no nearer finding Miss Cissie Winter than he had been of getting hold of Mrs X, his features took on an expression of the keenest disappointment, bordering almost on despair.

'Good heavens, Inspector! After raising my hopes, don't tell me now that you are really practically no farther on,' he lamented. Then sinking his voice, he went on slowly, 'If something isn't discovered soon I may tell you I don't know what I'm going to do. I'm getting to the end of my tether. I'm even getting short of cash. The insurance company won't pay—yet; they say it is not certain the stones will not be recovered. They say I must wait. But my creditors won't wait.'

He stopped and stared before him vacantly, and French, looking at him more keenly than he had yet done, was shocked to see how old and worn the man was looking. 'Even if the insurance company paid all, I don't know that I could make ends meet,' he went on presently. 'I'm beginning to see ruin staring me in the face. I thought I was strong and could scoff at reverses, but I can't, Inspector, I can't. I'm not the man I was and this affair has shaken me severely.'

French was somewhat taken aback by this outburst, but he felt genuinely sorry for the old man, who at the close of a life of comparative luxury and success was faced with failure and poverty. He gave him what comfort he could, pointing out that the discovery of Mrs X's identity was a real step forward, and expressed the belief that so well known a personality could not long remain hidden.

'I sincerely trust you are right,' Mr Duke answered, 'and I am ashamed of having made such a fuss. But do try,

Inspector,' he looked imploringly at the other, 'do try to push on the affair. I know you are,' he smiled, 'doing all that anyone could do, but it's so desperately important to me. You understand, I hope, that I am not complaining? I fully appreciate your splendid work in the face of great difficulties.'

French assured him that he himself was just as anxious to clear up the mystery as anyone else could be, and that he need not fear but that everything possible would be done to that end, and with further expressions of mutual amity they parted.

The inspector next turned his steps to the Comedy theatre. Rehearsals were in progress, and the building was open. Going round to the stage door, he spoke to the doorkeeper.

'No, sir,' the man said civilly, 'I'm not here long. Only about, nine months.'

'Who was before you?'

'A man they called Dowds, an old man. He was getting too old for the job. That's why he left.'

'Could you put me on to where I should find him?'

'I should try at the office, sir. I expect they'd have his address. To the right at the end of this passage.'

With some difficulty French found his way to the office. A young man glanced up from the desk over which he was bending. 'Well, sir?' he said briskly.

French explained his business. He was inquiring as to the whereabouts of the former actress, Miss Cissie Winter, and failing information as to her, he would be obliged for the address of the ex-stagedoor keeper, Dowds, who might be able to assist him in his main inquiry.

'Miss Cissie Winter?' the sharp young man repeated.

'I've heard of her, but she wasn't on here in my time. Any idea of her dates or plays?'

'Twelve or more years since she left the stage, I'm told. She played in *The Office Girl* and *The Duchess* and *Oh, Johnny!*'

The young man whistled beneath his breath as he sat thinking.

''Fraid I can't help you about the lady,' he declared at last. 'There are no records here of twelve years back. But I can put you on to Dowds all right, or at least I can give you his address when he left us.'

'Much obliged, I'm sure.'

The young man crossed the room, and taking a book out of a cupboard, turned over the pages rapidly.

'29 Babcock Street. It's off Charing Cross Road, about half-way down on the left hand side going south. You'll get him there if he hasn't moved.'

French, having noted the address, turned to go.

'Wait a sec',' said the young man. 'I'm not certain, but I believe Richard Jacques put out those plays you mentioned. If so, he could probably help you better than anyone. He does business at that new place he has taken over, the Aladdin in Piccadilly. You should try him.'

French thanked his new friend, and after again traversing the endless corridors of the huge building, found himself once more in the street.

At 29 Babcock Street the door was opened to him by a respectable-looking woman, who said that her husband, Peter Dowds, was within. His health was poor, but if the gentleman would come in, he would make shift to come down to see him.

French sat down to wait in the tiny parlour. Presently

a shuffling became audible in the hall, and the door, opening slowly, revealed a short but immensely stout man, whose small eyes blinked inquisitively at his visitor as the latter rose and wished him good-day.

'Good-day, good-day,' the man wheezed, as he steered himself across the room and sank into one of the chairs. 'It's the asthma,' he went on in a husky voice. 'It's always bad this time of year.' He stopped and sat panting, then went on, 'You wanted to see me?'

'Yes,' French admitted, 'but I'm sorry to find your asthma so bad. What do you do for it?'

The inspector had found from long experience that the time spent in discussing his illness with an invalid was not wasted. The pleasure he gave had the effect of creating a sympathy and good feeling which assisted him when he came to the second part of the interview, the favour he wanted for himself. He was not altogether a hypocrite in this. It was part of the technique of his business, and besides, he was a good-natured man who really did like giving pleasure. He therefore talked asthma and asthma cures for some minutes before turning to the subject of Miss Cissie Winter.

But in the present case the excellent impression which he undoubtedly produced brought him but little benefit. The stout old doorkeeper remembered Miss Winter well, and instantly recognised her photograph, but he knew nothing about her present whereabouts. She had gone off with some man, a man whom also he remembered well, as on many occasions they had chatted together while the former waited at the stage door for the lady's appearance. He was tall and well built, well on in middle age, and with the air of a professional or business man. His name, Dowds

believed, was Vane, but of this he was not positive. Asked
how he knew that the lady had gone off with this or any
other man, it transpired that he did not really know at all,
but that this had been the generally accepted theory at the
time. He had never learned the man's address, but he
seemed to have plenty of money and was liberal in his
tips. Since that time, about thirteen years previously, Dowds
had not heard or seen anything of either. Of Miss Winter
he had but a poor opinion. She might be a good actress,
but she was hard and mean and had a sharp tongue. What
the man could have seen in her he, Dowds, did not know,
but he had evidently been pretty completely bowled over.

When French had gleaned these particulars, he found he
had reached the end of the old doorkeeper's usefulness,
and he was soon on his way to his next call, the Aladdin
theatre in Piccadilly.

Mr Jacques was in the building, but engaged, and French
fretted and fumed for nearly two hours before being
ushered into his presence. But then he felt himself completely
compensated for his long wait. Like most others who came
in contact with him, French soon, fell a victim to the great
producer's winning personality and charm of manner. The
old gentleman apologised courteously for his engagement,
which, he explained, was a troublesome rehearsal, and then
listened with close attention to what French had to say.

But he could not tell so very much after all. He remembered Miss Winter, and after a search through some old
records was able to give some details of her life. He had
first seen her in the Tivoli theatre in New York, some
sixteen years previously, and had been struck by her acting.
She had somehow learned of his presence, for she had
followed him to his hotel, and explaining that she was

anxious to get a footing on the English stage, had asked him for a part in one of the plays she had heard he was then bringing out. He had agreed, and when she had completed her New York engagement, she had followed him to England, and he had starred her in *Oh, Johnny!* and certain other plays of that period. In all she had appeared in seven productions, and Mr Jacques had a high opinion of her capabilities.

Some three years later she had given him notice that she wished to leave the stage at the end of her then current contract. He had protested, telling her that she was ruining an extremely promising career, but she had insisted, explaining that she was going to be married. This he had not believed, though he had no definite reason for his opinion. It was generally accepted that she had gone off with some married man, but how this story arose he could not say. He had, at all events, completely lost sight of her. Her age when she left his company thirteen years earlier was twenty-nine, and her address was 17 Stanford Street, Chelsea.

'I'm afraid,' French said, 'that she has turned crook,' and he outlined her impersonation of Mrs Root.

'Of course I know nothing about that,' Mr Jacques answered, 'but I can at least tell you that no one could have carried out a scheme of the kind better than Cissie Winter. She had the brains and the nerve and the knowledge. I'm sorry to hear she has gone wrong, but if you are up against her, I can assure you you'll find her no mean antagonist.'

French smiled ruefully as he rose.

'I've discovered that already,' he admitted, 'but knowing what I know now, it can't be long until I have my hands on her.'

'I suppose I ought to wish you luck,' Mr Jacques declared, holding out his hand, 'but I don't know that I can. I thought a lot of the young woman once, and I'm sorry that she's in trouble.'

Inspector French, having cabled to the New York police asking for information as to the actress's early history, made his way to 17 Stanford Street, which he found was a better-class boarding house. But here he could learn nothing. The former proprietor was dead, and none of the present staff had been connected with the place for thirteen years, or had ever heard of Miss Winter.

Disappointed once more, he returned to the Yard and put through his earlier scheme. He arranged to have the lady's photograph inserted in the next number of the *Police Bulletin,* together with the best description of her that he could write, and a note that she was wanted. It was not a promising clue, but it was all he had left.

14

Tragedy

Some days later Inspector French was once again sent for by his chief. The great man seemed in an irritable frame of mind, and he began to speak before the other had well entered the room.

'See here, French,' he greeted him; 'here's a fresh development in that confounded Gething case. Read that.'

French stepped up to the desk and took the postal telegraph sheets his superior held out. They bore a message from the Chief of Police at the Hook, which had been sent out at 8.27 that morning.

'Captain of the S.S. *Parkeston* reports that tall, cleanshaven, white-haired man, apparently named Duke, committed suicide during passage from Harwich last night. Overcoat and suitcase found in cabin with letter addressed Miss Duke, The Cedars, Hampstead. Am sending letter with detailed statement.'

French was considerably surprised by the news. Though he had never felt actually cordial towards the old gentleman, he had respected him for his kindly conduct towards his subordinates and for the sportman-like way in which he had taken his loss. But it was evident the man had been hit harder than he had shown. French recalled the details of their last interview, the merchant's drawn, anxious face, his weary air, his almost despairing words, 'I'm getting to the end of my tether. I see ruin staring me in the face.' At the time, French had not taken the complaint as seriously as it had now proved to warrant. Mr Duke was evidently in difficulties which nothing less than the return of the stolen diamonds would solve, and French did not see how he could have done more to achieve that end than he already had.

'Unexpected, that, isn't it?' the chief remarked, 'though I don't suppose it will really affect the ease.'

'No, sir, I don't think it will,' French returned, answering the last part of the sentence first. 'But I don't know that it's so unexpected after all. Least-wise it is and it isn't. I mean, I'm surprised that a man of Mr Duke's character should take that way of escaping from his difficulties, but I knew he was in difficulties.'

The chief raised his eyebrows.

'You didn't tell me that.'

'The truth is, sir, that I didn't take what the old gentleman said seriously enough. I met him last week in Piccadilly, and he appeared anxious to hear my news and asked me to have a cup of coffee with him. He was pretty down in the mouth then, saying he was getting short of cash, and near the end of his tether, and so on. He was looking pretty old, too, old and worn.'

The chief grunted.

'As I say, I don't suppose it will make any difference,' he declared. 'But there's that girl to consider. I think you'd better go along and see her. After all, she should have some warning before she sees it in the paper.'

'That's so, sir. Then I shall go now.'

It was a job he hated, but there was no help for it, and having 'phoned to Miss Duke that he was going out on urgent business, he set off.

That his message had alarmed her was obvious. She met him with pale cheeks and anxious eyes, and once again the thought occurred to him that she knew something that she was holding back, and had feared her secret was the subject of his call.

But his news, when haltingly and with some awkwardness he had succeeded in conveying it, took her utterly by surprise. It was evidently quite different to what she had expected to hear, and the poor girl was terribly overcome. She gave a low cry, and sat gazing at him with eyes dilated with horror. The shock seemed utterly to have benumbed her, and yet French could not help thinking that her emotion contained also an element of relief. He was profoundly sorry for her, but his suspicion remained.

Presently she began to speak. Her voice was dull and toneless as she explained that she had known her father was lately terribly worried and unhappy, and that though he had made light of it, he had told her enough to show that financial trouble was at the root of his distress. He had said to her on one occasion that if only the insurance people would pay, things would be easier, but he had spoken cheerily, and she had had no idea things were so serious.

'When shall we get details?' she asked presently. 'Should I go over to the Hook?'

'I fear there would be little use in that,' French answered, 'and it would certainly be painful for you. Of course, I don't wish to dissuade you; if you think it would be an ease to your mind you should go. But in any case would it not be better to wait until you read your letter? Besides, the report from the Dutch police may show that a visit is unnecessary.'

She thought for some seconds, then agreed. French explained that the documents might be expected by the first post on the following morning, and promised to take them out to Hampstead immediately.

'In the meantime, Miss Duke,' he went on, with real kindness in his tone, 'it's not my business, of course, but would you not be better to have someone in the house with you—some lady friend, an aunt, a cousin? Or Mr Harrington? I mean, is there anything that I can do to take a message or send a wire?'

Her eyes filled with tears as she thanked him and asked him to telephone to the office for Harrington. It appeared that she had no near relations. She was an only child, and her father was now dead, and French knew that for many years her poor mother had been worse than dead, dragging out a colourless existence in a mental hospital at Otterham.

When he had put through his call, French took his leave. There was nothing more to be done until the details of the tragedy were received.

As he sat in the tube on his way back to the Yard, he was conscious of some misgivings as to the way in which he had handled the interview. He had done his best to make it easy for Miss Duke. This was, of course, the natural and the kindly thing to do, but was it his duty? Should he not rather have used the news as a lever to startle some admission out of the girl which would have given him the information which he suspected she possessed. If he had allowed a promising clue to slip he had neglected his duty and injured himself. And his chief was no fool. He would unfailingly see the possibility and ask what use had been made of it.

But though French felt thus a trifle uneasy, he could not bring himself to regret his course of action. He was not only a man of natural kindliness of heart, but he had the gift of imagination. He saw himself in the girl's place, and was glad he had not added to her trouble.

Next morning the report came from Holland, together with Miss Duke's letter. The former was a long document giving very complete details of the tragedy. The essential portions of it read:

'4th January.

'At 7.21 today a telephone message was received from the Harwich boat wharf office at the Hook that a passenger had disappeared during the crossing under circumstances which pointed to suicide. Inspector Van Bien was sent down to make inquiries, and he obtained the following information:

'Some little time before the boat berthed, the stewards, according to custom, went round the staterooms to arouse the passengers. There was no reply from stateroom N, a single-berth cabin on the port side, and when John Wilson, the steward in question, had knocked a second time, he looked in. The cabin was empty, but bore evidence of having been occupied. The bed had

195

been lain on, though not slept in, a large suitcase was on the floor, and various articles of a man's toilet were scattered about. The steward, thinking the traveller, whom he remembered to be a white-haired old man, was perhaps on deck, passed on. About half an hour later he looked in again, to find things in the same condition. He was engaged until after the boat berthed, but when the passengers were going ashore he went back to the stateroom, and again found everything as before. Becoming anxious, he reported the matter to the chief steward. The latter accompanied Wilson to cabin N, and they made a search. They found a half-sheet of paper and an envelope propped behind the tumbler in the little wooden shelf above the washhand basin. The former bore the words:

'"Financial embarrassments having made my life impossible, I am going to make an end of it tonight. I shall simply drop off the ship, and my death will be quick and easy. Please oblige by posting my letter.

'"R. A. DUKE.'

'The letter was addressed to "Miss Duke, The Cedars, Hampstead, London." Both note and letter are enclosed herewith.

'The tickets on this route are dealt with as follows: There is no check on passengers leaving the wharf, as this would entail too long a delay at the gangway. On coming on board, passengers apply at the chief steward's office, have their tickets either collected or punched, and get their berth numbers and a landing ticket. The landing tickets are collected as the travellers go ashore, and this constitutes the check that all have paid for their passage. On the occasion in question, 187 landing tickets were given out, and only 186 were collected, showing that one of the passengers who came aboard at Harwich did not go ashore at the Hook.

'A search of the ship revealed no trace of the missing man, nor had anyone seen him passing through the corridors or on the deck during the night. The chief steward recalled his application for his berth, which had been reserved in advance, and remembered having noticed that the old man was absent-minded, and seemed to be suffering from acute repressed excitement.

'The suitcase was found to contain articles of toilet and clothing suitable for an absence of three or four days, but nothing to throw any further light on the tragedy. We are sending it to you for transmission to Miss Duke, to whom presumably it belongs.'

When Inspector French had read the report he turned his attention to the letter. The envelope was square and of good quality paper, and the address was in Mr Duke's handwriting. French sat turning it over. He wondered . . . He would rather not, but on second thoughts he believed he ought . . . There might be something that would give him a hint . . .

He took a Gillette razor blade from his drawer, and inserting it beneath the gummed flap, worked it this way and that. In a moment the envelope was open, and he drew out a letter and cautiously unfolded it. It also was written by Mr Duke, and read:

'MY DEAREST SYLVIA,

'When you receive this you will have heard what I am about to do. My dear, I will not try to justify myself; I suppose I should be brave and fight to the end. But I just couldn't bear the ruin and disgrace which face me. Even, before the robbery things were not going too well. As you know, the war hit businesses like mine worse than most. Now, even if the insurance company paid, I shouldn't get clear; I should still be many thousands in debt. Sylvia, don't think too hardly of me, but I couldn't face it. Loss of position, friends, home, everything—and at my time, of life. I just couldn't.

'But chiefly I couldn't bear dragging you down with me. You will be free from that now. Your mother's jointure cannot be touched; it is hers—and yours. You will see that all expenses for her are paid, and the remainder will be yours. Of course the house must go, but you will have enough to live on. You will marry; I trust soon. Remember that it is my last wish and my last charge to you that you marry the man of your choice as soon as may be convenient. Though we have not always seen eye to eye, you have been a good daughter to me.

'Dear Sylvia, try not to take this too much to heart. I face the future, if there is one, without misgivings. Though the way I take may be the coward's way, it is the easiest and the best way for us all.

'Good-bye, my dearest girl, and if there be a God, may He bless you.

'Your devoted father,

'R. A. DUKE.'

Inspector French had a slight feeling of shame as he refolded this unhappy epistle and, working deftly and mechanically, regummed the flap of the envelope and stuck it down. He was disappointed to find that the letter contained no helpful information, and with a sigh he set out to bear his news to Hampstead.

Miss Duke and Harrington were anxiously awaiting him, and he handed the former both the report and the letter, saying he would wait if she cared to read them in another room. She remained calm and collected, but the pallor of her face and dark rings beneath her eyes indicated the tension under which she was labouring. She withdrew with a word of apology, Harrington accompanying her, and French sat thinking, wondering if a direct question, unexpectedly sprung upon them, might surprise one or other into some unguarded admission which would give him a hint of the secret which he believed they held.

But when they returned some half-hour later, Miss Duke momentarily disarmed him by holding out her letter.

'You had better read that,' she said. 'You may want to see it and there is nothing private in it.'

French was momentarily tempted to confess his action with the safety razor, but he saw that he must not divulge police methods, and taking the letter, he reread it and handed it back with a word of thanks.

'Did your father say he was going to Holland?' he inquired.

'Yes, it was one of his usual trips to the Amsterdam office. He expected to be away for two or three days. But I now think, he had made up his mind—about—this—before he left. He said good-bye—'

She paused, her lip trembling, then suddenly flinging

herself down on the sofa, burst into an uncontrollable flood of tears. 'Oh!' she cried brokenly, 'if only it hadn't taken place at sea! I can't bear to think of him—out there—' She sobbed as if her heart would break.

French saw that she had settled the matter of his procedure. In her present condition he could not probe her with subtle questions. There was nothing for it but to take his departure, and this he did as unobtrusively as he could, leaving her in Harrington's charge.

He wondered who would take Mr Duke's place in the firm, with whom he would have to deal if his efforts to trace the missing diamonds became successful, and determined to call at the office and make some inquiries. He therefore took the tube to the City, and some half-hour later was mounting the steps of the Hatton Garden establishment.

Mr Schoofs had already taken charge, and saw his visitor in his late principal's office. The business, he believed, would belong to Miss Duke, though he had no actual reason to say so. However, Messrs Tinsley & Sharpe of Lincoln's Inn were the deceased gentleman's solicitors, and no doubt fuller information could be obtained from them.

'I came over last night, and am just carrying on in the meantime,' he explained, 'and you can deal either with me or with Mr Tinsley.'

'Thanks,' French answered. 'Then I shall deal with you.'

'We're really closed for business today, you understand,' went on Mr Schoofs. 'I'm merely taking the opportunity to go through Mr Duke's papers and see how things stand. If only Harrington had had his partnership, it would be his job, but as it is, everything devolves on me.'

French, having replied suitably, made a move to go, but he lingered and went on:

'Unexpected, the old man going off like that, wasn't it? I shouldn't have thought he was that kind at all.'

Mr Schoofs made a gesture of commiseration.

'Nor was he,' he agreed, 'but it's not so surprising after all. You possibly didn't see him during the last week or two, but I can tell you, he was in a bad way; very depressed, and getting worse every day. I don't think he was well—I mean in health, and I think it reacted on his mind. He was worrying over the loss of his money.'

'Was he really bankrupt?'

Mr Schoofs had not the figures, but he very gravely feared it. It was a bad lookout for his daughter. Indeed, it was a bad lookout for them all. It was hard lines on elderly men when they had to give up their jobs and start life again. It was that damned war, responsible for this as well as most of the troubles of the times. It had probably made a difference to the inspector also?

'Lost my eldest,' said French gruffly, and turned the conversation back to the late principal. He was, it seemed, going to Amsterdam on routine business. He had no stones with him, and there was therefore nothing to suggest that his disappearance could have been due to other than suicide.

French had not really doubted the conclusions of the Dutch police, but the death by violence of a man bearing a packet of great value is always suspicious, and he was glad to be sure such had not obtained in this instance.

His next visit was to Messrs Tinsley & Sharpe, the Lincoln's Inn solicitors. Mr Tinsley was the sole surviving partner, and to him French was presently admitted.

It appeared that Mr Duke had left everything to Sylvia, 'Though, poor girl,' Mr Tinsley added, 'by all accounts that won't be much.' Mr Tinsley was executor, therefore any further dealings French might have about the robbery would be with him. Mr Duke and he had been old friends; in fact, he had been Mr Duke's best man, he didn't like to think how many years previously. He had been shocked by the change in the old gentleman when three days prior to his death he had called to see him. He seemed ill and depressed, and had said, 'I'm not feeling well, Tinsley. It's my heart, I'm afraid, and this confounded worry about money matters,' and had gone on to obtain the solicitor's promise to look after Sylvia 'if anything happened.'

'In the light of what has since taken place,' Mr Tinsley concluded, 'I am afraid he had made up his mind then that suicide was the easiest way out, though I was terribly surprised and shocked when I heard of it.'

'I am sure of that, sir,' French answered as he rose to go. 'Then if any further developments occur about the robbery, I shall communicate with you.'

He returned to the Yard, made his report, and when he had attended to a number of routine matters, found it was time to knock off work for the day.

15

The House in St John's Wood

It was one of Inspector French's most constant grumbles that a man in his position was never off duty. He might come home after a hard day's work looking forward to a long, lazy, delightful evening with a pipe and a book, and before he had finished supper some development at headquarters might upset all his plans and drag him off forthwith to do battle with the enemies of his country's laws. Not for him was the eight-hour day, overtime at high rates, 'on call' or country allowances, expenses . . . His portion was to get his work done, or take the consequences in lack of promotion or even loss of such position as he held.

'And no thanks for what you carry off either,' he would complain, 'though if you make a slip you hear about it before you're an hour older.' But his eye would twinkle as he said it, and most of his friends knew that Mr Inspector French was making an exceedingly good thing out of his job, and was, moreover, destined by his superiors for even greater and more remunerative responsibilities in the early future.

203

But on this evening his grouse was illustrated, if not justified. Scarcely had he sat down to his meal when a ring came to the door, and he was told that Constable Caldwell wished to speak to him.

'Let him wait,' Mrs French answered before her better half could speak. 'Show him into the sitting-room, Eliza, and give him the evening paper.'

French half rose, then sank back into his seat.

'Ask him if it's urgent,' he called after the retreating girl, partly from genuine curiosity, and partly to preserve the fiction that he was master of his own movements in his own house.

'It's not so urgent as your supper. Just let him wait,' Mrs French repeated inexorably. 'What difference will a minute or two make anyway?'

Her view, it soon appeared, was upheld by the constable himself.

'He says it's not urgent,' Eliza corroborated, reappearing at the door. 'He can wait till you're ready.'

'Very well. Let him wait,' French repeated, relieved that the incident had ended so satisfactorily, and for another fifteen minutes he continued steadily fortifying the inner man. Then taking out his pipe, he joined his visitor.

''Evening, Caldwell. What's wrong now?'

Caldwell, a tall heavy-looking man of middle age, rose clumsily to his feet and saluted.

'It's that there circular of yours, sir,' he explained. 'I've found the woman.'

'The deuce you have!' French cried, pausing in the act of filling his pipe and immediately keenly interested. 'Who is she?'

Caldwell drew his notebook from his pocket, and slowly

turned the well-thumbed pages. His deliberation irritated his quicker-witted superior.

'Get along, Caldwell,' French grumbled. 'Can't you remember that much without your blessed book?'

'Yes, sir,' the man answered. 'Here it is.' He read from the book. 'Her name is Mrs Henry Vane, and she lives in a small detached house in St John's Wood Road; Crewe Lodge is the name.'

'Good!' French said heartily. 'I suppose you're sure about it?'

'I think so, sir. I showed the photograph to three different parties, and they all said it was her.'

This sounded promising, particularly as French remembered that Dowds, the ex-doorkeeper at the Comedy, had stated that Miss Winter's admirer was named Vane. He invited the constable to sit down and let him hear the details, offering him at the same time a fill of tobacco.

Constable Caldwell subsided gingerly into a chair as he took the proferred pouch.

'Thank you, sir, I don't mind if I do.' He slowly filled and lighted his pipe, ramming down the tobacco with an enormous thumb. 'It was this way, sir. I had that there circular of yours with the woman's photo in my pocket when I went off duty early this afternoon. On my way home I happened to meet a friend, a young lady, and I turned and walked with her. For want of something to say, so to speak, I showed her the photo, not expecting anything to come of it, you understand. Well, the moment she looked at it, "I know that there woman," she said. "You what?" I said. "You know her? Who is she, then?" I said. "She's a woman that comes into the shop sometimes," she said, "but I don't just remember her name, though I have heard it," she said. I should say the young lady, her I was speaking to, worked in a drapery shop until a couple of weeks ago, though she's out of a job at the moment. "Well," I said, "I'd like to know her name. Can't you remember it?" "No," she said, she couldn't remember it. She'd only heard it once, and hadn't paid much attention to it.'

'Yes?' French murmured encouragingly as the constable showed signs of coming to an end.

'I said that if she couldn't remember, that maybe some of the other young ladies might know it. She wasn't having any at first, for I had promised to take her to tea and on to the pictures, and she was set on going. But when she saw I was in earnest, she gave in, and we went round to the shop she used to work in. After asking three or four of the girls, we found one that remembered the woman all right. "That's Mrs Vane," she said. "She lives up there in St John's Wood; Crewe Lodge is the name. I've made up her parcels often enough to know."'

'Good,' French approved once more in his hearty voice.

'I thought I had maybe better make sure about it,' went on the constable in his slow, heavy way, 'so I asked Miss Swann—that was the young lady that I was with—to walk round that way with me. I found the house near the Baker Street end, a small place and very shut in. I didn't want to go up and make inquiries, so I asked Miss Swann if she'd go next door and ask if Mrs Vane was in. She went and asked, and they told her to go next door; that was to Crewe Lodge. So when I saw it was all right, I put off going to the pictures for this evening and came straight here to tell you.'

French beamed on him.

'You've done well, Constable,' he declared. 'In fact, I

couldn't have done it better myself. I shall see that you don't lose by it. Take another fill of tobacco while I get ready, and then call a taxi and we'll go right out now.'

He rang up Scotland Yard, asking for certain arrangements to be made, with the result that by the time he and Constable Caldwell reached the great building, two plain clothes men were waiting for them, one of whom handed French a small handbag and a warrant for the arrest of Mrs Vane, alias Mrs Ward, alias Mrs Root of Pittsburg, U.S.A. Then the four officers squeezing into the taxi, they set off for St John's Wood Road.

Big Ben was striking half-past nine as they turned into Whitehall. The night was fine, but there was no moon, and outside the radius of the street lamps it was pitchy dark. The four men sat in silence after French had in a few words explained their errand to the newcomers. He and Caldwell were both in a state of suppressed excitement, French owing to the hope of an early solution of his difficulties, the constable to the possibilities of promotion which a successful issue to the expedition might involve. The other two looked upon the matter as a mere extra job of work, and showed a lamentable lack of interest in the proceedings.

They pulled up at St John's Wood Road, and dismissing the taxi, followed Constable Caldwell to the gate of a carriage drive which there pierced the high stone wall separating the houses from the street. On the upper bar of the gate were the words, 'Crewe Lodge.' To the right hand was a wicket gate, but both it and the larger one were closed. Inside the wall was a thick belt of trees through which the drive curved back, and, lit up through the interstices of the branches by the street lamps, the walls and gable of a small house showed dimly beyond. No light was visible from the windows, and, after a moment's hesitation, French opened the wicket gate and all four entered.

'Wait here among the trees, Pye and Frankland,' he whispered. 'Caldwell, you come on with me.'

The drive was short, not more than forty yards long, and the complete outline of the house was speedily revealed. It seemed even smaller than the first glance had shown, but was charmingly designed, with a broken-up roof, large bow windows, and a tiny loggia into which opened a glass panelled door. To be so near the centre of a great city, it was extraordinarily secluded, the trees and wall, together with some clumps of evergreen shrubs, cutting off all view of the road and the neighbouring houses.

The front of the house was in complete darkness, and instinctively treading stealthily, the two men moved round to the side. Here also there was no light, and they pushed slowly on until they had completed the circuit and once more reached the front door.

'Looks as if the place is empty,' French whispered as he pressed the electric bell.

There was no response to his repeated rings. The house remained dark and silent. French turned again to the constable.

'Call up those other two men,' he ordered, and soon Pye was posted at the corner between the front and side, and Frankland at that diagonally opposite, with orders to keep out of sight and to allow anyone who came to enter, but no one to leave the building.

Electric torch in hand, French then began a guarded survey of the doors and windows. Finally fixing on the door opening on the loggia, he made Caldwell hold the light while, first with a bunch of skeleton keys, and then with a bit of wire, he operated on the lock. For several minutes he worked, but at last with a snap the bolt shot back, and turning the handle, the two men cautiously entered the room and closed the door behind them.

They found themselves in a small, expensively-furnished sitting-room, evidently, a lady's. It was fitted up in a somewhat flamboyant and pretentious manner, as if costliness rather than good taste had been the chief consideration in its furnishing. It was unoccupied, but looked as if it had been recently used, there being ashes in the grate and books lying about, one of which lay open face downwards on a chair. On an occasional table stood an afternoon tea equipage with one used cup.

French did not remain to make any closer examination, but passed on to a tiny hall, off which opened three other rooms, and from which the staircase led to the first floor. Beneath the stairs was a row of clothes-hooks on which were hanging a man's garments, a couple of hats and coats, and a waterproof.

Rapidly he glanced into the other rooms. The first was a smoking-room, a man's room, furnished with dark-coloured, leather upholstery, and walls panelled in dark oak. Next door was a dining room, also small, but containing a quantity of valuable silver. The fourth door led to the kitchen, scullery, pantry, and yard. Here also there were evidences of recent occupation in the general untidiness, as well as in the food which these places contained.

Satisfied that no one was concealed on the ground floor, French led the way upstairs. In the largest bedroom, evidently that of the mistress of the house, there was a scene almost of confusion. Drawers and wardrobe lay open, their contents tumbled and tossed, while the floor was littered with dresses, shoes, and other dainty articles of feminine apparel. French swore beneath his breath when he saw the mess. Things were beginning to look uncommonly like as if the bird had flown. However, it was possible that someone might arrive at any minute, and he hurriedly continued his search.

Next door was a man's dressing-room and bedroom. Here there was not the same litter, nor was the unoccupied bedroom adjoining other than tidy, but in the maids' room, which he next entered, it was evident there had been a recent clearing out. Here the wardrobe drawers were pulled out and the door of a hanging press in the wall was standing open. Papers and a few obviously worn-out garments littered the floor. But the room differed from Madame's in that everything of value had been taken.

French swore again. There seemed no doubt that he was late. Mrs X, alias Mrs Vane, had taken fright and fled. If so, what hint, he wondered, had she received of her danger?

He stood for a moment in the disordered room, thinking. Under these new circumstances, what was his proper course?

First, it was obvious that he must make absolutely sure that this Mrs Vane was really the woman he sought. Next, he must learn if she had really gone, and, if so, why, and, if possible, where. If her departure was a flight, he must find out how or by whom she had been warned. Lastly, he must follow her to her hiding-place and arrest her.

But he must not end with Mrs Vane. Her husband must also be found. If she was Mrs X, the receiver of the stolen diamonds, possibly the murderer of old Gething, Mr Vane must be in it, too. It was inconceivable that he could have avoided becoming involved.

His first job must therefore be to make all the inquiries he could as to the mysterious occupants of Crewe Lodge. There were several obvious lines of research. First there was the house itself. People left the impress of their personalities on the houses they inhabited, and a careful search of this one must yield considerable information as to the pair. Next there were the servants. If they could be found, their testimony might prove invaluable. From the neighbours and local tradesmen and dealers he did not expect so much, but among them all some useful hints would surely be gleaned. Lastly, there were the house agents. They might or might not be able to help.

It was by this time nearly eleven, but he decided that his obvious duty was then and there to begin the search of the house, even if it meant an all-night job. He therefore called in Pye and Frankland, who were experienced in such work, leaving Constable Caldwell to patrol the grounds.

Then commenced an investigation of the most meticulous and thorough description. Taking the house room by room, the three men went over with the utmost care every piece of furniture, every book, every paper, every article of clothing. Hour after hour the search proceeded in spite of a growing weariness and hunger, and it was not until half-past six on the following morning that it was complete. Then in the growing daylight the three Yard men slipped out one by one on to the road, and joining forces round the corner, walked to the nearest tube station, and went to their several houses for breakfast. French rang up the Yard from the first exchange they came to, and arranged for a man to be sent to relieve Caldwell, who had been left in charge.

As French smoked his after-breakfast pipe before returning to the Yard, he jotted down in his notebook a list of the points which had struck him during the search. There was nothing that led him to either Mr or Mrs Vane, but there was a certain amount that was suggestive.

In the first place, it seemed evident that the departure of the lady had been sudden and unexpected. There was the evidence of the disordered bedrooms, of the used-looking sitting-room with the book evidently laid down where it could be picked up again without losing the place, of the ashes in the sitting-room fireplace and range, the used tea tray, and of the kitchen. There it appeared that cooking had been just about to begin, for a number of saucepans were on the range, and various kinds of food lay on the table as if ready for the saucepans. There was a good deal of food of various kinds about the kitchen and larder, and some wine and whisky in the dining-room sideboard. On the other hand, there was no evidence of any hurried departure on the part of the master of the house.

The date of the departure French thought he could roughly fix from the condition of the food. The milk, of which there was a bowl and two jugs, was sour, but not thick. Some fresh meat hanging in the larder was good. The bread was rather dry and hard. Some lettuces lying on a shelf in the scullery had gone limp. But some bunches of chrysanthemums standing in water in the sitting-room were quite fresh.

On the whole, he thought the evidence pointed to a flight some four days earlier, and this view was supported by another piece of evidence on which he had come.

In the letter box at the back of the hall door he had found a letter addressed 'Mrs Vane, Crewe Lodge, St John's Wood Road.' The postmark showed that it had been posted in London on the 3rd. It had, therefore, been delivered on the evening of the 3rd or morning of the 4th. But this was the 8th. Therefore the lady had gone at least four days earlier.

The letter itself had considerably intrigued him. It was simply a list of certain sales and purchases of stock, covering a large number of transactions, and running into some thousands of pounds in value. The items were not dated, and there was no accompanying letter nor any intimation of the sender. It was clear that someone was engaged in complicated financial operations, but there was nothing to indicate his or her identity.

That the Vanes were at least comfortably off seemed certain from the general appointments of the house. The furniture and fittings were heavy and expensive. The sitting-room was small, as has been stated, but French reckoned that the carpet would not have been bought for less than £120. Madame's dresses were of rich silks, and while no actual jewellery had been left behind, there were costly ornaments and personal knick-knacks. Moreover, the half-empty box of cigars in the smoking-room contained Corona Coronas. There was, however, no garage and no car, but it was obvious that a car might have been kept at some neighbouring establishment. Altogether it looked as if the couple had been living at the rate of two or three thousand a year. But this was a matter that could easily be tested, as the name of Mrs Vane's bank was among her papers.

One other point struck the inspector as curious. Neither the master nor the mistress of the house seemed to have literary tastes. There was a number of well-bound 'standard works' in a bookcase in the smoking room, but it was evident from their condition that they were there purely as part of the decorative scheme. Of actually read books in the smoking-room there were none. In the sitting-room were a number of the lighter type of novels, together with a number in French and Spanish with extremely lurid and compromising jackets. But among these, as out of place as an Elijah at a feast of Baal, lay a new copy of *The Concise Oxford Dictionary*.

There were several old bills in Madame's inlaid daven-port, but save for the names of firms with whom the lady had recently been dealing, French had learned nothing from them. In the sitting-room also was an excellent cabinet photograph of a lady who seemed to him the original of Mrs Root's steamer snapshot, and this he had slipped into his jacket pocket.

Having completed his notes, he knocked the ashes out of his pipe and set out upon the business of the day. Returning to St John's Wood Road, he interviewed Esler, the constable who had been sent to relieve Caldwell, and learned that no one had as yet approached the house. Then he began to call at the adjoining houses and nearer shops. At each he stated that he was looking for Mrs Vane, but that her house was shut up, and asked if anyone could tell him how he might find her.

Aware that in a great city neighbours might live beside each other for years without ever meeting, he did not hope for much result, and at the first two houses at which he called he did not get any. But at the third he had an unexpected stroke of luck. The maid who opened the door seemed to know something about the Vane household.

214

But she was suspicious, and on French's putting his usual questions, showed evident unwillingness to give away information. Keeping any suggestion of eagerness out of his manner, French went on conversationally:

'I wanted to see Mrs Vane about a question of the ownership of a field in the country near Canterbury, where she used to live. I represent Messrs Hill & Lewesham, the solicitors of Lincoln's Inn, and we want some information about the boundaries of her father's place. It's not exactly important, but it would be worth five shillings to me to get in touch with her, and if you could see your way to help me, you'd have very fairly earned it.'

The girl seemed impressed. She glanced back into the hall, came out into the porch, and drawing the door to after her, spoke rather hurriedly.

'I don't know much about it,' she explained, 'but I'll tell you what I can,' and she went on to say that on the previous Friday, that was five days earlier, Mrs Vane had got a cable that her husband in New York had met with a serious accident and was dying, and for her to go at once. She had packed hurriedly and driven off to catch the boat train for Liverpool, closing the house. As to Mr Vane himself, the girl knew nothing. She seemed to consider him a negligible part of the establishment. He was but seldom at home, and even then was rarely to be seen.

French asked her how it came that she knew so much about the family, and she explained that she and Mrs Vane's housemaid had become acquainted over her young gentleman's model aeroplane, which had flown over the dividing wall into the grounds of Crewe Lodge, and which had been ignominiously handed back by the girl in question. As a result of the incident an acquaintance had grown

up between the two, in the course of which much information as to their respective employers had been exchanged.
On that Friday evening Mrs Vane's maid had called the
narrator to the wall by means of a certain signal which
they had devised, and had hurriedly told her of her
mistress's sudden call to America, and also that the house
was being closed and the services of herself and the cook
dispensed with. 'She's in a most terrible fluster to catch the
boat train,' the girl had said, 'and we have to be out before
her so that she may lock up the house.' The girl had
breathlessly bid her friend good-bye and had vanished.

Though French was delighted to have learned these facts,
they were not in themselves all that he could have wished.
The story of the husband in New York might be true, in
which case a good deal of the theory he had been building
up would fall to the ground. It would, however, be an easy
matter to find out whether the lady really did sail on the
date in question. He turned back to the servant.

'I should like very much to find that friend of yours,' he
said. 'Could you give me her name and address?'

Her name, it appeared, was Susan Scott, but her address
was not known. For a moment French was at a loss, then
by judicious questions he elicted the facts that Miss Scott
spoke like a Londoner, and that she probably patronised
one of the several registry offices to be found in the region
surrounding the Edgware Road.

'Now there is just one other thing,' he added. 'Can you tell
me the name of the landlord or agents of Crewe Lodge?'

The girl was sorry she couldn't.

'Then of this house?' French persisted. 'As they are
close together, the two places may belong to the same man.'

The girl did not know that either, but she said that her

master would know, and that he had not yet gone out. French asked for an interview, and on stating his identity, received the information that the agents for both houses were Messrs Findlater & Hynd, of Cupples Street, behind the Haymarket.

Thinking he had got all the information he could, French paid over his five shillings to the maid and took his departure.

The next item on his programme was a visit to Mr Williams, and twenty minutes later he pushed open the door of the office in Cockspur Street. Mr Williams greeted him with what with him took the place of enthusiasm.

'Good-day, Inspector,' he exclaimed, 'I'm glad to see you. You bring me some good news, I hope?'

French sat down and drew from his pocket the cabinet photograph of Mrs Vane which he had found in that lady's sitting-room.

'I don't know, Mr Williams,' he answered quietly, 'whether that will be news to you or not.'

Mr Williams's eyes flashed with excitement as he saw the portrait.

'Bless my soul!' he cried. 'Have you found her at last? Mrs Root!'

'That's what I wanted to ask you. Are you sure it is Mrs Root?'

'Sure? Absolutely positive. At least, that's the woman who got my three thousand pounds, whatever her name may be Have you found her?'

'Well no,' French admitted. 'I've not found her yet. But I'm in hopes.'

'Tell me about it.'

'Unfortunately, there's not much to tell. I've got

information to the effect that this woman, the original of the photograph, left for New York last Friday. I don't know if it's true. If it is, the American police will get her on the ship.'

Mr Williams pressed for details, but French was reticent. However, before leaving he promised to let the other know the result of his further inquiries.

From Cockspur Street it was but a short distance to the office of the house agents, Messrs Findlater & Hynd. Here French saw Mr Hynd, and learned that the firm were agents for Crewe Lodge. But beyond this fact he learned little of interest and nothing helpful. The house had been taken five years previously by Mrs Vane, though Mr Vane had signed the lease. They were very desirable tenants, paying their rent promptly and not demanding continual repairs.

'One more call before lunch,' French thought, and a few minutes later he turned into the office, of the White Star, line, Here, though it did not exactly surprise him, he received some information which gave him considerably to think, and incidentally reassured him that at last he was on the right track. No steamer, either of the White Star or of any other line, had left Liverpool for America before the previous Saturday afternoon, and there was no boat train from Euston on the Friday night.

Mrs Vane was therefore without any doubt the woman of whom he was in search, and her departure was definitely a flight.

16

A Hot Scent

Inspector French had now so many points of attack in his inquiry that he felt somewhat at a loss as to which he should proceed with first. The tracing of Mrs Vane was the immediate goal, but it was by no means clear which particular line of inquiry would most surely and rapidly lead to that end. Nothing would be easier than to spend time on side issues, and in this case a few hours might make all the difference between success and failure. The lady had already had five days' start, and he could not afford to allow her to increase her lead by a single unnecessary minute.

He considered the matter while he lunched, eventually concluding that the first step was the discovery of the maid, Susan Scott. The preliminary spadework of this required no skill and could be done by an assistant, leaving himself free for other inquiries.

Accordingly he returned to the Yard and set two men to work, one to make a list of all the registry offices in the Edgware Road district, the other to ring up those agencies one by one and inquire if the girl's name was on their books. Then he went in to see his chief, told him of his discoveries, and obtained the necessary authority to interrogate the manager of Mrs Vane's bank on the affairs of that lady.

He reached the bank just before closing time and was soon closeted with the manager. Mr Harrod, once satisfied that his usual professional reticence might in this case be set aside, gave him some quite interesting information. Mrs Vane had opened an account with him some five years earlier, about the same time, French noted, as the house in St John's Wood Road had been leased. Her deposit had not been large, seldom amounting to and never exceeding a thousand pounds. It had stood at from four to eight hundred until comparatively recently, but within the past few months it had dwindled until some ten weeks earlier it had vanished altogether. Indeed, the payment of a cheque presented at this period had involved an overdraft of some fifteen pounds, and the teller had consulted Mr Harrod before cashing it. Mr Harrod, knowing Crewe Lodge and the scale on which the Vanes lived, had not hesitated in giving the necessary authority, and his judgment had proved correct, for some three days later Mrs Vane had personally lodged over £100. This had since been drawn upon, and there remained at the present time a balance of eleven pounds odd in the lady's favour.

All this information seemed to French to work in with the case he was endeavouring to make. The Vanes had apparently been living beyond their income, or at least Mrs Vane had been living beyond hers, and she was finding it increasingly difficult to make ends meet. He did not see that any other interpretation of the dwindling balance and the overdraft could be found. That overdraft represented, he imagined, part of the lady's ticket to America. Then a hundred pounds was paid in on the very next day, as he soon saw, to that on which Mr Williams had paid Mrs X her £3000. Here was at least a suggestion of motive for the robbery, and also the first fruits of its accomplishment. Moreover the subsequent withdrawal of all but a small balance, left doubtless to disarm suspicion, would unquestionably work in with the theory of flight. On the whole, French was well pleased with the results of his call.

But he was even more pleased to find on his return to the Yard that his assistants had located a registry office whose books included the name of Susan Scott. By some extraordinary chance, the very first call they made struck oil. The men, of course, had realised that there must be many Susan Scotts in London, but when they found that this one had placed her name on the firm's books on the day after Mrs Vane's departure, they felt sure that they were on the right track. They had not, therefore, proceeded further with their inquiry, but had spent their time trying to locate the inspector with the object of passing on the information with the minimum of delay.

The address was Mrs Gill, 75 Horsewell Street, Edgware Road, and thither before many minutes had passed Inspector French was wending his way. The registry office was a small concern, consisting of only two rooms in a private house in a quiet street running out of Edgware Road. In the outer were two young women of the servant class, and these eyed French curiously, evidently seeing in him a prospective employer. Mrs Gill was engaged with a third girl, but a few seconds after French's arrival she took her departure and he was called into the private room.

The lady was not at first inclined to be communicative. But when French revealed his profession and threatened her with the powers and majesty of the law, she became profusely apologetic and anxious to help. She looked up her books and informed him that the girl was lodging at No. 31 Norfolk Terrace, Mistletoe Road.

As it was close by French walked to the place. Here again his luck held in a way that he began to consider almost uncanny. A tall, coarsely good-looking blonde opened the door and announced in answer to his inquiry that she herself was Miss Scott. Soon he was sitting opposite to her in a tiny parlour, while she stared at him with something approaching insolence out of her rather bold eyes.

French, sizing her up rapidly, was courteous but firm. He began by ostentatiously laying his notebook on the table, opening it at a fresh page, and after saying, 'Miss *Susan* Scott, isn't it?' wrote the name at the head of the sheet.

'Now, Miss Scott,' he announced briskly, 'I am Inspector French from Scotland Yard, and I am investigating a case of murder and robbery.' He paused, and seeing the girl was duly impressed, continued, 'It happens that your recent mistress, Mrs Vane, is wanted to give evidence in the case, and I have come to you for some information about where to find her.'

The girl made an exclamation of surprise, and a look, partly of fear and partly of thrilled delight, appeared in her blue eyes.

'I don't know anything about her,' she declared.

'I'm sure you know quite a lot,' French returned. 'All I want is to ask you some questions. If you answer them truly, you have nothing to fear, but, as you probably know, there are very serious penalties indeed for keeping back evidence. You could be sent to prison for that.'

Having by these remarks banished the girl's look of insolence and reduced her to a suitable frame of mind, French got on to business.

'Am I right in believing that you have been, until last Friday house and parlourmaid to Mrs Vane, of Crewe Lodge, St John's Wood Road?'

'Yes, I was there for about three months.'

French, to assist not only his own memory but the impressiveness of the interview, noted the reply in his book.

'Three months,' he repeated deliberately. 'Very good. Now, why did you leave?'

'Because I had to,' the girl said sulkily. 'Mrs Vane was closing the house.'

French nodded.

'So I understood. Tell me what happened, please; just in your own words.'

'She came in that afternoon shortly before four, all fussed like and hurrying, and said she was leaving immediately for New York. She said she had just had a cable that Mr Vane had had an accident there, and they were afraid he wouldn't get over it. She said for cook to get her some tea while I helped her pack. She just threw her clothes in her suitcases. My word, if I had done packing like that I shouldn't half have copped it!. By the time she'd finished, cook had tea ready, and while mistress was having it, cook and I packed. I started to clear away the tea things, but mistress said there wasn't time for that, for me just to leave them and run out and get two taxis. She said there was a special for the American boat that she must catch.

So I got the taxis, and she got into one and cook and I into the other, and we drove away together, and that's all I know about it.'

'What time was that?'

'About half-past four, I should think. I didn't look.'

'Where did you get the taxis?'

'On the stand at the end of Gardiner Street.'

'Who gave Mrs Vane's taximan his address?'

'I did. It was Euston.'

'It was rather hard lines on you and the cook, turning you out like that at a moment's notice. I hope she made it up to you?'

Miss Scott smiled scornfully.

'That was all right,' she answered. 'We told her about it, and she gave us a fiver apiece, as well as our month's wages.'

'Not so bad,' French admitted. 'Who locked up the house?'

'She did, and took the key.'

'And what happened to you and cook?'

'We drove on here and I got out. This is my sister's house, you understand. Cook went on to Paddington. She lives in Reading or somewhere down that way. Mrs Vane said that when she came back she would look us up, and if we were disengaged we could come back to her. But she said not to keep out of a place for her, as she didn't know how long she might have to stay in America.'

French paused in thought, then went on:

'Was Mrs Vane much from home while you were with her?'

'No, she was only away once. But she stayed over three weeks that time. It's a bit strange that it was an accident, too. Her sister in Scotland fell and broke her collar bone, so she told us, and she had to go to keep house till she was better. Somewhere in Scotland, she said.'

'When was that?'

The girl hesitated.

'I don't know that I could say exactly,' she answered at last. 'She's back about six weeks or two months, and she left over three weeks before that, about a couple of weeks after I went. Say about ten weeks altogether.'

This was distinctly satisfactory. Mrs Vane's absence seemed to cover the period of Mrs X's visit to America.

'I should like to fix the exact dates if I could,' French persisted, 'or at least the date she came back. Just think, will you, please. Is there nothing you can remember by?'

The girl presumably thought, for she was silent for some moments, but her cogitations were unproductive. She shook her head.

'Did you stay in the house while she was away?'

'No. I came here and cook went home.'

This was better. The attention of a number of people had been drawn to the date, and someone of them should surely be able to fix it.

'On what day of the week did you go back?' French prompted.

The girl considered this.

'It was a Thursday,' she said at last. 'I remember that now, because Thursday is my night out, and I remembered thinking that that week I shouldn't get it.'

French was delighted with the reply. It was on a Thursday night, seven weeks earlier, that Mrs X had driven from the Savoy to Victoria, left her boxes there, and vanished. The thing was working in.

'What time of the day did she arrive?'

'In the evening.' Miss, Scott answered promptly this time. 'It was about half eight or a quarter to nine.'

Better and better! Mrs X left the Savoy shortly before eight, and it would take her about three-quarters of an hour to drive to Victoria, leave her trunks in the left luggage office, and get out to St John's Wood Road.

'Now,' French went on, 'if you or your sister could just remember the week that happened, I should be very much obliged.'

Susan Scott sat with a heavy frown on her rather pretty features. Concentrated thought was evidently an unwonted exercise. But at last her efforts bore fruit.

'I've got it now,' she said with something of triumph in her tone. 'It was the last week of November. I remember it because my brother-in-law got his new job in the first week of December, and that was the following Monday. I heard that much about his job that I ought to know.'

French had scarcely doubted that this would prove to be the date, but it was most excellent to have it fixed in so definite a manner. He felt that he was progressing in his weaving of the net round the elusive Mrs X.

'That's very good,' he said approvingly. 'Now will you tell me about Mr Vane.'

The girl sniffed.

'Him?' she said scornfully. 'There ain't much to tell about him. He didn't trouble us much with his company.'

'How was that? Did they not get on? Remember we're speaking in confidence.'

'Why, I never even saw him. He didn't turn up all the three months I was there. But I heard about him from cook. He was away all the time or next thing to it. When he did come, it was generally for two days. He would come late in the evening, so cook said, and stay for two days without ever going so much as outside the door, and then go away again in the evening.'

'You mean that if he came, say, on a Monday night, he would stay until the following Wednesday night?'

'Yes; or sometimes for three days, so cook said.'

'What time in the evening would he come and go?'

'About half-past ten he always came, and a little before eight he left.'

'Do you mean that he arrived and left at the same time on each visit?'

'Yes, always about the same time.'

'After dark?'

'No. Just at those times. It was the same summer and winter. At least, that's all what cook told me. We talked about it many a time. She thought he was balmy.'

French was somewhat puzzled by this information. The whole story had what he called with a fine disregard for metaphorical purity, a 'fishy ring.' At first it had looked uncommonly like as if Mr Vane were paying clandestine visits to his own house, and, if so, he might well be the man the old stage doorkeeper had spoken of, and still have another establishment elsewhere. But this last answer seemed to suggest some other explanation of Vane's mysterious movements. After a pause, French went on:

'Did it ever strike you he was trying to keep his visits secret?'

'I can't say it did,' the girl answered with apparent regret. 'Cook never said that. But,' more hopefully, 'it might have been that, mightn't it?'

'I don't know,' French rejoined. 'I'm asking you.'

Miss Scott didn't know either, but in her opinion the inspector's suggestion might well be the truth. French noted the matter as one for future consideration as he continued his interrogation.

'What was Mr Vane like in appearance? Did cook ever say?'

Cook, it appeared, had supplied information on this point also. Even French, who knew the ways of servants, was amazed at the detailed thoroughness with which these two had evidently discussed their employers' affairs. Mr Vane was tall, but stooped, with a sallow complexion, a heavy dark moustache, and glasses.

As French listened to this description an almost incredible idea flashed into his mind. He seemed to see a vision of the Duke & Peabody office in Amsterdam, and to hear again the voice of the dapper agent, Schoofs, saying: 'A tall man, but stooped, with a sallow complexion, a heavy dark moustache, and glasses.' Could it be? Could this mysterious Mr Vane be none other than his old acquaintance, Vanderkemp?

For a time he sat motionless, lost in thought, as he considered the possibility. It would certainly clear up a good deal that was mysterious in the case. It would account for Vanderkemp's actions previous to the murder, as well as his bolt to Switzerland; it would supply a cause for Sylvia Duke's perturbation and for the postponement of the wedding; and it would explain how Mrs Vane received her warning, Mr Duke having stated he would, without delay, tell Vanderkemp of the discovery of Cissie Winter. The choice of the name Vane even tended in the same direction. There were advantages in an alias beginning with the same, letter as the real name, lest an inadvertent initial on clothing or elsewhere should give the secret away. Moreover, the theory involved nothing inherently impossible. Vanderkemp was then, and had been for some time, ostensibly on an extended tour in the United States, so that, as far as he could see at present an alibi was out of the question.

At first sight it seemed to French as if he had hit on the solution of the mystery, but as he continued turning it over in his mind he became less and less certain. Several important points were not covered by the theory. First of all, it did not, in his opinion, square with Vanderkemp's personality. The inspector had a very exalted opinion of his own powers as a reader of character—with considerable justification, it must be admitted—and the more he thought of Vanderkemp's bearing during their momentous interview at Barcelona, the more satisfied he felt of the traveller's innocence. He found it hard to believe, further, that a man who had just benefited to the extent of over £30,000 would be able to deny himself at least a very slight betterment in his standard of living. But the real difficulty was to connect Vanderkemp with Miss Winter's escapade with the sixteen diamonds. How did she receive them? She was in the Savoy building all the time between the theft at Hatton Garden and the traveller's departure from London, and it was therefore impossible that they could have met. Nor did French think it likely that so dangerous a package would have been entrusted to other hands or to the post.

Here were undoubted objections to the theory, nevertheless French felt a pleasurable glow of excitement as he wondered if they could not be met and if he really had not reached the last lap of his long investigation. He determined that his first action on reaching the Yard would be to put the matter to the test.

Having arrived at this decision, he turned again to Miss Scott.

'I should like cook's address, please.'

Miss Scott did not know cook's address. She believed the woman lived somewhere down near Reading, but more than that she could not say, except that her name was Jane Hudson, and that she was small and stout and lively.

French felt that if he wanted the woman he could find her from this information. He scarcely hoped that she would be able to tell him more than the parlourmaid, but thought that it might be worth while to have her looked up on chance, and he decided to give the necessary instructions to one of his men on his return to the Yard.

By this time it was evident that Miss Scott had exhausted her stock of information, and he presently took leave of her, having asked her to ring him up if she heard or saw anything either of cook or of her former employers.

Returning to the Yard he rang up the Hatton Garden office, and having obtained Vanderkemp's last known address, sent a cable to the United States police, asking that inquiries should be made as to the man's whereabouts.

His next business was to find the man who had driven Mrs Vane to Euston. A few minutes' walk took him to Gardiner Street, and he soon reached the cab rank. Five vehicles were lined up, and he called the drivers together and explained his business. He took a strong line, demanding information as a right in his capacity of an officer of the C.I.D. It had immediate effect.

One of the drivers said that he and the man next on the rank were called to Crewe Lodge by a rather pretty girl about 4.30 on the afternoon in question. It looked as if the house was being closed. A lady, apparently the mistress, got into his friend's taxi and was driven off, then the girl who had called him and a friend—he took them to be servants—entered his car and followed. He set the girl down at some street off Maida Vale—Thistle Road or Mistletoe Road—he wasn't just sure, and took the other woman on to Paddington. The colleague who had driven the lady was not then on the stand, but he had been gone a considerable time and might turn up any moment. Would the inspector wait, or should the man be sent on to the Yard on his return?

French decided to wait, and in less than half an hour he was rewarded by the appearance of the car. Taximan James Tucker remembered the evening in question. He had followed his *confrère* to Crewe Lodge, and a lady whom he took to be the mistress of the house had entered his vehicle. The girl who had called him from the stand had told him to drive to Euston, and he had started off through North Gate and along Albert Road. But when he had nearly reached the station the lady had spoken to him through the tube. She had said that she had changed her mind, and would go on to St Pancras. He had accordingly driven to the latter station, where the lady had paid him off.

'Had she any luggage?' French asked.

Yes, she had two or three—the man could not be quite sure—but either two or three suitcases. No, there wouldn't be any note of them on his daily return as they were carried inside the vehicle. The lady got a porter at St Pancras, he believed, but he could not identify the man now. No, she had spoken to no one during the journey, and he could

231

not suggest any reason why she should have changed her mind.

Inquiries at St Pancras seemed to French to be the next item on his programme, and entering Tucker's vehicle, he was driven to the old Midland terminus. Where, French wondered, had his quarry been going? With Tucker's help he fixed a few minutes before 5.00 as the hour of the lady's arrival, and then, after paying the man off, he went to the time-tables to find out what trains left about that hour.

In the nature of the case—a woman making a hurried flight from the attentions of the police—he thought it more than likely that the journey would have been to some distant place. While a very clever fugitive might recognise that a change to another part of London was perhaps his safest policy, the mentality of the average criminal leaned towards putting as many miles as possible between himself and the scene of his crime. It was by no means a sound deduction, but in the absence of anything better, he thought the main line trains should be first considered.

He looked up the tables and was struck at once by the fact that an important express left at 5.00 p.m. It called at Nottingham, Chesterfield, Sheffield, and Leeds, and there were connections to Harrogate, Bradford, Morecambe, and Heysham for the Belfast boat. But any one of these places might be the starting-point of some further journey, and unless he got a lead of some kind it was quite hopeless to try to follow the traveller. Besides, she might not have gone by this train. There was a 5.5 stopping train to Northampton, a 5.35 to Nottingham, stopping at a number of intermediate places, and a 6.15 express to the north, not to mention local trains. No, he did not see that much was to be gained from the time-tables.

He made what inquiries he could at the station, exhibiting the lady's photograph to officials who were on duty when the trains in question were starting. It was, of course, a forlorn hope, and he was not greatly disappointed when it led to nothing.

As another forlorn hope, he wired to the police at Nottingham, Chesterfield, Sheffield, Leeds, Harrogate, Bradford, Morecambe, Heysham, and Belfast, saying that the woman referred to in page four of the previous week's *Bulletin* was believed to have gone to their respective towns, and urging that a vigilant lookout be kept for her.

French once more felt baffled. Again in this exasperating case he was left at a loose end. The information he gained always seemed to fail him at the critical moment. In something very like desperation he sat down that evening at his desk and spent a couple of hours going through his notes of the case, wondering if by any chance he could find some further clue which he had hitherto overlooked. After careful thought, he decided that there was still one line of research unexplored—an unpromising line, doubtless, but still a line. That list of dealings on the Stock Exchange: could anything be made of that? Would, for example, the secretaries of the various firms be able to tell him who had carried out the transactions in question? If so, it should lead to Mrs Vane or to someone who knew her intimately. He was not hopeful of the result, but he decided that if next day he had no other news he would look into it.

233

17

A Deal in Stocks

Full of his new idea, French on arrival at his office on the
following morning took from his archives the letter addressed
to Mrs Vane which he had found in the box on that lady's
hall door and spread it out before him on his desk.

As he looked down the list of sales and purchases of
stock, he was struck once again not only by the surprising
number of the transactions, but also of the diversity of the
stocks dealt in. There were British War Loan, Colonial
Government and foreign railway stocks, as well as those
of banks, insurance companies, stores, and various indus-
trial concerns—some five-and-twenty altogether. He
wondered from which of them he would be most likely to
obtain the desired information.

Finally he selected James Barker and *The Daily Looking
Glass*, and taking the latter first, he went to the registered
offices of the company and asked to see the secretary. His
question was a simple one. In his investigations of the
affairs of a suspect, he had come across a memorandum
of the sale of £895 19s. 8d. worth of *Daily Looking Glass*

ordinary stock. Could the secretary please inform him either of the parties to the transaction or of the stockbroker through whom it was carried out?

The secretary was dubious. He asked French the date of the sale, and when the latter replied that he did not know, dilated on the complexity of the search. This ignorance as to time, together with the constantly varying value of the stock, made the sale very difficult to trace; in fact, he was not sure that the information could be obtained. French in his turn dilated on the urgency and importance of the matter, with the result that two clerks were set to work and a report promised for the earliest possible moment.

So far so good, but this was not enough. French went on to James Barker's, where he set similar inquiries on foot. Then, anxious to leave no stone unturned, he asked the same questions at the registered office of the Picardie Hotel.

The latter was the first to reply. The secretary telephoned to say that he had had a careful search made, and that no transaction covering the exact amount in question had taken place. Nothing within eight pounds of the figure given by Inspector French had been dealt with.

He had scarcely finished the conversation when the secretary of James Barker rang up. He, too, had made a careful search for several years back, and he, too, had found that stock of the amount mentioned by the inspector had not changed hands during the period. On the 2nd March previously a sale had taken place of slightly over a pound more than the inspector's figure, £1 2s. 1d. to be exact, but with the exception of this there was nothing very close to it. An hour later came a similar reply from the Picardie Hotel. No transaction could be traced within ten pounds of the amount mentioned by the inspector.

Could the discrepancies, French wondered, represent broker's commission, stamp duties or tax of some kind? To make sure of this would, he thought, be a tedious business, involving research through the books of a considerable number of the companies concerned. He was rather ignorant of the business of stockbroking, and he had no idea of the scale of the brokers' fees nor how these were paid. He thought, however, that if in the case of, say, six companies, a note were made of the names of those concerned with all transactions of amounts approximating to those mentioned in Mrs Vane's letter, and if the same broker, seller, or purchaser occurred in the deals of each company, he would be justified in assuming that person had some connection with Mrs Vane. It was somewhat complicated as well as unpleasantly vague, but it did at least represent a clue. French decided he would get on with it, though exactly how he did not see.

After some thought he decided he would put his problem before a stockbroker friend of his own. George Hewett was junior partner of a small firm with offices in Norfolk Street off the Strand, and French, having made an appointment for fifteen minutes later, put the list in his pocket and set off to walk along the Embankment.

His friend greeted him as a long-lost brother, and after lighting up cigars, they discussed old times as well as the testamentary affairs of one Bolsover, deceased, which had involved a Chancery action in which Hewett had given evidence. That subject exhausted, French turned to his immediate business. He handed his list to the other, and telling his story, ended up by asking for an expert opinion on the whole affair.

The stockbroker took the paper and glanced rapidly

down it; then he began to re-read it more slowly. French sat watching him, puffing the while, at his cigar. Finally the other made his pronouncement.

'Hanged if I know, French. It is evidently a statement of someone's dealings in the money market, but it's not in the form a professional man would use. In fact, I never saw anything quite like it before.'

'Yes?' French prompted. 'In what way is it different from what you're accustomed to?'

Hewett shrugged his shoulders.

'I suppose if I said in every way, I shouldn't be far wrong. First place, there are no dates for the transactions. Of course if the statement was only intended to show the net result of the deals the dates wouldn't so much matter, but a stock-broker would have put them in. Then it's impossible to get at any idea back of the sales. You see here that 4% War Loan was sold and 5% War Loan was bought; Great Westerns were sold and North-Easterns bought, while Australian 6% was sold and British East Africa 6% bought. These stocks there was are all pretty much the same in value, and nothing to be gained by selling one and buying another. Same way no sensible man would sell Alliance Assurance and buy Amalgamated Oils. You get what I mean?'

'Quite. But mightn't the operator have been ignorant or misled as to the values?'

'Of course he might, and no doubt was. But even allowing for that, he's had a rum notion of stock exchange business. Then these small items are unusual. What does "balances" mean? And why are "telegrams" shown as a sale and not a purchase? I don't mind admitting, French, that the thing beats me. It's the sort of business you'd expect to be done on the stock exchange in Bedlam, if there is one.'

'I tried to get at the operator through the secretaries of some of those companies, but that was no good.'

'Which ones?'

'*The Daily Looking Glass*, James Barker, and the Picardie Hotel.'

'And they couldn't help you?'

'They said no transactions of those exact figures had been carried out. The nearest were within a few pounds of what I wanted. I wondered would the amounts include brokers' fees or stamp duty or taxes of any kind which would account for the difference?'

'I don't think so.' Hewett pored in silence over the paper for some seconds, then he turned and faced his visitor. 'Look here,' he went on deliberately, 'do you want to know what I think?'

'That's what I came for,' French reminded him.

'Very well, I'll tell you. I think the whole thing is just a blooming fraud. And do you know what makes me sure of it?'

French shook his head.

'Well, it's a thing you might have found out for yourself. It doesn't add. Those figures at the bottom are not the sum of the lines. The thing's just a blooming fraud.'

French cursed himself for his oversight, then suddenly a startling idea flashed into his mind. Suppose this list of sales and purchases had nothing whatever to do with finance. Suppose it conveyed a hidden message by means of some secret code or cipher. Was that a possibility? His voice trembled slightly, as with a haste verging on something very different from his usual Soapy Joe politeness he took his leave.

He hurried back to the Yard, eagerly anxious to get to work on his new inspiration, and reaching his office, he spread the list on his desk and sat down to study it. It read:

STOCK AND SHARE LIST

	Bought			Sold		
	£	s.	d.	£	s.	d.
1. War Loan 5%	328	4	2			
2. Australia 6%				568	5	0
3. Great Western Ord. ..				1039	1	3
4. Associated News Ord. ..	936	6	3			
5. Aerated Bread	713	9	2			
6. Barclay's Bank	991	18	1			
7. Alliance Assurance ..				394	19	10
8. Lyons				463	17	5
9. Picardie Hotel				205	14	11
10. Anglo-American Oil. ..				748	3	9
11. War Loan 4%				403	18	10
12. British East Africa 6% ..	401	3	9			
13. L. & N. E.	292	1	1			
14. Brit. American Tobacco ..	898	5	7			
15. Army & Navy Stores ..				1039	0	4
16. Lloyd's Bank				586	10	10
17. Atlas Assurance				922	4	5
18. Telegrams					16	7
19. Maple				90	19	6
20. Mappin & Webb	463	4	5			
21. Amalgamated Oils	748	5	7			
22. War Loan 4½%				568	2	3
23. Canadian Govt. 3½% ..	958	5	6			
24. Balances		17	3			
25. Metroplitan Railway ..	812	10	4			
26. *Daily Looking Glass* Ord. ..				895	19	8
27. J. Barker				371	18	11
	£6935	12	1	£9127	18	2
				6935	12	1
				£2192	6	1

The first question which occurred to French was whether, assuming the list did contain some secret message, this was hidden in the names of the stocks or in the money, or in both?

Taking the former idea first, he began trying to form words out of certain letters of the names, selected on various plans. The initials, W, A, G, A, A, . . . were not promising, even when read bottom upwards, J, D, M, B, C . . . Nor were the final letters, downwards and upwards, any better. Those next the initials and the penultimates were equally hopeless, nor did diagonal arrangements promise better.

French tried every plan he could think of, working steadily and methodically through the various cases of each, and not leaving it until he was satisfied that he was on the wrong track. He came on no solution, but he did make one discovery which seemed to indicate that the message, if such existed, was contained in the money columns rather than in the names. He noticed that in the majority of cases the names of the various stocks began with one of the earlier letters of the alphabet, and where this did not obtain, the stock in question was one of the first of that kind of stock to be quoted. He picked up a *Daily Mail* and looked at the financial page. The stocks were divided under various headings, British Stocks, Overseas Dominions, Home Railways, Canadian and Foreign Railways, and such like. The first division was British Stocks, and the first item in it was War Loan 5%. But the first item on Mrs Vane's list was War Loan 5%.

The second item on the list was Australia 6%, and referring to the *Daily Mail* once more, French saw that Australia 6%'s was the first item on the second division. This was sufficiently interesting, but when he found that the next five items, Great Western, Associated News, Aerated Bread,

Barclay's Bank, and Alliance Assurance were each the first of their respective divisions, he felt he had stumbled upon something more than a coincidence.

He re-examined the list on this new basis, only to find his conclusions verified. Apparently the person writing it had simply copied down the stocks given in some paper—probably the *Daily Mail*. In order to obtain variety and to make an unsuspicious-looking list, he had not simply copied them consecutively; he had taken the first out of each division. Then he had gone over the divisions again, using the second name in each case, and so on until he had obtained the whole twenty-five names that he had required. It had not been done with absolute accuracy, but there was no doubt of the general method. From this it followed that any message which the list might convey was contained in the money columns, and French accordingly transferred his attention to the latter.

The amounts extended from 16s. 7d. up to £1039, and varied surprisingly between these extremes. There were none in the £100's or the £600's, but all the other hundreds were represented. Speaking broadly, there were more of the £800's and £900's than of the lower numbers. But he could not see where any of these facts tended.

There being no obvious line of research, he began a laborious and detailed investigation into the possibilities of substitution, that is, one of those ciphers in which a number or other sign is used to denote a letter. It was clear that single numbers were insufficient for this purpose, as in that case only ten letters of the alphabet could be used. Some combination was therefore involved, and French tried various schemes of addition to meet the case. But though he got three men to assist him in the details of his various tests, he could not find anything which gave the least suggestion of an intelligible combination.

While engaged in this manner, he noticed that so far as the pounds were concerned there were no less than three similar pairs, numbers 2 and 22, 3 and 15, and 10 and 21. He examined these pairs for some time, and then he suddenly made a discovery which seemed to show that at last he was on the right track. He had put the figures down beside each other, so:

	£	s.	d.
No. 2	568	5	0
No. 22	568	2	3

when suddenly he noticed that if the shilling and pence of each item were added the result would be the same: 5 0=5; 2 3=5. Eagerly he turned to the other pairs and wrote them out similarly,

	£	s.	d.
No. 3	1039	1	3
No. 15	1039	0	4

and,

	£	s.	d.
No. 10	748	3	9
No. 21	748	5	7

Here he saw at a glance that the same thing obtained, the pounds alone, and the pence and shillings added together, making two similar pairs, and therefore presumably standing for the same word.

242

This discovery restored all his eager interest. It seemed definitely to prove three things, each several one of which afforded him the liveliest satisfaction. First, these combinations of figures proved that there really was some underlying scheme, and that in its turn involved the hidden message; secondly, they showed that he, French, was on the direct road towards a solution; and thirdly, they indicated a code or cipher built up of pairs of numbers, a frequent combination, embracing many well-known varieties of cryptogram.

His next step was, therefore, to rewrite the list in dual column, the pounds in front, the pence and shillings added together behind. This gave him a new jumping-off place in the following:

328–6
568–5
1039–4
936–9
713–11, and so on.

On this he started his three men, making them try to work out keys on squares and parallelograms, as well as in other well-established ways. Then the pounds figure proving too large for this, he tried adding the various digits of these figures together. In this way, 328 became 3 2 8 or 13, and so he compiled a second list beginning:

13–6
19–5
13–4

243

But in spite of all his own and his men's efforts he was unable to find any clue to the key. They worked until long after the usual quitting time, and at length he had to agree to an adjournment for the night.

Next day he again attacked the problem, but it was not until well on in the afternoon that he made an advance. Tired and dispirited, he had sent for a cup of coffee to clear his brain, and after it he had, contrary to his custom, lighted his pipe, while he leaned comfortably back in his chair still turning the matter over in his mind. He was beginning to think the puzzle insoluble, when suddenly an idea flashed into his mind, and he sat up sharply, wondering if he had hit on the solution.

He had been considering numerical ciphers of which the key is some book. These consist usually of sets of three numbers, the first representing the page, the second the line on that page, and the third the word on that line. But he recognised that one of these latter numbers might be a constant, that is, that the word should always be on, say, the fifth line of the page, or that it should be the first or second of the line. In this way the cipher could be worked with pairs of numbers. The difficulty in these cases was of course to find the book which each of the communicating parties used.

So far had he progressed when he got his great idea. Where had he seen a book which seemed strangely out of keeping with its fellows? Of course! That was it at last! The *Concise Oxford Dictionary* in Mrs Vane's sitting-room!

As he thought over this he felt more and more certain that he had reached the explanation. Not only was there the fact of the book being there, but a dictionary was obviously not only the kind of book best suited for the purpose, but also that best suited for a dual number system. The first number would represent the page and the second the word on that page. The idea, further, was confirmed by the fact that while the figure for the pounds—or pages—ran from 1 to about 1000, that for the shillings and pence—or words on the page—never rose above 30. There was no doubt, French thought, that he had got it at last.

At Scotland Yard all things are procurable at short notice. He rang up a subordinate and gave urgent instructions that a *Concise Oxford Dictionary* was to be obtained immediately and sent up to him.

Five minutes later he was eagerly turning over the leaves. It took but a second or two to find page 328, and another second to count down to the sixth word. It was 'French.'

Without waiting to consider whether this might refer to himself, in which case he had found the solution, or merely be a coincidence, in which case he hadn't, he hastily went on to the next number. Page 568, word 5, was 'On.'

'French on.' Still it might make sense or it might not. He looked up No. 3.

The fourth word on the 1039th page was 'Your.' 'French on your' was going all right, but when he turned up No. 4 and found that the ninth word on page 936 was 'Track,' all doubt was at an end. 'French on your track.' He had got it with a vengeance!

The remaining words came easily until he came to number 17, Atlas Assurance £922 4s. 5d. The ninth word on page 922 did not make sense. But he had gone so far that this further problem could not long hold him up. After a very few seconds he saw that if he added the shillings and pence of the following line—which showed no figure in the pounds column—to those of the £922, he found the word he wanted. It simply meant that there were more than thirty words preceding that in question on that page of the dictionary. 19 and 11, or 30, was the largest number one line of shillings and pence would show, therefore a larger number than 30 required two lines of shillings and pence to one of pounds. The word 'telegrams' had evidently been written as a blind, and he soon saw that the item 'balance' was wanted for a similar purpose. After this a few minutes sufficed to turn up all the words, and presently he sat back and looked at the completed result of his work.

'French on your track rendezvous victory hotel lee d s if i fail take your own ticket boat leave s on twenty six t h.'

This as it stood was clear, but he rewrote it, putting in stops and capitals, and joining the broken words.

'French on your track. Rendezvous Victory Hotel, Leeds. If I fail take your own ticket. Boat leaves on twenty-sixth.'

So they were trying to escape by sea, Mrs Vane and the person who had sent her the warning! Who that person was, French had but little doubt. Almost certainly it was Mr Vane, and if so, it seemed to him also beyond reasonable doubt that Mr Vane was the murderer. At all events, whether or not, the person who had sent cipher directions to Mrs Vane regarding their joint flight was the person he wanted. He chuckled to himself as, he thought that he would soon know all about it now. He would soon find the boat they were sailing in, and then he would have them in the hollow of his hand.

But would he? As his eye fell on the almanac hanging above the chimney-piece he swore. Inexorably it reminded him that this was the twenty-sixth. The steamer had left on that very day!

But be that as it might, his procedure was clear. He must find the boat. For a moment he sat considering ways and means, and then his attention was attracted to the wording of the last phrase of the message: 'Boat leaves on twenty-sixth.' This surely suggested a clue—that the service was other than daily. Had the latter obtained, the phrase would have been, 'Take next Thursday's boat,' or words to that effect. If his deduction was correct, it meant that the steamer was a sea-going ship, not merely a cross-Channel packet. This view, moreover, was to some extent supported by the probability that the fugitives would almost certainly make for a distant rather than an adjacent country.

From where, then, in the neighbourhood of Leeds, did steamers start to distant lands? Liverpool was, of course, the obvious answer, but it need not necessarily be Liverpool. From Hull and Grimsby, or even Manchester and Goole, ships left for foreign ports. It would be necessary to make a list of all the ocean-going steamers which left all the ports near Leeds on the current date.

Late though it was, French stuck to his task. A study of the shipping news revealed the fact that seven steamers were booked to leave Liverpool and Hull and the ports adjoining. From Liverpool there was a White Star liner to Boston and Philadelphia, a Lamport & Holt boat to Buenos Aires and Rosario, a Booth liner to Para and Manáos, and a Bibby liner to Egypt, Colombo and Rangoon. From

Hull, a Finland liner sailed to Helsingfors and a Wilson boat to Copenhagen, while another Wilson liner left Grimsby for Christiansand. Besides these, there were doubtless numbers of cargo boats, some of which might take passengers, but these were the only regular liners, and French determined to try them first.

He called up the head office of each of the lines in question and asked had any persons named Vane booked passages on their ships leaving on that day, and if not, could they tell him if a couple answering the description which he gave had done so. There was a considerable delay in getting replies, but when he received that from the Booth Line he did not grudge the loss of time. It stated that a Mr and Mrs Vane, of Crewe Lodge, St John's Wood Road, had booked passages to Manáos by the *Enoch,* which left Liverpool at 3.00 p.m. that afternoon; further, these persons had gone on board at Liverpool, and as far as the head office knew, had actually sailed.

French was a trifle hazy about the Booth Line. He knew that Manáos was in South America—Brazil, he imagined, but whether the steamer sailed there direct or made intermediate calls at which it might be overtaken and at which an arrest might be made, he did not know.

He telephoned to have the information sent up to him. 'The last lap!' he thought contentedly, as he pictured the arrival of the steamer at Manáos and the descent of the fugitives on to the wharf into the clutches of the waiting police. And for him it would mean not only the completion of a peculiarly worrying and difficult case, but undoubted kudos, if not actual promotion.

18

The S.S. 'Enoch'

In the vast organisation of Scotland Yard the indexing of information on every available subject has been brought to something more than a fine art. If French had wished to know the number of inhabitants of Prague, the favourite recreations of the Elder Brethren of Trinity House, or the width of the Ganges at Allahabad, some notes or books of reference would immediately have been forthcoming which would have fully supplied the desired information. How much more when the question was merely one of trains and steamers. He had not long to wait for an answer to his telephone, and this revealed the fact that the Booth liner *Enoch*, which had left Liverpool on the previous afternoon, called at Havre, Oporto, Lisbon, Madeira, and. Para, before completing her voyage to Manáos by a sail of a thousand miles up the Amazon. Moreover, she awaited at Havre the arrival of the Southampton boat, the connection of which left Waterloo at 9.30 on the night of the 27th.

'Tonight!' French thought as he hastily glanced at his watch. It was just 8.42. *What* a stroke of luck! He would travel by it, and with any reasonable good fortune he would have these Vanes safe in his clutches before another dozen hours had passed.

As a man of action French was unsurpassed. Within five minutes he had called an assistant, a keen, efficient young sergeant named Carter, and instructed him to join him that night on the 9.30 Continental train from Waterloo, had sent another keen, efficient helper post-haste to have extradition warrants and other necessaries sent to the same train, and had rung up for a taxi to take him home to tell his wife of his change of plan and to put two or three things together, for the journey. In short, thanks to his energy, the hands of the Waterloo station clock had scarcely reached 9.25 when he and Sergeant Carter reached the platform from which the boat train was about to start. Awaiting them was Manning, the other keen and efficient assistant, who handed over warrants for the arrest and extradition of Mr and Mrs Vane, passports, English and French money, as well as an introduction to the French police at Havre.

'Good, Manning! That's all right,' French approved as he took over the munitions of war. In another couple of minutes the train drew slowly out of the station, and increasing its speed as it passed the myriad lights of South London, was soon roaring through the darkness of the open country beyond.

Fortunately, the night was calm and the boat was not crowded, so that the detectives were able to get berths and a sleep to prepare them for their toils on the following day. They reached Havre on time, and jumping into a taxi were driven to the berth of the *Enoch*, which was some distance down the docks. French hurried on board and asked to see the Captain, while Carter remained at the gangway lest the quarry, seeing French and knowing his appearance, might take fright and attempt to slip ashore.

Captain Davis saw French immediately.

'Sit down, Mr French,' he said pleasantly when he had examined the other's credentials, 'and let me know what I can do for you.'

French took the proferred seat as he drew from his pocket Mrs Vane's photograph as well as her description and that of her husband.

'I'll tell you, Captain,' he answered. 'I'm after a man and woman who are wanted for murder and robbery. They call themselves Mr and Mrs Vane, though I don't know if this is their real name or even if they are married. I have learned that they booked with you from Liverpool to Manáos, but I only found that out last night, so I came over by Southampton in the hope of making an arrest. There,' he passed over his photograph and papers, 'are the descriptions.'

The Captain glanced at him as he took the papers. He did not speak until he had looked through the latter, then he said gravely:

'I'm afraid, Mr French, they've been one too many for you this time. A Mr and Mrs Vane did book passages and even came on board at Liverpool, but they left the ship almost immediately and didn't turn up again. I assumed that some accident had prevented their return, and that they would follow by Southampton as you did, but from what you tell me it looks as if they had learned you were on their track and made a bolt for it. But we had better see the purser. He will tell us details.'

French was aghast. Once again had happened to him

what he had so often previously experienced. When he was most sure of himself and most confident of success, that was the time of failure! How often had he taken a sporting chance, doubtful of himself and his ability to meet a situation, and the occasion had resulted in a brilliant coup. And how often, alas, had his certainty of success ended in disaster!

By the time the purser arrived, he had to some extent recovered his equanimity. 'Mr Jennings—Inspector French of the C.I.D.,' the Captain introduced them. 'Sit down, Jennings, and hear what the inspector wants. It's about that Mr and Mrs Vane that came aboard at Liverpool and left again before we sailed. Ask him what you want to know, Mr French.'

Mr Jennings was a shrewd, efficient-looking man of about forty, and as French began to speak he felt a comfortable assurance that at least he would receive in answer to his questions concisely-worded statements of accurately observed facts.

'It's this way, Mr Jennings,' he explained. 'These Vanes are wanted for murder and robbery. I traced them to your ship, and crossed last night from London, hoping to arrest them here. But the Captain tells me I have missed them. Perhaps you'll give me any information you can about them.'

'There's not much to tell,' the purser answered. 'They came aboard about noon on Thursday, and Mr Vane showed me their tickets and asked for their stateroom. The tickets were singles from Liverpool to Manáos, all O.K. An upper deck stateroom, No. 12, had been reserved at the London office, and I gave the number to their cabin steward and saw him leading the way there with the luggage. About half an hour later they came back to my office and asked what time the ship sailed. I told them three o'clock. Mr Vane said they had to go ashore to complete some business, but would be back in good time. They then left in the direction of the gangway.'

'Did you actually see them go ashore?'

'No, you can't see out on deck from the office.'

'Yes? And then?'

'After dinner their cabin steward asked me if I knew anything, about them. He said they hadn't been down for dinner, and he couldn't find them anywhere about the ship. We had a look round, and then I spoke to Captain Davis, and he had a thorough search made. They have never been seen since, and they're certainly not on board now.'

'They couldn't have hidden somewhere and slipped ashore here in Havre?'

'Quite impossible. There's not the slightest doubt they missed the boat at Liverpool.'

'Intentionally or unintentionally?' the Captain interjected.

'I don't know anything about that,' Mr Jennings replied, 'but they certainly did not sail with us. Perhaps, Inspector, they learned when they went on shore that you were after them?'

'Impossible,' French declared. 'I did not myself know where they had gone until last night.'

He felt ruefully sure that the whole thing was part of the elaborate laying of a false trail, but he did not see that anything was to be gained by discussing this with the ship's officers. He pushed his papers towards the purser.

'Can you recognise the parties from those, Mr Jennings?'

A glance at the photograph sufficed. The original was

undoubtedly that Mrs Vane who had for a brief half-hour boarded the *Enoch*. And the description was that of Mr Vane also. French was forced to the conclusion that his quarry had indeed, in the Captain's words, been too many for him. He swore bitterly beneath his breath.

'You say they left some luggage in their stateroom,' he went on. 'Could I have a look at it?'

'Of course. But, you know, they may still be here. On several occasions I have known passengers to miss the ship at Liverpool and follow on here. They may turn up at any minute.'

'If they do, so much the better,' French answered. 'But I won't bank on it. If you don't mind, I'll have a look at the luggage now. What time do you sail?'

'In about half an hour.'

'That will just give me time. Meantime I have a man at the gangway, and he'll spot them if they come along.'

There were four large suitcases in the roomy and comfortable stateroom set apart for the Vanes, as well as a number of articles of toilet and apparel which might well represent the first hurried attempt at unpacking. The suitcases were locked, but French soon opened them with his bunch of skeleton keys. And here he got confirmation of his theory that all this journey to Manáos was merely a carefully thought out plant. The cases were empty. Dummy luggage brought in to bolster up the trick. But there was nothing in the cabin to give any hint of where the fugitives had really gone.

'I needn't wait for them to turn up,' French said grimly. 'Those empty suitcases give the show away.'

'I'm afraid it looks like it,' the purser admitted. 'Sorry we didn't know about it sooner.'

'Can't be helped. That's what we Scotland Yard men are up against all the time.' He bid the friendly purser good-day and slowly left the ship.

But he did not leave the wharf. Though he thought it unlikely, there was still just a chance that the quarry had missed the ship and were following on. He would make sure.

But though he waited until the *Enoch* cast off and swung her bows round towards the open sea, there was no sign of any late arrivals, and when he had once seen the liner under way he turned disconsolately to his satellite.

'It's all U P., Carter, as far as this trip is concerned. They've given us the slip about proper. Goodness only knows where they are by this time; perhaps half-way to the States. Let's find a telegraph office and report to Headquarters.'

A few minutes later French had sent a long wire to his chief at the Yard. Then at a loose end, he turned to Sergeant Carter.

'Well, Carter, what shall we do with ourselves now? Here's ten o'clock and we can't get back until the evening. We have the whole day to play round in.'

Except that he believed he could do with a bit more breakfast, the sergeant's ideas were nebulous. French laughed at him.

'It's what I was thinking myself,' he admitted, 'but it's a bad time. These folk over here have no notion of what a good breakfast means, and it's a bit early for their lunch. However, we'll see what we can do.'

They went into a small restaurant and asked for coffee and ham and eggs. This proving too much for the waiter, the proprietor was summoned. He had a little English and at last understood.

'But yes, messieurs,' he cried, waving his hands. 'The ham, the eggs, the omelette; is it not so? He bowed low. 'Immediately, messieurs. Will messieurs be pleased to be seated.'

Messieurs were pleased to be seated, and in an incredibly short space of time a smoking omelette arrived, garnished with chip potatoes and onions, together with coffee and delicious rolls and butter. To this the hungry men did full justice, and Carter's estimate of the French, which had been low, went up several points. They took their time over the meal, but eventually it was finished, and the problem of how to fill in their time once more became insistent.

'We might go round and see some of these coast places,' French suggested. 'St Malo or some of those. Or I dare say we could work across somehow to Dieppe and catch the afternoon boat to Newhaven. What do you say?'

Carter voted for going to the station and looking into the possibilities, and they walked slowly up the town, fascinated by the foreign life of the busy port. Havre is a fine city with good streets, shops, and public buildings, but it is not an interesting town, and by the time they reached the station, a mile and a half away, they felt they had seen enough of it.

An examination of the time-tables showed that they were too late for Dieppe—the English boat would have left before they could possibly get there—and St Malo, they discovered, was not in that part of the country at all, but miles away to the south-west. Trouville was only eight or ten miles away across the bay, but Trouville in winter did not seem an attractive prospect.

'Tell you what,' French said at last. 'We've got an

introduction to these French johnnies. We'll go and look 'em up, and perhaps see something of their police station.'

Sergeant Carter, delighted with his superior's condescension, hurriedly agreed, and a few minutes later the two men found themselves ascending the steps of a large building which bore over the door the legend 'Gendarmerie.' Here French tendered his introduction, with the result that he was shown into the presence of and politely welcomed by the officer in charge.

'I regret the Chief is out of town at present,' the latter said in excellent English. 'He will be sorry not to have seen you. I hope that presently, you will give me the pleasure of your company at lunch, and in the meantime let me know if there is anything I can do for you.'

French explained the circumstances. He would not stay for lunch, as he had but a short time since finished an excellent breakfast, but he would be most grateful if the other would tell him how best he could spend the time until his return boat to Southampton.

'That's not until midnight,' answered the Frenchman. 'You don't know this country?'

'Not at all. It was just that if there was anything to see within reach, we might as well see it.'

'Of course, naturally. Well, monsieur, were I in your place I should certainly go to Caen. It is an interesting old town, well worth a visit. There is a steamer all the way, but you would scarcely have time for that; it is rather slow. I should recommend you to go to Trouville by steamer—it's just across the bay—and then go on from there to Caen by rail. In the time at your disposal I really do not think you could do anything better.'

French thanked him, and the other continued, 'The

257

steamer sails according to the tide. Today,' he glanced at an almanac, 'it leaves at midday. You should get to Caen about two, and you could dine there and come back in the evening in time for your boat.'

At ten minutes to twelve French and his satellite reached the wharf, having delayed on their walk down town to consume bocks in one of the many attractive cafés in the main streets. They took tickets and went on board the little steamer. The day was cold though fine, and there were but few travellers. They strolled about, interested in the novel scene, and at last finding two seats in the lee of the funnel, sat down to await the start.

Midday came, and with leisurely movements the horn was blown, the gangway run ashore, and the ropes slacked. The Captain put his lips to the engine-room speaking tube, but before he could give his order an interruption came from the shore. Shouts arose, and a man in the blue uniform of a gendarme appeared running towards the boat and gesticulating wildly. The Captain paused, the slackened ropes were pulled tight, and all concerned stood expectant.

The gendarme jumped on board and ran up the steps to the bridge, eagerly watched by the entire ship's company. He spoke rapidly to the Captain, and then the latter turned to the staring passengers below.

'Monsieur Fr-r-ronsh?' he called in stentorian tones, looking inquiringly round the upturned faces. 'Monsieur Fr-r-ronsh de Londres?'

'It's you, sir,' cried Carter. 'There's something up.'

French hastened to the bridge and the gendarme handed him a blue envelope. 'De monsieur le chef,' he explained with a rapid salute, as he hastened ashore.

It was a telegram, and it contained news which, as it

were, brought the inspector up all standing. It was from the Yard and read:

'Liverpool police wire Vanes went aboard *Enoch* and did not go ashore again. Mackay was watching ship for Henson and saw them. They must still be on board. Follow ship to Oporto or Lisbon.'

'Come ashore, Carter,' French cried rapidly, rushing to the side. The boat was actually moving, but the two men, jumping, reached the wharf amid the execrations of the Captain and staff.

'Here, officer,' he called, beckoning to the gendarme, who had watched the proceedings with a horrified interest, 'how do you get quickly to Headquarters?'

The man bowed, shrugged his shoulders, and indicated in dumb show that he did not understand. French hailed a passing taxi and pushed his companions in.

'Monsieur le chef!' he cried to the bewildered gendarme, producing and tapping the telegram. 'Monsieur le chef?'

The man understood. A smile dawned on his perturbed countenance, and with a rapid flow of French he gave the required address. In ten minutes they were once more at the gendarmerie, French still clamouring for 'Monsieur le chef.'

He was shown into the room of the same polite officer whom he had previously met.

'Ah,' the latter said, 'so my man was in time. You got your telegram?'

'Yes, sir, I did, and greatly obliged to you I am for your trouble. But I can't make head or tail of the thing. Those ship's officers this morning were absolutely positive the wanted couple had not sailed.'

The officer shrugged his shoulders.

'Doubtless,' he said smoothly. 'All the same I thought you should have the message, lest you should wish to follow up the steamer as suggested.'

'I have no choice,' French returned. 'It is an order from Headquarters. Perhaps, sir, you would add to your already great kindness by telling me my route. With this confounded difference of language I feel myself all at sea.'

The officer, who had seemed bored as to the movements of the Vanes, became once more the efficient, interested consultant. The obvious route, he said, was via Paris. It was true that you could get across country to pick up the international express at Bordeaux, but Paris was quicker and more comfortable. Fortunately, French had returned in time to catch the midday train to the capital. It left at 12.40, and he could easily reach the station and book in the twenty minutes which remained before that hour.

His time from the receipt of the wire until the Paris express pulled out of Havre station had been so fully occupied that French had not been able seriously to consider the message sent. Now, seated in the corner of a second-class compartment with Carter opposite, he drew the flimsy sheet from his pocket and re-read it carefully. He understood the reference to Mackay and Henson. Detective-Sergeant Mackay was one of the best men of the Liverpool detective staff, and he was on a very similar job to French's own. He was watching the outgoing steamers in the hope of capturing one Charles Henson, who with a couple of others had made a sensational raid on a country bank, and after murdering the manager, had got away with a large haul from the safe. French knew Mackay personally, and he was satisfied that if he had said the Vanes had gone on board and remained there, they had done so.

He wondered how it came that Mackay had not at the time recognised the Vanes as a wanted couple. Probably, he thought, the man had been so much occupied with his own case that he had not read up the particulars in the *Bulletin*, which, after all, was a magazine intended more for the rank and file than for men on specialised duties. However, the fact remained that Mackay had missed his chance, though his habit of detailed observation had enabled him to some extent to redeem his error.

But if it was true that the Vanes had not left the ship at Liverpool, what became of the statements of the Captain and Purser? It was not likely that these men could be hoodwinked over such a matter. They were experts; moreover, they were dealing with a ship with whose every part they were familiar. To the Vanes, on the other hand, the ship would be strange, and they would be ignorant of its routine. Under these circumstances it was absolutely out of the question that the pair could have hidden themselves on board. No, if they were there, the Captain would have known of it. French could not devise any explanation of the matter. The whole thing seemed a contradiction.

He had, however, to settle his own plans. The kindly French police officer had helped him by 'phoning the local office of the Booth Line and finding out the itinerary of the *Enoch*. This was Saturday, and on the afternoon of the following day, Sunday, the steamer was expected to reach Leixoes, the port of Oporto. She would remain there that night and the next day, leaving Leixoes about 8 o'clock on the Monday evening. Next day about noon she was due in Lisbon, where she would remain for two days. After that her first call was Madeira.

French had intended to meet her in Lisbon, but it now occurred to him that he might be able to make Oporto in time to join her there. He had bought a railway guide in Havre, and he now proceeded to look up the trains. The route, he saw, was to Bordeaux by the Paris-Orleans line, then on by the Midi to the Spanish frontier at Irun, and so by Medina and Salamanca to Oporto. The first through train from Paris after their arrival at 4.35 p.m. was the 10.22 p.m. from the Gare Quai d'Orsay, and this reached Oporto at shortly after midday on the next day but one, Monday. Oporto to Lexioes was only half an hour's run, so he had six or seven hours' margin. Oporto, he decided, was his goal.

They were fortunate in securing sleeping berths between Paris and Bordeaux, and there was a restaurant car on the train to Irun. They waited an hour at the frontier station, and French blessed the intelligence of Manning, who had had their identification papers made available for Spain and Portugal as well as France.

French on his trip from Chamonix to Barcelona had been amazed by the illimitable extent of the earth, but his feelings of wonder on that occasion were as nothing compared to those he now experienced. The journey from Irun to Oporto was absolutely *endless*; at least he thought so as interminable mile succeeded interminable mile, while day turned into night and night more slowly turned back into day. It was cold, too, through the high tableland of Spain—bitterly cold, and the two men could not get the kind of meals they liked, nor could they sleep well in

262

the somewhat jolting coaches. But all things come to an end, and at half-past one on the Monday, about an hour late, the train came finally to a stand in the Estacao Central of Oporto. There was plenty of time, and the travellers went straight to the Porto Hotel for a short rest before setting out to find the tramway to Leixoes.

French was immensely struck with the picturesque, old world city, nestling on the steep, hilly banks of the Douro, and he marvelled to feel quiver at every horse-hoof the great high level Dom Luez bridge, which throws its spidery steel arch in a single span of nearly 600 feet across the placid river flowing far beneath. Then after passing down the steeply-inclined streets to near the water's edge, he and Carter boarded the tram and set off seawards along a road skirting the right bank of the stream.

In spite of the business which had brought them so far, both men gazed with intense interest at the unwonted sights they passed, the semi-tropical vegetation, the long, narrow, four-wheeled carts with their teams of oxen, the mole constructed across some three-quarters of the mouth of the Douro to increase the scour through the remainder, then, passing a stretch of sandhills, they finally reached the houses of Leixoes, with lying below them the harbour contained within its two encircling stone piers, and, blessed sight, the *Enoch* lying at anchor therein.

They made a bargain with a dusky boatman for what seemed to French a fortune of reis, and ten minutes later they had ascended the ladder and were once more on the steamer's deck.

19

French Propounds a Riddle

If Captain Davis experienced surprise on seeing, French reappear at the door of his cabin, he gave no indication of his feelings.

'Good-afternoon, Inspector,' he greeted him quietly. 'Come aboard again? You should have stayed with us, you know.' He smiled quizzically. 'It would have been much less tiring than going all that way round by land, and for the matter of that, a good deal cheaper. Found your criminals?'

'Well, I've not,' French answered slowly,'—yet. But I hope to soon. Captain, I've had a wire from the Yard that those people are on board after all.'

The Captain frowned.

'No doubt the Yard is a wonderfully efficient organisation,' he said gravely, 'but when it comes to telling me who is or is not aboard my ship—well, I think that is a trifle, shall we say, thick? How do they profess to know?'

'I'll tell you. I got a wire shortly after the ship left Havre on Saturday, and it said that one of the Liverpool detectives,

Sergeant Mackay, was watching your ship before she sailed. He was looking out for a man also wanted for murder, not this Vane—a different person altogether. He saw the Vanes going on board, though, of course, he did not realise they also were wanted. But he saw them right enough, at least, he was able to convince the Yard as to their identity. Mackay waited until the ship sailed, and he states the Vanes did not go ashore. I know Mackay personally, and he is a most careful and accurate officer. I am satisfied that if he makes this statement it is true. Now, none of your people saw them go ashore, and with all due respect to you and your purser, the suggestion is that they're still on board. The wire ended by instructing me to follow up the ship either here or to Lisbon, and investigate further.'

'You've certainly followed us up all right, but having overtaken us I should like to ask, if it is not an indiscreet question, what you propose to do next?'

French saw that if he was to retain the help of Captain Davis he would have to be careful how he answered.

'There, Captain, I was going to ask for your kind help, though I feel I have troubled you more than enough already. I'll tell you what I was thinking over in the train. Suppose for argument's sake the Yard is right, and that these people really are on board. It is obvious from your search that they're not here in their own characters, therefore they must be posing as two other people. That, I take it, is what the people at the Yard had in mind also.'

'Well?'

'This is not such an unlikely supposition as it sounds. The woman is, or rather was, an actress, and we know she is a clever one. Not only was she well thought of when on the stage, but she has recently carried off successfully a far stiffer test than that. She crossed from New York to Southampton on the *Olympic*, and convinced the people on board that she was English, and then she went on to London and convinced the people there that she was an American. I have seen the people in each case—critical, competent people who know the world—and each lot ridiculed the idea that she was not what she seemed. If she could do that, she could surely manage another impersonation. A comparatively simple disguise would do, as there would be nothing to make you or the purser suspect.'

The Captain was listening with considerable interest, but it was evident that his ruffled feelings were not yet entirely smoothed down.

'That may be all very well,' he admitted, 'but you have not taken into consideration the evidence of the bookings. 176 passengers booked from Liverpool, and in almost every case their tickets were taken and their staterooms reserved several days in advance. The exceptions in all cases were men. 176 passengers turned up, Mr and Mrs Vane among them. But there were only 174 passengers on board when we left Liverpool. You follow what I mean; that all the other passengers on board are accounted for?'

'I see that,' French admitted slowly, 'and you may be right. It certainly doesn't seem easy to answer what you say. At the same time, in the face of the instructions I have had from the Yard, I daren't do other than go on and sift the thing further.'

'Naturally, but how?'

'I don't know. I don't see my way clear as yet. For one thing, I shall have to meet every woman on board, with the special object of trying to penetrate any disguise which may have been attempted. If that fails I may give up the search or I may try something else. I suppose you can take me on as far as Lisbon at all events?'

'With pleasure.' The Captain seemed to have recovered from his momentary irritation. 'Let me know if there is anything I can do to help you. Though I confess I think you're on a wild-goose chase, I'll give you every facility I can.'

'Thank you, Captain. You will understand that whatever I may think myself, I am not my own master in the matter. The only thing I should like at present is a chat with the purser over the passenger list.'

'That, at all events, is easily arranged,' answered Captain Davis as he touched a bell.

The purser had not observed French's arrival, and professed amazement on finding him on board.

'I begin to wonder if the ship's not haunted,' he smiled as he shook hands. 'Mr and Mrs Vane we leave behind at Liverpool, and you say they're aboard at Havre. You we leave behind at Havre—I saw you myself on the wharf—and here you are aboard at Leixoes! What distinguished stranger are we to expect to find on board at Lisbon?'

'I hope there'll be a clearance of four at Lisbon,' French rejoined. 'Though it sounds impolite, nothing would please me better than to change to a homeward bounder in company with my Sergeant and Mr and Mrs Vane.'

'What? Do you still think they're on board?'

'The inspector still thinks so,' the Captain intervened, 'and he wants to talk to you about it. Better take him to your cabin and give him any help you can.'

'Right, sir. Will you come along, Mr French?'

Mr Jennings, in spite of his obvious competence, had a

pleasant, leisurely manner which conveyed to the many who sought his counsel that though he might be busy enough at other times, he was not too hurried at that moment to give them his most careful and undivided attention. So he listened to French's story, and so he took out the passenger list, and set himself to discuss the personalities of those enumerated thereon.

'I'll deal with the women first,' French explained. 'You say that there are sixty-seven on board, as against about twice as many men. Besides, I have more information about Mrs Vane than her husband. Now, if you don't mind, let's get on with them.'

The purser ran his finger down the list.

'Miss Ackfield is the first,' he explained. 'She is a lady of between fifty and sixty, I should say. You can easily see her, but in my opinion there is not the slightest chance that she could be otherwise than what she seems.'

French noted the particulars.

'Right,' he said. 'Next, please.'

'The next is Miss Bond. She's also pretty well on in years, but she couldn't be your friend because she's at least four inches taller.'

'Very good.'

'Then there is Mrs Brent. She is a young girl. Her husband is on board, and they are evidently newly married. She's too young.'

They worked on down the list, provisionally eliminating the unlikely. Mrs Cox was too tall, Miss Duffield too short, Mrs Eaglefield too stout, Miss Fenton too thin, and so on. In the end they had reduced the number to ten, of which French had to admit that not one seemed in the least promising.

There was indeed one couple who had at first appealed to him, a Mr Pereira da Silva, and his daughter, Miss Maria da Silva, because they kept almost entirely to their cabins, mixing but little with the life of the ship. Mr da Silva, a man of over seventy, Mr Jennings thought, was an invalid, and had come on board with difficulty, leaning on a stick and his daughter's arm. He was practically confined to bed, and Miss da Silva was assiduous in her attention to him, reading to him and keeping him company when many another similarly placed daughter would have been on deck or in the saloon, amusing herself among the other passengers. The two had their meals together, and the lady, though friendly enough when she did go on deck or when occasionally she sat in the saloon, was but rarely seen. This was, thought French, a likely enough ruse for the fugitives to adopt, and his suspicions were strengthened by the fact that Miss da Silva's general appearance was not unlike that of Mrs Vane. But Mr Jennings soon demolished his house of cards. The da Silvas were obviously Brazilian. They, or rather the girl, for the old man had been too feeble even to deal with the business of the tickets, spoke fluent Portuguese, the Portuguese of a native, and her English was not only broken, but was spoken as a Portuguese alone speaks it. Besides, she looked like a Portuguese. They lived at Rio, so Mr Jennings had gathered, and had visited England to see Mr da Silva's brother, a London merchant. They had booked to Para, near where other relatives lived, and from where they would return to Rio. They had taken tickets and reserved their staterooms some time before the Vanes.

French was disappointed. He booked on to Lisbon on chance, then not wishing to be seen, he retired to his cabin,

leaving Sergeant Carter to watch the ladder leading to the
shore boats.

As he sat smoking beside the open porthole, he kept on
racking his brains for some method of solving his problem,
but at last it was a chance word of the Purser's that gave
him his idea. Mr Jennings had dropped in just after the
ship, pushing out between the two great stone moles of
the harbour, had dipped her nose into the deep, slow-
moving Atlantic swell, and he had said: 'Talking of
disguises, it's a pity you couldn't disguise yourself and
come into the saloon tonight, Mr French. We are having
our first sing-song, and you would have a good chance
then of seeing the lady passengers.'

'That's rather an idea,' French had replied. 'Could you
not hide me somewhere, say, near the door of the saloon
through which those attending must enter, so that I could
see each as she passed?'

Mr Jennings had believed it might be possible, and had
promised to see what could be done. And then as he was
taking his leave, the idea flashed into French's mind, and
he had called him back.

'Don't trouble about that business in the meantime,
Mr Jennings. Would it be convenient to you to call back
again in half an hour? I shall have something to ask you
then.'

Jennings glanced at him curiously, but all he said was
'Right-o!' as he went on his business. After the allotted
span he came back, and French spoke earnestly.

'Look here, Mr Jennings, if you could do something for
me you'd put me under a heavy debt of gratitude. I'll tell
you what it is. First I want you to smuggle me into the
saloon before the concert begins, without anyone having

seen me. I want to sit in some place where I can't be seen by a person entering until he or she is right inside the room. Is that possible?'

'Why, yes, I think so. I'll fix it for you somehow. I take it your notion is that if the lady sees you so suddenly and unexpectedly she will give herself away?'

'Quite, but there is something else, Mr Jennings. That scheme would only work if she knows my appearance, but I don't think she does. I want someone to read this out as an item. Will you do it?'

He handed over a sheet of paper which he had covered with writing during his half-hour's wait. It read:

'RIDDLE.

'A prize of a 5-lb. box of chocolates is offered
for the best answer to the following riddle:
'If she is Winter in Comedy,
Ward in *Olympic*,
Root in Savoy, and
Vane in Crewe,
What is she on the *Enoch*?'

Mr Jennings looked somewhat mystified.
'I don't quite get you?' he suggested.
'Woman's aliases and the places where she used them.'
Something like admiration showed in the purser's eyes.
'My word! Some notion, that! If the woman is there and hasn't smelt a rat, she'll give herself away when she hears that. But why won't you read it yourself?'

'If she makes a move to leave I want to be out before her. If she leaves, it will mean that her husband is not present, and I want to get her before she can warn him. Carter'll be on the same job.'

'Well, I'll read it if you like, but frankly I'd rather you had someone else to do it.'

'What about Captain Davis?'

Jennings glanced round and sank his voice.

'If you take my advice, you'll leave the old man out of it altogether. He just mightn't approve. He treats the passengers as his guests, and bluffing them like that mightn't appeal to him.'

'But I'm not bluffing them,' French retorted with a twinkle in his eye. He drew a pound note from his pocket and passed it over. 'That's for the chocolates, and whoever puts in the best answer gets it. It's all perfectly straight and above board. Whether we get the woman over it or not no one need ever know.'

The purser smiled, but shook his head doubtfully.

'Well, it's your funeral. Anyway, I've said I'll go through with it, and I will.'

'Good!' French was once more his hearty, complacent self. 'Now there is another matter if this one fails. Mrs Vane may stay in her cabin. I want you to check the women present by your list, and give me a note of any absentees. Then I shall go round their cabins and make some excuse to see each.'

The purser agreed to this also. 'I'll send you some dinner here, and at once,' he added as he rose to take his leave, 'then I'll come for you while the passengers are dining, and get you fixed up in the saloon.'

'Better send Carter here, and he can dine with me while I explain the thing to him.'

When Mr Jennings had gone, French stood in front of

his porthole gazing out over the heaving waters. Daylight had completely gone, but there was a clear sky and a brilliant full moon. The sea looked like a ghostly plain of jet with, leading away across it, a huge road of light, its edges sparkling with myriad flashes of silver. His cabin was on the port side, and some three miles off he could dimly trace the white line of surf beating along the cliffs of the coast. The sea looked horribly cold, and he turned from it with a slight shudder as the door opened and Sergeant Carter entered.

'Ah, Carter, Mr Jennings is sending us in some dinner. We'll have it together. I have a job on for tonight,' and he explained his plan and the part his subordinate was to play therein. Carter said, 'Yes, sir,' stolidly to everything, but French could see he was impressed.

Shortly before eight, Mr Jennings appeared and beckoned his fellow-conspirators to follow him. They passed quickly across the deck and along some passages, and reached the saloon unobserved. There they found that the purser had placed two arm-chairs for their use close to the door, but hidden from outside it by screens. From French's chair the face of each person who entered the room would be visible, while Carter's was arranged so that he could see all those of the seated audience which were out of French's immediate purview.

The concert was timed for half-past eight, and before that hour little groups of people began to arrive. French, with a novel open on his knees, sat scrutinising unostentatiously each person as he or she entered. Once he stared with increased eagerness, as a dark, stoutish woman entered with two men. It seemed to him that she bore some resemblance to the photograph, but as he watched her foreign

gestures and as he listened to her rapid conversation in
some unknown language, he felt sure she could not be the
woman he sought. He called a passing steward, and learned
from him that she was the Miss da Silva whom he had
already suspected and acquitted in his mind.

As the time drew on the saloon gradually filled, but
nowhere did he see anyone whose appearance he thought
suspicious. When the hour arrived, the proceedings were
opened with a short recital by a well-known pianist who
was making the voyage to Madeira for his health.

French was not musical, but even if he had been he
would have paid but scant attention to the programme.
He was too busily engaged in covertly scrutinising the faces
of the men and women around him. He was dimly
conscious that the well-known pianist brought his contri-
bution to an end with a brilliant and highly dexterous feat
of manual gymnastics, that two ladies—or was it three—
sang, that a deep-toned basso growled out something that
he took to be a Scotch song, and that a quiet, rather pretty
girl played some pleasant-sounding melody on a violin,
when his attention was suddenly galvanised into eager life
and fixed with an expectant thrill on what was taking
place. Mr Jennings had ascended the platform.

'Ladies and gentlemen,' the purser said in his pleasantly
modulated voice, 'while possibly it may be true that the
days of riddles have passed, and while it certainly is true
that the middle of a concert is not the happiest time for
asking them, still perhaps you will allow me to put this
one to you. It is a topical riddle concerning our voyage
made up by one of our company, and he offers a prize of
this large box of chocolates for the best solution. The riddle
is this, and I can let anyone who cares to consider it have

a copy: "If she is Winter in Comedy, Ward in *Olympic,* Root in Savoy, and Vane in Crewe, what is she aboard the *Enoch*?'"

The audience listened with good-humoured attention, and for a moment Mr Jennings stood motionless, still smiling pleasantly. The little buzz of conversation which usually sprang up between the items had not yet begun, and save for the faint, all-pervading murmur of the engines, the gently swaying saloon was momentarily still. Then through the silence came a slight though unexpected sound. Miss da Silva's handbag had slipped off her knee, and the metal hasp had struck the parquet floor with a sharp tap.

French glanced at her face with a sudden thrill. It had gone a queer shade of yellowish brown, and her hand, hanging down by her side, was clenched till the knuckles showed the same livid brownish hue. She evidently had not noticed her bag fall, and in her fixed and staring eyes there grew the shadow of a terrible fear. No one but French seemed to have noticed her emotion, and a man beside her stooped to pick up the bag. At the same time the silence was broken by a stout, military-looking old gentleman, who with some 'Ha, ha's!' and 'Be Gad's!' adjured the company to set about solving the puzzle, and conversation became general. Miss da Silva rose quietly and moved rather unsteadily towards the door.

For French to get up and open the door for her was an act of common politeness. With a slight bow he held it as she passed through, then following her immediately, he closed it behind him.

They were alone in the passage leading to the companion-way, and as he glanced keenly at her face he felt no further doubt. Disguised by some adroit alterations to hair and eyebrows, and, he believed, with a differently-shaped set of false teeth, a darkened complexion and glasses, there stood before him the original of the photographs. He laid his hand on her arm.

'Miss Winter,' he said gravely, 'I am Inspector French of Scotland Yard. I arrest you on a charge of being concerned in the murder of Charles Gething and the theft of precious stones and money from Messrs Duke & Peabody's on the 25th of November last.'

The woman did not reply, but like a flash her free arm went to her mouth. French grasped wildly and caught it. She gulped, and at the same moment reeled. French, himself trembling and with beads of perspiration on his forehead, laid her gently on the floor, where she lay unconscious. He hastily stepped back into the saloon, and moving quietly to where he had seen the ship's doctor sitting, whispered in his ear. Sergeant Carter got up at the same moment, and a second later the two detectives stood looking down with troubled faces, while Dr Sandiford knelt beside the motionless figure on the floor.

'Good God!' he cried at once, 'she's dead!' He put his nose to her lips. 'Prussic acid!' He gazed up at his companions with a countenance of horrified surprise.

'Yes; suicide,' said French shortly. 'Get her moved to my cabin before anyone comes.'

The doctor, ignorant of the circumstances, looked at the other with a sudden suspicion, but on French's hurried explanation he nodded, and the three men bore the still form off and laid it reverently on the sofa in the inspector's stateroom.

'When you've examined her, tell the Captain,' French said. 'Meantime Carter and I must go and arrest the poor creature's husband. You might show me his cabin when you're through.'

A few seconds sufficed the doctor for his examination, and then in silence he led the way to a cabin on the boat deck. French knocked, and instantly opening the door, passed inside, followed by the others.

It was a large, roomy stateroom, fitted up as a private sitting-room, an open door revealing a bedroom beyond. The room had a comfortable, used appearance. Books and papers lay about, a box of chessmen and a pack of cards were on a locker, while in a lounge chair lay a woman's crochet work. On a table stood an empty coffee cup and the smell of a good cigar was heavy in the air.

In an arm-chair under the electric light, clad in a dressing-gown and slippers, sat an old gentleman, the cigar in one hand and a book in the other. He seemed a tall man, and his long hair was pure white. He wore a long white beard and moustache, and had bushy white eyebrows. He sat staring at the intruders with surprise and apparent annoyance.

But as his eyes settled on French's face their expression changed. Amazement, incredulity, and a growing horror appeared in rapid succession. French advanced, but the other sat motionless, his eyes still fixed on his visitor's with a dreadful intensity, like that of an animal fascinated by a snake. And then French began to stare in his turn. There was something familiar about those eyes. They were a peculiar shade of dark blue that he recalled very clearly. And there was a mole, a tiny brown mole beneath the corner of the left one, which he had certainly seen not long previously. So, for an appreciable time both remained motionless, staring at one another.

Suddenly French recalled where he had seen that shade of iris and that mole. With a murmur of amazement he stepped forward. 'Mr Duke!' he cried.

The other with a snarl of anger was fumbling desperately in his pocket. Like a flash, French and Carter threw themselves on him and caught his arm as it was half-way to his mouth. In the fingers was a tiny white pilule. In another second he was handcuffed, and French's skilful fingers had passed over his clothes and abstracted from his pocket a tiny phial containing a few more of the little white messengers of death. At the same moment Captain Davis appeared at the door.

'Shut the door, if you please, Captain,' French begged. 'The Yard was right after all. This is the man.'

A few sentences put the Captain in possession of the facts, and then French gently and with real kindness in his tones broke the news of Miss Winter's death to his unhappy prisoner. But the man expressed only relief.

'Thank God!' he cried with evidently overwhelming emotion. 'She was quicker than I. Thank God she was in time! I don't care what happens to myself now that she's out of it. If it wasn't for my daughter'—his voice broke—' I'd be thankful it was over. I've lived in hell for the last few months. Wherever I turn I see Gething's eyes looking at me. It's been hell, just *hell*! I shouldn't wish my worst enemy to go through what I have. I admit the whole business. All I ask is that you get on and make an end quickly.'

The whole scene had been enacted so quickly that French, after his first moment of overwhelming surprise, had not had time to think, but presently, after the immediate exigencies of the situation had been met, the mystery of this amazing denouement struck him even more forcibly. He felt almost as if he had glimpsed the supernatural, as if he had been present and had seen one raised from the dead. Mr Duke was dead, at least so until a few minutes earlier he had unquestioningly believed. The evidence of that death was overwhelming. And yet—it was false! What trick had the man played? How had he managed so completely to deceive all concerned as to the events of that mysterious crossing from Harwich to the Hook? French felt it would not be easy to control his impatience until he learned how the thing had been done, and the more he thought of the whole problem, the more eager he grew to be back at the Yard so that he might once again attack it, this time with the practical certainty of clearing up all the features of the case which still remained obscure.

The next afternoon they dropped anchor in the Tagus off Lisbon, and there French transferred with his prisoner to a homeward-bound liner. On the third morning after they were in Liverpool, and the same night reached London.

20

Conclusion

Given the key of the identity of the murderer, it was not long before Inspector French had unearthed all the details of the murder of Charles Gething and the theft of the diamonds, and had arranged them with a due regard to their proper bearing and sequence. And he found, as he had so often found before, that what had seemed a complicated and insoluble mystery was really a very simple happening after all. Briefly the facts which came out, partly as the result of a renewed investigation, and partly from Mr Duke's confession, were as follows:

Reginald Ainsley Duke had lived a happy and contented life until a terrible calamity befell him—his wife's brain gave way, and with splendid physical health she had to be removed to an asylum, a dangerous and incurable lunatic. Though he had never been passionately in love with her, they had been sincerely attached, and for some time he was crushed beneath the blow. But in his case, as in others, time softened the sharpness of his grief, and this terrible period of his life gradually became a hideous though fading nightmare. Then he saw Miss Cissie Winter act at the Comedy, and feeling attracted to her, he arranged a meeting. The attraction proved to be mutual, and other meetings followed, as a result of which he fell violently, overwhelmingly in love with her. To his unbounded and ecstatic delight, he found his passion was returned.

Their problem then was a common one. Obviously they could not marry, so after much thought they did what a good many other people would have done in their place—set up an unconventional household. Their difficulty was Duke's daughter. Had it not been for her, they would have taken no trouble to hide their predicament. But Duke did not want any stigma to rest on her, and with Miss Winter's approval he decided to live a double life and keep two establishments. A simple disguise being necessary, he took for his model Vanderkemp, partly because the traveller was somewhat of his own height and build, and partly in the hope that were he at any time followed from the office to his second dwelling, he might be mistaken for Vanderkemp. With the help of the actress, he evolved a make-up, consisting of a wig, a false moustache and glasses, and exchanged his own upright carriage for Vanderkemp's stoop. As Duke he retained his own personality, as Vane he wore the make-up. Their plan had met with such success that no suspicions were aroused. To his daughter he explained his frequent absences by saying he had to keep in constant touch with the Amsterdam branch, and the servants at Pennington, the forerunner of Crewe Lodge, were given to understand he was a traveller for a firm of engineers.

The arrangement worked successfully until the war began to interfere with the profits of his business, and then the keeping up of his two homes became a burden greater than he could bear. For a time he struggled on, but an insidious temptation had begun to haunt him, and the greater his difficulties grew the stronger it became. Here was he virtually in control of the business. His partners gave it but little attention. Peabody was old and doddering, and Sinnamond was well-off and spent most of his time travelling. A little juggling with figures, a few slight alterations to the books, and he would have all the money he wanted. He resisted with all his strength, but even in doing so he saw fresh ways in which the thing could be carried out—with absolute safety, as he believed—and eventually he fell. His plans worked as he had expected, his financial difficulties were met, and he congratulated himself that all would be well.

But there was one thing on which he had not reckoned. He forgot that a man cannot start a deceit or a swindle and stop when he likes. He soon discovered that each falsified entry required some further manipulation to buttress it up, and in spite of all his efforts he found himself becoming more and more deeply involved. And then came the inevitable unforeseen catastrophe. His head clerk, Charles Gething, began to suspect. He made an investigation, confirmed his suspicions, and with characteristic straightforwardness showed his discoveries to his employer, declaring that his duty required him to call in the other partners.

Duke, seeing he was up against it, played for time by stoutly swearing that Gething had made a mistake and promising him a complete explanation and proof that all the books were in order, if the clerk would only wait until he got some balancing figures from the Amsterdam office. He left that evening—for Crewe Lodge, and there he told Miss Winter the whole story. That astute lady saw that though through the simple expedient of wearing a wedding ring she had covered up their first departure from orthodoxy, this was a different matter. Here discovery would mean prison for her lover and destitution for herself. It did not take her long to make up her mind that there should be no discovery.

Exercising all her arts, she succeeded after a struggle in bringing Duke round to her way of thinking, and the two set their wits to work to devise a scheme by which to safeguard themselves. Miss Winter supplied the main idea of the plan; Duke, who was thorough rather than brilliant, worked out the details. In short, the scheme was to stage a robbery at the office, murder Gething, get hold of as many stones as possible, and then make a leisurely departure for distant and more healthy spheres.

Miss Winter had a complete and first-hand knowledge both of Brazil and the United States. Her father was English, but having as a young man been sent to Rio as representative of his firm, he had settled down there, married a Portuguese wife, and made his home in the Brazilian capital. His daughter had a genius for acting, and on her parents' death while she was yet in her teens, she succeeded in getting a start on the Rio stage. After five years, she accepted an engagement with an enterprising New York manager who had seen her act during a visit to Brazil. Two years later she came to London, and had there met Mr Duke as already stated.

This knowledge of Brazil and America supplied the foundation of her scheme. Brazil represented an ideal country to which to retire after the crime, and their first care was to arrange a line of retreat thereto. They were well known in the neighbourhood as Mr and Mrs Vane and had no difficulty in getting the certificates and letters of recommendation necessary to obtain their Brazilian passports. Having received the passports, Duke forged similar certificates and letters in the names of da Silva, and having with the aid of Miss Winter's theatrical knowledge made themselves up in character, they applied at the same office a second time, obtaining two more passports in the assumed names. Thus they had two sets of Brazilian passports in the names of Vane and da Silva respectively.

The next point was to procure some ready money immediately after the crime, to enable the fugitives to purchase the necessary tickets to Brazil, and for the host of other expenses which were certain to arise. With this object, the visit of Mrs Vane to New York was arranged. She was to travel there by one line and immediately return by another. During the voyage home she was carefully to observe the passengers, and select the most suitable person she could find to impersonate. She was to make friends with this woman, find out all she could about her, and observe her carefully so as to obtain as much data as possible to help on the fraud. On arrival at Southampton she was to see her prototype off at the station, ascertaining her destination, then going to some hotel, she was to make the necessary changes in her appearance, proceed to London in her new character, and put up where she was unlikely to meet the other. On the next day she was to interview Williams, and if all had gone well up to this point she was to telephone to Duke from a public call office, so that he could proceed with his part of the affair. Finally she was to meet him at 9.45 on the next evening on the emergency staircase of the Holborn Tube station to obtain from him the portion of the spoils destined for Williams.

In the meantime, Duke was to pacify Gething by promising him a full explanation of the apparent discrepancies, together with a sight of the actual cash needed to put matters right, on the receipt of certain letters from America. He was also to get together as large a collection of stones as he possibly could. He was then to ask Gething to meet him at the office on the evening in question—the evening of the day of Miss Winter's first interview with Williams— to go into the whole matter and see the proofs that all was right. Having thus got Gething into his power, he was to murder him, take out the diamonds and some money that was also in the safe, and having handed over to Miss Winter the few stones for Williams, go home as quickly as possible with the remainder.

Though this scheme seemed to them good, the conspirators were not satisfied with it, and they added on three additional features to safeguard themselves still further in the event of suspicion being aroused.

The first of these was an alibi for Mr Duke. He arranged that he would dine and spend the evening at his club, with his solicitor, leaving at a certain definite prearranged hour. By suitable remarks to the solicitor and the club, porters, he would fix this hour, and by similar remarks to his servants he would establish the time at which he reached his house. The interval between would be sufficient to enable him to walk home, and he would take care to inform the police that he had so occupied it. But in reality he would taxi from near the club to near the office, commit the murder, and return to Hampstead by tube.

The second safeguard took the form of an attempt to throw suspicion on to Vanderkemp. In carrying this out, Duke himself typed the secret instructions which brought the traveller to London, and he gave Gething orders to see Vanderkemp on his arrival, send him on his wild goose chase to the Continent, and hand him some of the notes of which he had reason to believe the bank had the numbers, and which he afterwards swore were stolen from the safe.

Events after the crime moved so well from the conspirators' point of view that they did not at first put their third safeguard into action. Indeed they began to think that even retirement to Brazil would be unnecessary, and that they could continue their life in London as formerly. But the chance remark of Inspector French to Duke that he had discovered that the elusive Mrs X was Miss Cissie Winter showed that their house of cards was falling to the ground, and immediate flight became imperative. Duke, afraid to visit Crewe Lodge, wrote the warning in a cipher on which they had previously agreed. But by one of those strange chances which interfere to upset the lives and plans of mortals, just after he had posted it the guilty pair met in a tube train. Loitering in a passage till they were alone, Duke gave his news by word of mouth. Then Miss Winter made the slip which compassed their downfall—she forgot about the cipher letter which Duke had said he had sent, and fled, leaving the letter to fall into the hands of the police.

Duke then proceeded to carry out his third safeguard—to fake a suicide in order to account for his disappearance. This he did by means of a trick which they had carefully worked out beforehand, and which they also intended to employ on the Booth liner to put the detectives off in case suspicion should be aroused. In his personality of Duke, he bought at Cook's office a return ticket from London to Amsterdam via Harwich, engaging his berth for that night and impressing his identity on the clerk. He then went on to Liverpool Street and in his personality of Vane he took a return ticket from London to Brussels by the same route. As Duke he had the passport he used on his occasional visits to Amsterdam. As Vane he had obtained a passport for Holland and Belgium some eighteen months earlier, when he and Miss Winter had gone there for a short holiday.

As Duke he travelled down on the boat train to Harwich, choosing his carriage so that he would be among the first on board. He gave up his ticket at the office, received his landing ticket, and was shown to his cabin. There he arranged his things and left the note for his daughter. Then he put on his Vane make-up, slipped out of the cabin unobserved, and joining the last stragglers from the train, presented his second ticket and was shown to the cabin he had reserved as Vane. As Vane next day he went ashore leaving behind him incontrovertible evidence of the death of Duke.

At Rotterdam he took tickets for return via Hull, and travelling to Leeds, put up at the Victory Hotel until the date of the sailing of the *Enoch*. He and Miss Winter joined forces in the train between Leeds and Liverpool, and on going on board the liner they attempted to throw any pursuing detective off the scent by carrying out the same ruse by which Duke had faked his suicide. They had taken two sets of tickets—one set at Cook's to Manáos in the name of Vane, and the other at the Booth Line offices to Para in the name of da Silva, and had engaged staterooms and tried to impress their personalities on the clerks on each occasion. They had further provided themselves with sets of large and small suitcases. The small ones, in which they packed their clothes and the diamonds, they labelled 'da Silva,' the large ones they labelled 'Vane.' They then put the 'da Silva' suitcases inside the 'Vane,' went on board as Vane, and were shown to their cabin. As Vane, they went back to the purser and said they were going ashore. They went out on deck in the direction of the gangway, but instead of crossing it they regained their cabin, made up as the da Silvas, took out their small da Silva suitcases, and slipping unseen from the cabin, returned to the Purser as having just come on board.

The scheme as a whole worked out according to plan—save for Miss Winter's lapse in omitting to wait for and destroy the cipher letter—but though the principals did not know it, a coincidence took place which came within an ace of wrecking it. When Sylvia and Harrington were driving home from the East End on the night of the crime they saw Mr Duke turn out of Hatton Garden into Holborn. He was hurrying anxiously along the pavement with very different mien to his usual upright, leisurely bearing. There was something furtive about his appearance, and his face, revealed by a bright shaft of light streaming from a confectioner's shop, was drawn and haggard. Fearing some ill news, Sylvia had stopped the taxi and hurried after him, but before she had reached the pavement he had disappeared. She did not, however, take the matter seriously until at breakfast the next morning he told her of the crime. Even then it never occurred to her to suspect him; in fact, she had forgotten the incident, but when he went on to state, as it were casually, that he had been at his club all evening and had walked directly home from there, she remembered. She realised that he was lying, and suspicion was inevitable. In desperation lest Harrington should unwittingly give away information which might put the police on her father's track, she rang him up and arranged an immediate meeting at which she warned him of the possibilities. That afternoon Harrington called to tell her how things had gone at the office, and then she had overwhelmed him by insisting on the postponement of the wedding until the affair should be cleared up. When, however, she learned that French suspected Harrington and herself of knowing the criminal, she thought the postponed marriage might give direction to his investigations, and to avoid this she gave out that the ceremony had once again been arranged. The poor girl's mind was nearly unhinged thinking of what she should do in the event of the police making an arrest, but fortunately for her she was not called upon to make the decision.

It remains merely to say that some weeks later Reginald Ainsley Duke paid the supreme penalty for his crimes, and his daughter, hating London and England for the terrible memories they held, allowed herself to be persuaded for the third time to fix the date of the wedding with Charles Harrington, and to seek happiness with him on his brother's ranch in Southern California. The firm of Duke & Peabody weathered the storm, and the surviving partners did not forget the Gething sisters when balancing their accounts.

By the same author

Inspector French
and the Cheyne Mystery

When young Maxwell Cheyne discovers that a series of
mishaps are the result of unwelcome attention from a
dangerous gang of criminals, he teams up with a young
woman who is determined to help him outwit them. But
when she disappears, he finally decides to go to Scotland
Yard for help. Concerned by the developing situation,
Inspector Joseph French takes charge of the investigation
and applies his trademark methods to track down the
kidnappers and thwart their intentions . . .

'*Freeman Wills Crofts is among the few muscular writers of
detective fiction. He has never let me down.*'

DAILY EXPRESS